NUECES BLOOD

ALSO BY MARK GREATHOUSE

The Frontier Chronicles

Perilous Trails

Wyoming Calls

Longhorns North

Warpath

The Tumbleweed Sagas

Nueces Justice

Nueces Reprise

Nueces Deceit

Nueces Blood

NUECES BLOOD

TEXANS PREPARE FOR WAR

THE TUMBLEWEED SAGAS
BOOK 4

MARK GREATHOUSE

WOLFPACK
PUBLISHING
— EST 2013 —

*Dedicated with love to my wife, Carolyn, and to our two sons,
Mike and Matt.*

THE NUECES STRIP

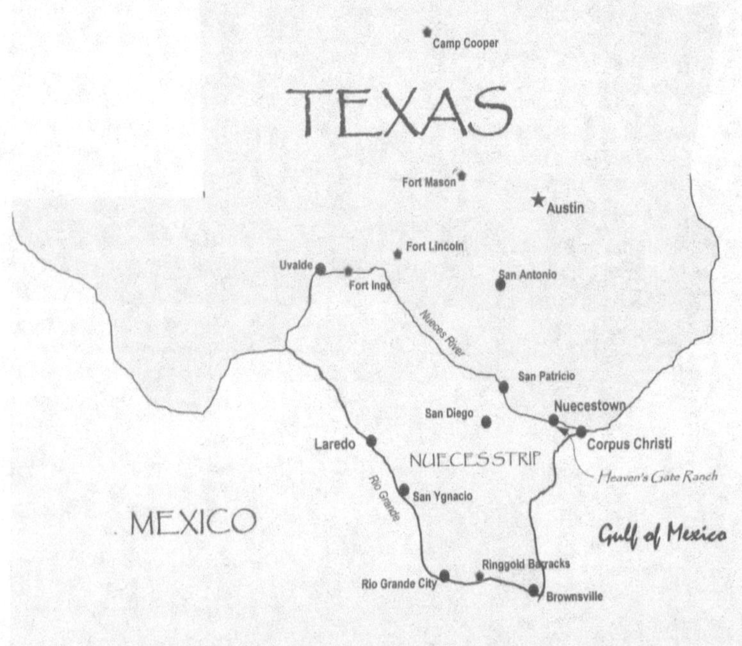

The vast Nueces Strip serves as the primary setting for the Tumbleweed Sagas. The Strip was also called Wild Horse Desert, owing to the millions of Mustangs that roamed its prairies. *(Sketch by Mark Greathouse)*

NUECESTOWN

Nuecestown, Texas, established in 1852 by English and German settlers, was developed by Corpus Christi founder Colonel Henry Kinney along the Nueces River as a ferry crossing. Mostly thanks to the railroad passing it by, it's now a "ghost town" marked only by historical markers. All that remains is a preserved schoolhouse and the old Nuecestown Cemetery. *(Sketch by Mark Greathouse)*

THE CAST

Lucas "Long Luke" Dunn – *Before gaining notoriety as one of the greatest Texas Ranger captains ever, Luke escapes the Great Famine in Ireland to seek his fortune on Texas' Nueces Strip. He gains repute as Indian fighter and respected lawman. Later conflicted between being lawman and rancher. Comanche call him Ghost-Who-Rides.*

Elisa Corrigan Dunn – *Marries Luke Dunn after losing her family to frontier rigors, including fighting off Comanche. She and Luke build Heaven's Gate ranch and a life on the frontier.*

Scarlett Rose – *Red-headed prostitute from Laredo seeking to overcome her past, including bad choices of men, to run a legitimate business.*

Doc Andrews – *The formerly alcoholic Nuecestown doctor is the conscience of the town.*

Three Toes – *Comanche Chief, son of famous Penateka Comanche War Chief Santa Anna and favored by Buffalo Hump. He develops a friendship with Luke that contradicts tribal ways.*

Bernice & Agatha – *Nuecestown town gossips with hearts of gold who run the local boarding house.*

Horace Rucker – *Retired US Army Colonel turned preacher. Veteran of Mexican American War who fights off ghosts of his past to gain self-respect and to support his family.*

Brevet Captain Gordon Belknap – *West Point graduate assigned to fighting Indians in Texas. Gains experience with Luke and Three Toes. Becomes renowned Indian fighter.*

Horatio Thorpe – *One of the wealthiest men in Texas, descended from a Carolina plantation family, builds his own plantation on the Texas Gulf plains. Uses power of money to greedily influence Texas politics and commerce.*

Samuel – *As one of Horatio Thorpe's slaves, he serves as office "gatekeeper" and trusted messenger in Thorpe's Austin office.*

William Meaney – *Sheriff of Corpus Christi, hired by Colonel Kinney to replace George Whelan. Meaney lends a bit of respect to the lawman role by dressing well. But it belies his toughness.*

Jaime Sanchez – *Works as vaquero at Luke Dunn's Heaven's Gate Ranch. Becomes valuable asset to Luke in dealing with threats to the Nueces Strip. His wife, Julia, helps Elisa with ranch chores.*

Boland Richards – *As Indian fighter, trader, and erstwhile mountain man, Bol made a name for himself in the Texas War of Independence, though he forever resents Texas joining the United States.*

Walker Carson – *Two-bit cowboy turned incompetent bank robber, Carson's frustration with trying to succeed in life leads him on a path fraught with ever-more desperate attempts to make a name for himself until he meets Luke Dunn.*

Edward Thorpe – *Horatio Thorpe's son, heir to his vast wealth, and committed to preservation of the Union.*

Rex & Stephen Rucker – *Horace Rucker's sons attending the US Military Academy at West Point have opposing views on the slavery issue.*
Zeke Bose & Cal Withers – *Anti-slavery protesters stirring up folks in southern Texas.*

Jubal Strong – *Cousin to the outlaw "Bad Bart" Strong whom Luke brought to justice back in 1856 near Laredo. Strong journeys from Wyoming to ostensibly protect his family "honor" by seeking vengeance on Luke.*

Sheriff Stills – *Cantankerous sheriff of Laredo known for tobacco-spitting skills.*

HISTORICAL CHARACTERS

Colonel Henry Lawrence Kinney – *Entrepreneur, rancher, and trader. Founder of Corpus Christi, originally as a trading post, and a leader in the settlement and economic development of the eastern part of the Nueces Strip.*

John Salmon "Rip" Ford – *Soldier, elected official, newspaper editor, and Texas Ranger, Ford was critically important to taming the Texas frontier. He was a renowned Indian fighter and led a campaign against Mexican rebel Juan Cortina. He would later be intimately involved with secession, fighting in the War Between the States, and post-war redevelopment. He assembled the last great force of Texas Rangers before the War Between the States.*

Sam Houston – *One of the most illustrious leaders of Texas, from soldier leading Texas to independence, to politician serving as president of the Republic of Texas, US senator, and Texas governor. Dreamed of conquering Mexico and becoming US president. His decisions directly impacted formation of the Texas Rangers.*

Benito Juarez – *Part indigenous Indian, he became president of Mexico by the succession mandated by its Constitution when moderate liberal President Comonfort was forced to resign. He remained in the presidential office until his death in 1872.*

Juan Nepomuceno "Cheno" Cortina – *Mexican rancher, politician, military leader, outlaw, and folk hero who did not accept the terms of the Treaty of Guadalupe-Hidalgo and fought against settlers, US soldiers, and Texas Rangers on the Nueces Strip.*

THEME

BLOOD

Carnage; slaughter of many people, as in battle; butchery; massacre

INTRODUCTION

Nueces Blood: Texans Prepare for War is the fourth of The Tumbleweed Sagas. The Nueces Strip of 1859-1861 could be said to be afire with growth, as ranches and farms spread ever westward and communities sprang up seemingly overnight. As the telegraph expanded its reach, it became an ever-greater contributor to commerce. Family, community, commerce, and faith were increasingly the primary contributing factors to settling the frontier, though romantics might yet attribute the winning of the west to a gun or spirit of adventure.

The Strip was still mostly a vast prairie of tall grasses and loamy sands that stretched as far as the eye could see and beyond. The grasses often grew high enough to reach a horse's withers. The Nueces Strip, called "Wild Horse Desert" by some, reached south from the Nueces River all the way to the Rio Grande. Its eastern boundary was the Gulf of Mexico. At its northern extreme was the little town of Uvalde near Fort Inge. Laredo with its nearby Fort McIntosh was generally regarded as the main outpost of the western Nueces Strip. Corpus Christi founder

Colonel Kinney had a road built from Corpus to Laredo and another to San Antonio. They were rough but serviceable.

Mottes, or small clusters of live oak or mesquite, offered occasional shade relief on the sunbaked prairies. The often-dry creek beds and arroyos eventually filled with rainwater and emptied into Nueces Bay and...farther to the east... Corpus Christi Bay. Flash flooding was an ongoing fear. Summers? Well, they tended to be hot and humid. Weather was pretty much whatever you wanted, if you waited long enough.

The abundant animal life on the Nueces Strip featured deer, javelina, fox, coyote, and even mountain lion. At one point, horses were more numerous on the Strip than any animal, including humans. Occasionally, spotted ocelots and even wolves could be sighted by the practiced eye. Come spring, wildflowers swept across much of the land-scape painted like a huge rainbow, with scarlet sage, hibis-cus, daisies, poppies, lilies, and the ubiquitous bluebonnets. Groves of cypress, juniper, and palmetto could be found mostly farther south toward Brownsville. Cactus along with yucca and agave abounded.

If you were on foot, it was advisable to keep an eye and ear peeled for rattlesnakes. They tended to blend in fairly well with their surroundings, so their rattle was often folks first and only warning of an impending attack. The rattlesnake spawned many a "Texas-ism" like "he's so bad he has rattlesnake fangs and twice the venom."

No discussion of the Nueces Strip can ever be complete without mention that much of the most significant fighting of the Texas War for Independence was fought on and just north of the Nueces Strip back in 1835 and 1836, and it was scene to the first fighting of the Mexican American War of 1846. The Strip was officially ceded to the United States by the Treaty of Guadalupe-Hidalgo in 1848, though Texas had already laid claim to it.

The plentiful and accessible longhorn could be called the "low-hanging-fruit" of the Nueces Strip economy. They were a hardy breed that could withstand the South Texas heat, fend off disease-carrying pests, and carry just enough meat on their bones to make them reasonably profitable to raise. Originally brought from the Iberian Peninsula by early Spanish priests, the longhorns eventually escaped the mostly failing missionaries, proliferated, and roamed wild and free across the prairies. Millions of the beasts soon covered Texas and especially the excellent grazing lands of the Nueces Strip. They competed with the wild mustangs that had also been introduced by the Spaniards. Of course, there were the indigenous buffalo, millions of the beasts. They were a staple of the Indian way of life. The Texas prairies provided plenty of feed for all.

The factor that would ultimately win the west was the family—the larger, the better as children grew up in the face of all manner of lurking dangers. Families established the ranches and farms popping up not only throughout the eastern portions of the Nueces Strip but across Texas as a whole. The territory east of the 98th meridian sliced through the very heart of Texas that was fast becoming an economic juggernaut, and the Strip was no exception. Its economy was based on growing cotton and raising longhorns and horses. Cotton was bundled and hauled to port for transport to markets in Louisiana and points east while cattle were driven to Kansas and Missouri railheads to be shipped to the packing houses of the Midwest. Indians were pushed ever westward, as tribes were overcome by a cocktail of socioeconomic forces and disease.

To the west of the aforementioned 98th meridian was the Comancheria. Indigenous tribes of Comanche, Kiowa,

Apache, Ute, and more rode free across this vast region that extended into New Mexico and north into the Texas Panhandle.

Texas was not immune to the potential social, political, and economic upheaval of slavery. By 1860, the number of slaves in Texas was roughly 180,000, or close to a third of the population. There was a lingering fear of a slave revolt, especially as tempers began to flare concerning slave versus free states and the very institution of slavery had come to near boiling over as an issue. The word of John Brown's raid on the armory at Harper's Ferry and the violence in Kansas only added fuel to the fire. The Nueces Strip was not immune.

The far reaches of the mostly untamed prairies of the strip beckoned to principled men like Luke Dunn. While the frontier grew ever westward, there was ongoing worry about the threats posed by Comanche, Kiowa, and Lipan Apache, as well as the rogue marauding bandits from south of the Rio Grande. This all served to keep early Texans on this wild and often lawless frontier ever vigilant. It was easy to make the case for calling up companies of Texas Rangers to patrol the Nueces Strip, as they took it upon themselves to go where the military found it politically undesirable. On the other hand, the legislators in the state capital in Austin often were unable to pull together the financial means to fund the necessary companies of Rangers. They had to rely on the US Army, which could be chancy at best, as it was subject to the politics of whomever was in power and perceiving real or imagined threats.

In *Nueces Deceit*, Texas Ranger Captain Luke Dunn had been making significant headway in bringing justice to the Nueces Strip and just beginning to enjoy the resurgence of the Rangers as a force fighting to bring the law to the region. *Nueces Blood* takes us to the events and accompanying dynamics in southern Texas leading up to the War Between the States. He and Elisa had grown Heaven's Gate ranch both in terms of land holdings and livestock, and the Dunn family had added a daughter to join with their twin boys in creating their family.

Blood shed by both innocent and evil men colored the Nueces Strip. The obsessive mastermind of a government fraud is revealed and a revenge-driven Mexican rebel must be brought to justice. Lesser but no less dangerous lawbreakers don't make Luke's efforts any easier. Luke remains ever-conflicted over his roles of rancher and Texas Ranger. Danger lurked, whichever Luke chose. Prairie fires, blizzards, floods, stampedes, desperate killers, rustlers, and savages were part and parcel whether lawman or rancher. Just about anywhere he rode, death could be reaching for his bridle reins. While Luke had built considerable notoriety and created enemies by virtue of his success in bringing lawbreakers to justice, he also established reliable allies. When Texas Ranger Commander John "Rip" Ford called to form companies of Texas Rangers, Luke would be pressed to making a future-altering decision. But, by 1860, there's a sense of future troubles lingering in the air.

While the "Cast of Historical Characters" provides some helpful true-to-life framework to the life and times on the Texas Nueces Strip, woven into The Tumbleweed Sagas are actual settlers of the frontier as drawn from the author's family ancestry. Peter Dunn immigrated from Ireland in 1850 and established a blacksmith shop in Corpus Christi, John Dunn ranched and grew many acres of cotton, and Nicholas Dunn was a rancher, drover, livestock speculator, and Comanche fighter of some repute. Such real-life characters, coupled with actual events, have served to reinforce the historical setting for The Tumbleweed Sagas.

My poet/novelist cousin, Mary Maude Dunn Wright

(pseud. Lilith Lorraine), in writing the preface to her father "Red John" Dunn's biography back in 1932, posed the question, "Not in the spirit of judging their actions by artificial standards which in their day had no existence, but by asking ourselves if we were in their places, should we have acquitted ourselves as well, and by putting to ourselves the still more potent question: how well have we kept the birthright that they have given us, how well have we safeguarded the liberties that they purchased through untold privations, how courageously are we meeting the problems that confront us today; in short when we stand before the tribunal of remote posterity, to whom shall the laurel be awarded…?" Y'all might think on that.

NUECES BLOOD

PROLOGUE

LUKE'S SIX-FOOT-THREE height had earned him the nickname "Long Luke" from some, but he was partial to the name the Comanche called him: Ghost-Who-Rides. His ruggedly handsome Irish face framed a well-tended fiery-red mustache. Seven years had now passed since he'd immigrated from County Kildare back in Ireland. Luke had flirted with joining rebellious clan factions back in his homeland, learned the use of claymore and firearms, and developed a quite self-righteous sense of right and wrong. He naturally gravitated to the lawman profession upon his arrival in Corpus Christi. Having a few cousins who had already immigrated to America, Luke had the advantage of being introduced to Colonel Kinney, the founder of Corpus Christi. Thus, his law enforcement career had gotten underway first as a deputy sheriff and a bit later as a Texas Ranger.

Luke became increasingly familiar with the landscape and people of the Nueces Strip. He generally wore a weather-beaten, broad-brimmed tan hat with a simple leather band. He usually wore a buckskin vest or a coat over a blue shirt with gray trousers stuffed into well-worn cowboy boots. His gun belt accommodated two Colt Navy revolvers plus plenty of ammunition. When on duty as lawman, he pinned the Texas Ranger badge to his shirt, where it stood out so as to be impossible to miss.

This was the man with whom Elisa had found true love and married. Their family seemed to be growing faster than double-struck lightning, having quickly been blessed with twin boys and a daughter. But it was also the way it was on the Texas frontier, as large families ensured the ultimate cohesion that marked building civilized communities where disease, dangerous critters, hostile Indians, and lawbreakers tended to create numerous challenges to life. Importantly, civilization was winning.

Luke was faced with a critically important decision concerning becoming a special agent Texas Ranger under Rip Ford, commander of the Texas Rangers throughout the state. Luke had already raised a company of more than two dozen men at Ford's request and established grizzled Texas War for Independence veteran Bol Richards as its leader. Luke was initially miffed that Ford didn't choose him to lead the company, but the request to serve as a special agent that would take better advantage of his skills was very tempting. His thoughts turned to his personal conflict over being a rancher and family man versus lawman. He was ever more fully understanding the nature of the longhorns. As his ranching skills had developed, he couldn't help appreciate how the qualities of being a Texas Ranger paralleled those of being a cowboy. Both professions demanded powers of observation, alertness, loyalty and, most importantly, resourcefulness. In addition, he'd developed critically important skills such as excellent marksmanship and becoming a fine horseman. Plus, he was considered intelligent. He thought on the psychology of managing longhorns, and likened dealing with those sometimes-unpredictable beeves to wrangling with lawbreakers. Indeed, the similarities he brought to ranching and bringing justice to the Nueces Strip made his conflict between the two roles all the more challenging to choose between—if, in fact, a choice was necessary.

ONE
RANGERS ON THE FRONTIER

ELISA LOOKED DEEPLY into her husband's eyes as she stared across the table. She thought she had him figured out, then he'd go and surprise her. They'd had this conversation before. Perhaps, he'd work out the answer before somebody got lucky and took his life, took him from her. She didn't cotton much to the idea of widowhood at age eighteen.

"I'm sort of on the fence, Lisa." Lisa was Luke's affectionate name for Elisa. She, in turn, called him Lucas. "My heart is here. I fully enjoy the family and ranch life at Heaven's Gate. But my inner sense of justice calls me to be a Texas Ranger to protect what we and our neighbors have built." There was always the "but" part.

Elisa understood how important it was that Luke make his decisions on his own for whatever the right reasons were. He needed to be fully happy, as a happy man would be a happy husband and by extension a happy wife and family. She understood his passion for law and justice, though she yearned to keep him ever near. She dared not share her latest news with him just yet—that she was pretty sure she was pregnant with their fourth child. "You've got to make the decision, Lucas. You've always made good decisions, love, so you know I'll support whatever you decide."

In a way, Luke wished she'd tell him to give up the Rangers. It would be so very easy for him to fully commit to ranching and home life. But would he be truly happy, would it totally fulfill him? Would there be a hole lurking in his soul that constantly drew him to correct the wrongs of the world, to bring hope to the broken and justice to the breakers? "Doesn't appear to be full time, Lisa, but it could pull me away for days or weeks at a time, depending on the assignment." In his mind, he was grateful that they could afford Jaime and even a second *vaquero*. Along with Jaime's wife Julia, it considerably lightened the burden on Elisa.

"Why don't you go out for a ride, Lucas? Get some fresh air." She smiled and gave him a light kiss. "You know it does wonders for clear thinking."

★★

"You say Luke Dunn sent you?" Bol Richards gave the young man before him a visual once-over.

"Yes, sir."

"You ever have any lawman experience?"

"No, sir."

"You ever been in a gunfight?"

"Once, sir."

"Did you win?"

"No, sir."

Richards figured since Walker Carson was standing alive and well before him, he couldn't have lost too badly. "You have any weapons other than that 1851 Colt peashooter?"

"No, sir."

"You own that horse and tack?"

"Yes, sir."

"You can stop calling me sir." Richards snuck in a wry smile. "Address me as captain." Richards was apprehensive, but would do as Luke had asked. "Let's see to getting you outfitted."

"Yes, sir, Captain." Carson was trying a little too hard, but it couldn't hurt. An experienced veteran like Richards could be a great mentor for the young man, and Luke surely realized that.

"We're headed to Brownsville in a couple of days, so stay around me and learn what you can. Most of our company is made up of men who've been in battles on both sides of the law, so it's gonna be a bit raw around here and folks might not have much patience. I'm thinkin' it wouldn't be fair to you to throw you to the wolves. First off, we'll get you a new Colt, a Bowie knife, and a Sharps rifle. I assume you've got some money?"

"Yes, Captain, I have some money." Walker thought it best not to tell the source of his small cache of money as paid by Horatio Thorpe.

At Elisa's urging, Luke had saddled his big gray stallion, Big Horse, and began an aimless trek around their Heaven's Gate ranch. The weather was delightful for the end of autumn. He rode tall in the saddle, though he didn't sing any of the Irish ballads he was wont to enjoy when riding about. Now, he was trying to concentrate on weighty decisions. The fall roundup had gone smoothly, and they managed to get several head of cattle to market. The profit would see them through the winter and beyond.

He soon came upon one of the many arroyos that meandered through the ranch, formed at the whim of heavy rains and rushing waters over the dry sandy soil. Big Horse's sudden snort gave him pause to break out of his thinking about Ford's Texas Ranger offer. There, lying beneath a carved-out side of the arroyo, was a body. It was out of view of even the buzzards and apparently hadn't yet been discovered by four-footed scavengers.

Luke scanned the area. There appeared to be no one around. Anyone on horseback would be visible. He listened intently, but the only sound was the rustling of the wiregrass waving in the light breeze. He dismounted and cautiously walked over to what was obviously a dead man. He bent over and turned the body face up. A dead body on his ranch was not to be taken lightly. From the black tunic, cross on a long necklace, and white collar, he judged the man to be a Catholic priest. He had taken a couple of bullets to his chest. The collar had been torn lose. There was no sign of a struggle and no sign that the priest had been armed.

Luke felt a sadness well up within. He'd seen a lot of dead folks in his line of work, but the apparent murder of this man of the cloth had a deeper effect on him.

From his practiced view, Luke guessed that the priest had been shot at least a couple of days before. The bullets had gone clean through. There were no signs of a struggle and the fact that there was not much blood led him to believe the priest had been shot elsewhere and the body deposited in the arroyo. He looked around for any sign, and it didn't take long to discover a trail of hoof prints of a horse coming and going. He could tell the horse was carrying a heavy load by the depth of the indentations of the horse's hooves in the soil relative to other horses. Once he'd made the assumption that the priest had been murdered elsewhere, his next concern was in finding the scene of the crime. He decided to follow the deeper track, which appeared to be heading to the Corpus Christi to San Antonio Road along the banks of the Nueces River. The road was about a mile away.

First, he had to handle the distasteful duty of wrapping the body in a blanket and tying it behind his saddle. The early stages of decomposition didn't help the task. He did his best to be respectful of this man of the cloth.

The trail was easy to follow, thanks to Luke's practiced eye. Clear hoof prints and recently broken blades of grass helped. Soon enough, he found himself on the road. Again, there were no signs of a struggle. He dismounted and headed over to some cypress and pecan trees along the river bank. He hadn't gone far before he found dried blood on the trunk and on the grass and roots around one of the trees. There were plenty of random hoof tracks, as though a horse had been startled and reared up. Luke guessed that the priest had been mounted when he was attacked. The force of the bullets at close range apparently blew the priest from his horse. There was also sign of the priest's horse, but it had likely run off.

Luke soon found two holes in the trunk of a nearby cypress, now home to the two bullets that had apparently passed through the victim. It occurred to Luke to see what caliber bullet had been used, as he figured he could narrow down who the murderer might be. He unsheathed his Bowie knife and carefully dug into the trunk. He was soon able to extricate what appeared to be a couple of .44-caliber slugs. Despite the caliber being common to a lot of weapons on the Nueces Strip, the bullets would help to narrow down his search. Luke's sleuthing pretty much confirmed in his mind that the priest was shot at the cypress grove along the river and then moved to the arroyo where he'd found the body. He was left to ponder what motive the killer might have had.

Luke sighed audibly and began the short ride to nearby Nuecestown. To his mind, this appeared to be a robbery and murder, though he didn't expect the priest would have been carrying much of value.

As he approached the town, he encountered none other than his friend, Corpus Christi Sheriff Bill Meaney. "Bill, glad to see you."

"Whatcha got there, Captain Dunn?" Naturally, he'd already seen that Luke had a dead body draped across his horse.

"Found this priest's body dumped in an arroyo on my ranch. I tracked hoof prints back to the attack scene but found no clues as to who killed him or why. The killer used a 44-caliber bullet, but that's not much help. The priest's horse, if he had one, was gone."

"Damn, that's the third murdered clergyman I've heard about around these parts in the past two months, Luke." Meaney shook his head. "Let's borrow a buckboard and take the body back to the parish in Corpus."

"You say three priests in the past two months, Bill?"

"Yep. All seem to be waylaid along the San Antonio or the Laredo roads. I'm thinking someone is carrying some deep hatred for priests." Meaney reached into the pocket of his vest. "This gold coin was left at one of the killings."

"Think that was meant to be a sign?"

"Twenty dollars is a lot to leave behind."

"I didn't see any coin back up the road where this priest was shot, but neither was I looking for it. Guess I'll go back and be certain. I do feel that I ought to warn Pastor Rucker. He's not a priest, but he should be on guard."

After duly warning his friend Rucker, Luke rejoined Meaney and they rode together toward Corpus Christi.

They stopped along the way to make a longer, more detailed examination of the murder scene, and then they rode to the arroyo where Luke had found the body. After a bit of digging, Luke found a gold coin. "This killer has an expensive signature, Bill. Gotta wonder what his message is." Luke passed the coin to Meaney. "You might contribute this to the parish, Bill. Ought to cover burial."

"I'll put my ear to the ground and see whether there's anyone been talking about being unhappy with the Catholic Church. I expect we can narrow it to someone with enough money to throw away gold coins." Meaney smiled sardonically. "Unless, of course, the killer is throwing around stolen loot."

"Let me know what you find out, Bill. I'll keep my ears open between here and San Patricio." He nodded to his friend. "Looks as though I'll be taking up Rip's offer to serve as a special agent Texas Ranger. He's putting the new company under Bol."

"Damn, Luke. Glad to hear it." Meaney gave Luke a big grin of congratulation before turning away.

With all in order, Luke turned Big Horse and headed back to his ranch to share his decision with Elisa. With all that was stirring on the Nueces Strip, he felt the ever-present pull of bringing justice to the region. The mystery of the murdered priests had reignited his passion for bringing justice to the prairies and towns he'd come to know so well.

Luke needn't have said a word. Elisa could read the look on his face as he rode up to the house. This was the real man she married, torn between ranching and Rangering but tending to choose the latter. His sense of bringing justice to the Nueces Strip was beyond strong.

She wouldn't tell him just yet that she was once again with child. Her love for Luke far transcended her personal wants and needs. He'd need to be reassured that he was making the right decision. She'd known better than to think she could change him when she'd fallen in love and become his wife. The man she loved had just ridden home, and was bedding down his horse. He'd be in her arms soon enough, loving arms to be sure. She felt an almost electric surge course through her body at the thought of his body pressed against hers. Her loins convulsed involuntarily. She wished he'd hurry getting his horse stabled.

TWO
ONCE A WHORE?

THE CARRIAGE WAS brand new and delivered a reasonably smooth ride despite the rough road between Austin and San Antonio. Horatio Thorpe would spend a couple of days in San Antonio to rest up before making the final leg of his journey to Corpus Christi. He was traveling light, and the driver Samuel had found for him seemed capable. He wasn't a professional gunman like some of the others he'd hired.

Thoughts of his plantation estate, Magnolia, were pushed into the distant past. By now, his remaining son Edward had become aware that the huge plantation had actually been put up for sale. Magnolia had been in the Thorpe family for three decades and had been exceedingly profitable. Even the burial plot on the property with its graves of his wife Martha and his son and daughter, did not touch his long-ago steeled heart. After all, it was all about Horatio Thorpe and his personal wealth, power, and influence. Nothing else mattered save what fed his ego, his own measures of self-worth.

Thorpe was convinced that signs pointed to the United

States being ripe for significant political, social, and economic upheaval. John Brown's raid at Harper's Ferry had given just an inkling of what was to come. With nearly 200,000 slaves residing mostly on plantations in eastern Texas, eventual violence was a real possibility. This meant that nearly a third of Texas inhabitants were in bondage. He'd decided to liquidate his holdings. He'd already investigated buying up prime ranching lands in Colorado and Wyoming. In his studied opinion, the tentacles of the slavery issue would not likely extend that far. He had a huge stake in Texas and its politics but, with that damnable Texas Ranger Commander Rip Ford and his minions inching ever closer to rooting out his schemes, Horatio needed to tie up any loose ends, keep his assets protected, and get out of the state.

It's said that every powerful man has a fatal flaw, a weakness that could ultimately spell his doom. Thorpe's fatal flaw was that he had an obsession other than power—it was sex. And it went well beyond his string of brothels. He was deeply obsessed with a whore he'd met in Laredo. He'd been chasing Scarlett Rose for nearly four long years, and she kept eluding his grasp. Every hired thug he'd sent to bring her to him had failed, and most of those failures were attributed to one man: Texas Ranger Captain Luke Dunn. If it was the last thing he ever did, Horatio was determined to have that damned Laredo whore for himself and teach the Texas Ranger a lesson. Obsession indeed. It had become personal, and he was taking matters into his own hands.

Thorpe hadn't used a gun since the Mexican American War when he found himself defending the power base he'd worked so hard to build. He'd marched himself down to Corpus Christi and signed on with General Zachary Taylor. His money bought him a colonel's rank, though Taylor quickly recognized that Thorpe's value was in his influence rather than his battlefield expertise. The man could acquire supplies that were otherwise next to impossible to obtain. Unfortunately, Thorpe's faculty with supplying troops earned him the enmity of fellow officers, the ones that had earned their ranks by dint of performance on the battlefield. More than one threat was made on his life.

One early evening during the war, he'd just finished dinner when a major requested entry to his tent. Thorpe thought nothing of it, even though the officer in question had been known to be angry with the special privileges afforded to Thorpe. The major had been recently passed over for a promotion and considered Thorpe the cause. True or not, any scapegoat would do. At the subsequent court-martial, it was said that the meeting went as follows.

Thorpe looked up as the major entered. "At ease, Major. How can I help you?"

"You sorry-assed son of a bitch." The officer drew his revolver and fired at near point blank range. Incredibly, he missed.

Thorpe grabbed the gun on the table before him and fired before the major could get off a second shot. The wounded officer dropped his gun, turned, and sought to escape. However, the shots brought several enlisted men to Thorpe's tent, and they subdued the major. Importantly, the men had been recipients of a bit of Thorpe's largesse, so were not pleased that anyone would threaten their colonel. They beat the major unmercifully with whatever was handy.

The beating might have normally mitigated the major's sentence upon conviction at court-martial, but that wasn't to be. Even an appeal to General Taylor fell on deaf ears, and the major was summarily executed.

Despite justice having been served, it left a lasting

impression on Thorpe. His fear from that incident forward was such that he began to require that any officers meeting with him be unarmed. He was pretty fair with a revolver in his own right, but reluctant to use it on another person. This attitude followed him back into his world of business and politics.

Now, as he found himself rumbling along the road to San Antonio, he thought on what it might take to lure Scarlett Rose into his lair. In his mind, once a whore, always a whore. He'd dangle enough money in front of the damned Laredo whore that it'd be impossible for her to refuse him.

As for the Texas Ranger, that would likely take more work. The men he'd hired, including one of his own sons, had failed. He kept reminding himself how each failure was linked to the damnable Texas Ranger. Now, with his spy having been killed and no longer serving as a mole in Rip Ford's Austin headquarters, Thorpe was frustratingly clueless as to whether Dunn had been set on his trail. Ford had figured out his schemes, and Dunn had or was in the process of destroying his illegal operations piece by piece. Thorpe had at least another ten days on the road before he reached Corpus Christi. There was plenty of time to develop a strategy to kill the Texas Ranger.

Life was good for Scarlett Rose. Her seamstress business was established, friendships were blossoming, toddler daughter Margaret was growing and yearning to be a helpmeet, and her days of prostitution were long behind her and ever fading from memory. Now and then, she'd remember Sheriff Whelan, his evolving love for her, and how he ultimately gave his life to save hers. She recalled the long-ago wildness with the exciting desperado Dirk

Cavendish and fighting off the predations of the Mexican bandit and hider Carlos Perez. She was grateful both men were dead, brought to justice at the hands of the law. The mere thought of Perez, the horror of his touch, still caused shivers of repulsion to flow through her body.

Scarlett would never forget Horatio Thorpe's son Gascon and his attempt to rape her. She'd come far too close to succumbing to the handsome young man's charms. Gascon had met his end by a bullet from Luke Dunn's guns, a consequence of his trying to ambush the Texas Ranger. But the sins of the son caused her to recall the father and his obsession. Her only lingering fear was Horatio Thorpe. And he was the remaining link the removal of which could help her to totally sever her links with her whoring past. She was now a legitimate business woman.

Of course, there was one more thing that sat in the inner recesses of Scarlett's mind. She wanted a family of her own. Yes, she'd had Margaret, the consequence of a jail cell rape by Sheriff George Whelan, but she wanted so much more. Was it too much to ask? She was still young, a very desirable young woman. Was there a man out there somewhere for her? A real man?

A grateful Bol Richards found Walker Carson to be a fast learner. Luke had been a good judge of potential. It seemed the young man mostly needed someone to show confidence in him. Carson turned out to be a crack shot with the Sharps rifle and handled his newly acquired Colt Navy revolver respectably. The other Rangers in the company quickly accommodated the young man, sparing him the teasing and hazing that they might have been tempted to subject a more wet-behind-the-ears greenhorn to.

Most of Richards's company were experienced with life on the frontier and took their roles as Texas Rangers with due seriousness. As a fast learner, Carson quickly won their respect.

The sun had just crested the horizon and begun to burn off the mid-November night's chill. Twenty-four men sat astride their horses before Captain Bol Richards. Richards's practiced eyes scanned the company. There was minimal consistency appearance-wise. They each had a horse and tack, Texas Ranger badge, Sharps rifle, one or more Colt revolvers, Bowie knife, broad-brimmed cowboy hat, vest, saddlebags, and bedroll. The company had three pack mules loaded with supplies, especially plenty of ammunition. Richards himself had traded most of his frontier buckskins for more traditional garb. He hung onto the fringed buckskin jacket that he saw as his trademark holdover from days fighting Santa Anna's Mexican soldiers and wild Indian savages.

"Rangers, we're gonna ride into Corpus Christi this morning. We must assure the citizens that they will be protected. Colonel Kinney and some local dignitaries will review us, and then we'll be riding out toward Brownsville. Seems we're to have a meeting with a fellow named Juan Cortina." Richards smiled as he delivered the last sentence. It wouldn't likely be the sort of interaction most folks would imagine a meeting to be. The idea would be to deliver a show of Texas strength on the border—something the US Army had singularly failed to accomplish. Seemed as though only the Texas Rangers could manage to have an effective impact on folks like Cortina. The Rangers might be outnumbered five to one or greater, but would invariably defeat their opponents.

Richards took a final scan of the company, turned his horse, and headed toward Corpus Christi with his Rangers following behind in a column of twos. They only had a couple of miles to cover as they'd formed up the company on the bluff overlooking Nueces Bay near Tule Lake.

The company was impressive-looking. As they rode toward the reviewing area Kinney had set up, Scarlett Rose decided to walk up the street. She had heard of the review and the adventurous mission the Texas Rangers would be undertaking. She dressed in a pretty pink dress with ruffles across the bodice and carried a parasol. Her fiery-red hair flowed in waves across her shoulders. She turned just as the company began to ride past. Walker Carson's horse reared a bit, and it was enough to draw her attention to the young man. He easily controlled his mount, but his eyes locked on Scarlett's. He felt some animal magnetism from deep within. She smiled...winsomely. In his peripheral vision, Richards caught the synergy at work. He smiled inwardly.

Once Colonel Kinney's review was completed, Richards led the men out of the city. The entire show had been aimed at giving the fine citizens of Corpus Christi a sense of security. Mission accomplished. However, instead of heading south toward Brownsville, he turned the column northwestward toward Nuecestown.

"Captain, might I ask where we're headed?" Carson was naturally curious as to Richards's intention. Likely, he spoke for the thinking of the rest of the company. The company was enthused at the prospect of kicking bandits and Indians out of Texas.

Richards smiled. "You'll see soon enough. Be patient, Mr. Carson." He turned to the company. "When we get into action, don't ever ask questions about command decisions. That could get you into a heap of trouble."

"Yes, sir." The advice had been delivered just loudly enough that Carson could benefit without being totally embarrassed before the rest of the company.

Roughly an hour later, Richards turned the company through the arched gateway to Heaven's Gate ranch. Now Carson understood. Richards picked up the pace to an orderly canter and soon drew his charges up in front of the Dunn home.

Luke and Elisa had heard them approach and stood on the gallery to greet them.

"Texas Rangers Company C reporting, Captain Dunn." Richards proudly saluted, as his men fanned out in a single line facing the house.

"Damn handsome-looking company, Captain Richards. I wish you Godspeed on your mission." Luke spoke loudly enough for all to hear. "I'm proud of you all. It's great to see the men who will bring justice to the Nueces Strip and peace to all of Texas." He could only hope that their mission would be as effective as hoped. As he thought on that, he caught Carson's eye and nodded recognition to the young man, who nodded respectfully in return. Per frontier etiquette, folks never waved in this and most sorts of situations.

Richards stepped forward so as to be out of earshot of his men. "Captain, I deeply appreciate the trust you've placed in me. I'll do my best not to disappoint you and Texas." He turned toward Elisa. "Ma'am, you've got a fine husband and great Texas Ranger here. Please do take good care of him."

Elisa blushed. "You can count on that, Bol. Y'all are welcome back here at Heaven's Gate any time." In her heart, she could only trust in God that the Rangers and especially Luke would be safe on any assignments that Rip Ford might yet make for them.

Richards saluted, turned his mount, and led the company back up the trail from Heaven's Gate and the road south to Brownsville.

For Walker Carson, he found a deeper respect for Richards and another life lesson embodied in the phrase "thanking those that brung ya."

Thorpe, as per usual, found San Antonio much to his liking. Once settled into his hotel room, he decided to venture out to his favorite local brothel. Before leaving, he gave himself a once-over in the full-length mirror near the bed. He'd been doing a bit of fasting and was convinced it was beginning to pay off. He'd soon be needing a tailor to make adjustments to his suits. His confidence boosted, he headed out for a night on the town, or more accurately a night on a woman.

As he strolled up the avenue, he thought back to when he was first married and how he and Martha enjoyed their passions. As he craved ever more power and control, he'd begun to find deepening satisfaction in the easy control he could enjoy over women simply with money. He enjoyed using that control on the more attractive of his female slaves on Magnolia as his personal concubines. There was more than one mulatto slave on the plantation that folks might think looked remarkably like Horatio Thorpe. Of course, it went without saying that Martha took notice. She had initially tried to overcompensate but soon enough gave up and drew away from him. She bore him three children, but consumption would take her soon enough and at a prime age. Sadly, a son and daughter predeceased her. Horatio couldn't have cared less. He'd long since mentally departed their relationship and the plantation life for the elixir of power found in the Texas state capital.

Thorpe would savor a bit of debauchery this otherwise lonely evening in San Antonio. As was his habit and given that he was the secret owner of the brothel, he demanded and received only the very best whore in the house. In his mind, there was no question: once a whore, always a whore. He was confident that he'd easily win over Scarlett Rose. It was so strong in his mind that he found himself challenged to fully enjoy the bounty of sex at hand. Obsessions seemed to be that way.

THREE
COMANCHE SURVIVAL

IN HIS HUNTS for game around the headwaters of the Brazos River, Penateka Comanche Chief Three Toes felt as though the Great Spirit was trying to communicate with him. It was a sensation that ran deep within his soul. He thought about his friend Ghost-Who-Rides, Texas Ranger Captain Luke Dunn, with whom he'd shared many adventures and learned to respect. While he'd been thoroughly enjoying intimacy with young Cactus Flower and the more mature Bird Woman, he was now faced with them both being pregnant. The chief was nothing if not fertile. Given all he'd been through, his hand-to-hand battle with the mountain lion, his enduring of torture by White men, and his leading of successful raids on settlers, he was also justly proud of his prowess in lovemaking. But the raids had become ever fewer and far between, owing mostly to an insufficient number of remaining warriors with which to mount attacks.

On the one hand, he missed enjoying the pinnacle of his standing with his Penateka Comanche brothers, which he had when he owned six hundred ponies and had five wives. And it had been too long since he'd counted coup and taken scalps. Each eagle feather in his war bonnet revealed his great prowess as warrior and chief among his people.

They were dependent on Three Toes's ability to bring home game. They wisely stayed on the move, as their safety seemed to depend on never lingering too long at any one place.

Despite the pregnancies and the presence of the teen boy, Laughing Crow, the chief continued to fully enjoy the sexual pleasures afforded by Cactus Flower and to a lesser extent by Bird Woman, who were both eager participants. Instinctively, they sought to propagate the race, to produce new warriors to sustain the tribe. Times were desperate for the Comanche. Three Toes seriously considered taking a third wife if he could find a suitable woman. The territory was not exactly teeming with prospects.

Three Toes took long walks and meditated frequently. It engendered a sense of hope, though he found himself ever more willing to accept the White man's ways. Clinging to the old customs was increasingly untenable.

In his walks, the chief often found himself challenging the strength of the Great Spirit with whom he'd sought counsel all his life. He wondered, too, at the cross that hung on the bone bead necklace around his neck that Luke's wife, Elisa, had given to him. She assured him of its ultimate strength. He pondered why these crosses could be found in the burned-out remains and lingering death of many White man's settlements? What was the nature of its strength? Why and what did the White victims of the Comanche pray in their final moments of life? Perhaps one day, Three Toes would see Luke and Elisa again and learn more.

"What are you thinking about, my chief?" Bird Woman

seemed to sense when Three Toes's mind drifted off into some far away spirit place.

"I think on future of Comanche."

"No lose hope?"

"Must always hope, Bird Woman. Comanche waste much of bounty Great Spirit gave us. Now, Comanche must rebuild." He kept telling himself this, as though repetition would make it come true.

Laughing Crow came running into the encampment. "Mighty Chief, bluecoats close."

Three Toes considered breaking down the camp, but there likely wasn't time. They'd camouflaged the camp pretty well, so they'd have to trust that it would be adequate. "Everyone stay silent."

They soon heard the noises of a sizable troop of soldiers moving up the arroyo feeding into the nearby Brazos River. Voices, the sound of horse hooves, the clinking of swords, squeaking of saddle leather, and flapping of the unit standard grew ever louder. They saw the first a mere fifty yards away, and the soldiers were already looking in the direction of the encampment.

The sergeant who was riding a few yards in front of the column called over his shoulder. "Captain Belknap, lookee here, sir."

Cactus Flower and Bird Woman stood behind Three Toes, while Laughing Crow cowered behind their small teepee. What the chief saw brought a smile of guarded relief to his face.

Captain Belknap rode forward toward their camp with four soldiers. "Three Toes?" He had difficulty recognizing the chief right away due to the still-fresh scars on his face.

"Lieutenant Belknap?" The chief moved toward the officer.

To the surprise of his men, Belknap dismounted and

embraced Three Toes. "It's Captain Belknap, now, Chief. It's good to see you."

The soldiers were stunned at what they were seeing. Having been convinced by considerable indoctrination that the only good Indian was a dead Indian, the captain's actions were hard to fully grasp.

"Lieutenant Nelson, have the men bivouac up the canyon a piece. Sergeant Johnson, remain here with me." The men moved on behind the lieutenant, each wearing an inquisitive if not dumbfounded expression as they rode past. "Sergeant, I'm sure you remember our friend Three Toes."

The sergeant was pleased to see that his protégé officer had learned to accept the Comanche chief. "It is good to see you, Chief. Where are all your people?" So much had happened in the handful of months since the troop had been to Utah and back that they'd missed out on Texas Ranger Rip Ford's successes in routing the northern Comanche tribes up on the Canadian and Red Rivers.

"We live." Three Toes really didn't have much to say in response to the sergeant's question. "You welcome to share Comanche fire." It was about as sincere and welcoming an invitation as a Comanche chief might offer. Even Cactus Flower and Bird Woman stepped forward to stand at either side of Three Toes, and Laughing Crow came out from his hiding place with his chest thrust out to show his bravery.

Belknap looked at the sergeant. "Sergeant, I sense an opportunity here. Please let Nelson know that we'll share the chief's hospitality this evening."

The sergeant nodded and rode off up the canyon.

"And Sergeant? Ask Nelson to join us once the men are settled." The implication was that Nelson might learn something about the Comanche in an up close and personal environment that he'd be unlikely to learn anywhere else.

Luke had been thoroughly enjoying the opportunity to work the ranch. Heaven's Gate was continuing to grow. With aggressive property acquisition using cash and minimum debt, the Dunn spread had stretched to a bit more than five thousand acres and featured nearly four hundred longhorns and fifty horses. Luke was training half the horses as cutting horses, as they fetched a fair price from ranchers. He'd helped Elisa plant about a half-acre of vegetables and a flower garden, all of which served food on their table as well as bait for the deer that kept the family in venison for the foreseeable future.

Cattle prices were good, and Luke's cousin up the road a piece shared what he'd been learning about buying and selling livestock. Given present economics, Heaven's Gate was turning a respectable profit.

Sam Houston had been sworn in as governor, and Texans had high hopes for even greater economic revival, especially if the slavery issue could be resolved. Folks seemed to be stubbornly holding to positions on both sides and it tended to haunt most conversations. In plantation-dominated eastern Texas, big money lobbied to continue slavery and lobby to admit states where slavery was permitted. Where talk of leaving the Union arose, there tended to be overwhelming support by Texans. They were an independent lot anyway. The many German immigrants on the other hand tended to be against slavery and very much pro-union. They had primarily immigrated to central Texas not far from the capital, though their voice in Austin wasn't nearly so strong.

Luke rode in with Jaime after a long day checking live-stock around Heaven's Gate and bedded their horses for the night. Luke was relieved to have not found any more bodies of priests, though he warned Jaime to be on the look-out. "I'm not sure who or why, Jaime. Whoever is killing priests must be holding some deep hatred."

"I'll check with my cousins, Señor Dunn. Sometimes they hear things that the Anglos miss." He winked friendly-like, as the barriers between and among races and cultures often produced unexpected perspectives. They were tied into their own networks of friends and families.

Luke nodded to his *vaquero* and headed toward the house.

Elisa heard the jangle of spurs as he neared the house and climbed the front steps. She had dinner ready and waiting for she and Luke to savor. She'd even placed a couple of lighted candles on the table to add just a touch of romance. The twins and their baby daughter were bedded down early.

Luke saw the low light and took in the aromas of fine cooking before he even reached for the door latch. He availed himself of the water bowl by the door, washing up especially well. He knew Elisa had something on her mind. As folks might say, this wasn't Luke's first rodeo. But he figured he had an edge. He'd had the foresight to gather a bouquet of Indian Blanket and Mexican Hat. The vivid combination of reds and yellows would brighten the dining table.

He doffed his hat and stepped into the parlor. "How's the sweetest, most beautiful woman in Texas?"

"Just Texas?" She laughed. "Welcome home, cowboy. How's Heaven's Gate today?"

Luke sidled up behind her and wrapped his well-muscled arms around her. The bouquet found its way into her hands. He'd likely have wrapped around her twice given his size, and she'd have enjoyed it twice as much. His hands found her belly and paused. He stepped back, turned her toward him, and looked quizzically into her eyes. The flowers dropped to the floor.

Elisa looked up at her man. "What?" she said softly.

"Again?" Luke smiled.

She nodded. "I think God wants us to have a big family, Lucas Dunn."

He brought her close and they held each other tightly, letting love course through the moment.

Of a sudden, there was a sizzling sound. "Uh-oh, we'd better eat, Lucas. Wouldn't do to have a burned dinner." She pulled away and motioned to him to sit at the table. He obliged, picking the flowers up from the floor on his way and dutifully stuffing them in a vase.

He sat back and watched her as she piled the bounty of her cooking labors on a couple of plates. She had even baked the to-die-for cornbread she was becoming famous for. Luke watched her every move in wonderment at how this hard-working petite young woman he'd married, who'd born him three children already, remained so incredibly beautiful and sexy. She had found a way to make perfume from flower petals and, along with her natural beauty, created an irresistible allure that never failed to draw him in. Luke fully appreciated how lucky he was.

They ate slowly. Except for Elisa excusing herself once to feed Andrea Ann, they enjoyed a quiet romantic dinner.

After they finished the meal, Luke got up to start clearing the table, but Elisa stopped him. She gave him the most wanton sexy look he'd ever seen cross her delicately beautiful face.

"Leave it for later, Lucas." She took his hand and led him over to the mountain lion skin laying before the fireplace. Along the way, bits of her clothing dropped to the floor. Half-naked, she turned to him and began to unbutton his shirt. She drew close and absorbed the sensation of his skin against her full breasts. They dropped to the floor. Luke's lips forced hers apart, and she yielded to him. His hands caressed her body, sending near-orgasmic shivers coursing through her. Their carnality knew no bounds as they absorbed each other in heated passion. Their ardor spewed forth in seemingly limitless crescendos, and they made love until exhaustion forced them to simply lie in each other's arms by the warmth of the fire for what would seem to be forever.

Luke awakened to find Elisa's place next to him in the bed empty. He didn't remember ever having left their carnal lust on the mountain lion skin. The sounds and aromas of eggs and bacon wafted up from the kitchen, and he could hear Peter and John prattling about something. He dressed quickly and strolled into the kitchen, hugging each of his boys and giving Elisa a brief but loving kiss. Last night was still very much on his mind.

"Sit down, cowboy, and I'll serve up some grub." She laughed at her feigned camp cookie talk.

As Luke sat, he couldn't help but notice the envelope next to his place setting. Texas Ranger Commander Rip Ford had sent something official. He smiled, as Elisa had undoubtedly received it the day before and hadn't wanted it to interrupt their evening. She was a smart lady.

"I guess he has an assignment, Lucas."

Luke opened the envelope, read the letter, and set it aside.

Elisa looked questioningly at him. "What's it about?"

"Horatio Thorpe is headed our way. Rip wants me to keep an eye on him."

"Is that all?"

Luke sighed. "Thorpe is a very wealthy, very powerful man, Lisa. He's been up to no good, but the law hasn't been able to gather enough evidence to arrest him. Thorpe's used to getting whatever he wants, and lately I've been a thorn in his rather large backside. Rip says the man is obsessed with Scarlett Rose and blames me for many of his problems. Bern Culthwaite, Roy Biggs, and Thorpe's son Gascon were all hired to get me out of his way so he could feed his lustful obsession."

Elisa stepped behind Luke and massaged his shoulders to relax him a bit. "So, it's more than keeping an eye on him."

Luke nodded.

The journey to Brownsville was slow going. Richards's Rangers were primed for the action they anticipated against the Mexican rebels Juan Cortina had been deploying along the border. Their objective would be to force Cortina's bandits to stay south of the Rio Grande, inflicting whatever damage might be necessary. The mission was complicated somewhat by Cortina's frequent dalliances on his mother's ranch a few miles west of Brownsville. At any sign of trouble, he'd slip south into Matamoros.

The column was into its fifth day when it approached the little hamlet of Norias. The town would eventually serve as a shipping point and division headquarters for the King Ranch, but for now it was simply a sleepy cluster midway between Brownsville and Corpus Christi. Bol Richards was concerned that the place seemed unusually quiet. He pulled up before what seemed to be the main building, a sort of combination hut, store, and saloon. Richards did a double-take as he realized that the man who seemed to be asleep on the bench in front of the store was dead. He'd been shot.

Richards had no sooner dismounted for closer inspection than a young man staggered through the doorway. He was bleeding from a wound caused by a bullet that had grazed his forehead.

"Whoa! Who are you and what's happened here?" Richards had his revolver at the ready and was backed up by a bristling array of rifles in the hands of his Rangers.

The man leaned back against the wall and slowly slid to the ground. He looked up at the Texas Ranger captain. "Apache. Twenty or more." He wiped some of the blood from his head. He was a bit dizzy but tried to describe what had happened. "Came out of nowhere. Shot us up pretty good. Stole a bunch of guns and ammuni..." He passed out.

"Carson! See to this man. The rest of you see if there are other victims of those damned savages."

Three more victims were found, two killed and one other wounded. Three women were hunkering in a nearby hut and were unharmed. The women tended to the wounded men, and at least one was deeply grieved at the loss of her husband. It was beginning to appear that Company C of the Texas Rangers would be diverted from their trip to Brownsville.

Richards had been looking to use his finely honed tracking skills and was finally getting a chance. He regretted the circumstances, but promised the Norias residents that he'd bring the Apache to justice, that Apache blood would be spilled.

It wouldn't be difficult picking up the Apache trail. If there were as many warriors as the folks in Norias were describing, they'd have a tough time hiding any trail. He knew that people under duress often exaggerated their descriptions of attackers, but even if it were only a half dozen warriors, they'd be leaving plenty of signs.

★★

Three Toes couldn't grasp what the White man's army was thinking by sending Belknap on such a long journey to the faraway place they called Utah and then having him return to Texas. In fact, the chief was wondering what the blue-coats were doing in Texas at all, since the Texas Rangers had already been quite effective at battling his Comanche people.

"Where are you heading, Three Toes?" Belknap was genuinely curious as they sat around the campfire. A mild chill had swept in from the northeast as the first signs of winter began to descend upon the region.

Three Toes took a long and thoughtful pull on the pipe they were passing. "West, away from agency camps and White settlers. Where do you go, Captain?"

"I've been assigned to Fort Ringgold near Rio Grande City. You know of it?"

The chief smiled. "Yes. Ghost-Who-Rides and Three Toes have been to Laredo. Almost went to Rio Grande City."

"Your smile tells me that your visit was good." Belknap studied the life experiences written across Three Toes's body and embedded in his eyes. The scars spoke of a survivor, of both a wily tough foe and trusted friend.

"Twice we defeat men you call outlaws."

Having met and even fought together, Belknap was invariably amazed at Three Toes's experiences and his unusual relationship with Luke Dunn. The chief seemed the antithesis of the Comanche way of life until one saw the scalps hanging from his lodge pole, the multiple wives, a penchant for torturing victims, and a passion for keeping lots of horses. Belknap felt that he, like Luke, had developed a special relationship with Three Toes built out of a trust and respect similar to what the chief established with Luke. "Time is passing quickly, Chief."

The chief understood Belknap's implication. He sighed deeply. "Yes, Captain. And Comanche time will come."

Belknap read the chief's response as a for-better-or-worse answer and decided not to press further. They went on to make small talk until they parted ways to their separate camps. By morning, they'd all be gone on their own journeys.

FOUR
RETRIBUTION

IT WASN'T what Horatio Thorpe had expected. The telegraph message had finally caught up with him between San Antonio and San Patricio. He was confident that his son Edward would have headed back to Philadelphia after burying his mother and being told that the family plantation, Magnolia, was to be sold.

"Son of a bitch," he thought to himself. Somehow, Edward had assembled the resources to purchase Magnolia for himself. This put a different perspective on Thorpe's mission. While residually amazed at his son's apparent financial prowess, he was relieved to now have the ready assets to purchase property beyond the reach of the divisive politics of Washington, DC while enabling him to maintain power and influence by virtue of his other extensive business holdings. His shipping business was thriving and modest string of brothels remained profitable. He seemed to have extricated and distanced himself neatly from the Indian agency scam he'd engineered. He lamented that his man Peter O'Rourke was no longer accessible as a mole in Rip Ford's office, owing to his killing at the hands of

Apaches. It left him a bit blind as to Texas Ranger operations.

He'd have to get a message of congratulations back to Edward, though in his heart he lamented that his son failed to see the danger to the plantation way of life that lurked on the horizon. Thorpe had visions of some future time, when Magnolia would fall prey to an armed slave uprising or, equally bad, take over by federal forces.

Meanwhile, he remained determined to take the Laredo whore as his own and settle the score with Luke Dunn. It wouldn't be easy, as the Nueces Strip was now swarming with Texas Rangers, and Dunn was a worthy opponent by any measure.

Richards had picked up the trail of the Apache right quickly. From what they'd learned from the victims in Norias, the savages couldn't be more than a couple of hours ahead. They had run pretty hard due south for a couple of miles before having been brought to a slower pace by the couple of cattle they'd stolen and the weight of the extra guns and ammunition they'd swiped from the general store. Richards's intuition held that the Apache would make camp by mid-afternoon, as they were highly unlikely to suspect that they were being followed.

After about four hours, Richards brought the company to an abrupt halt. He looked long and hard at the ground to his right. The pony tracks revealed that the Apache had split up. "Sons of bitches," he muttered.

"What is it, Captain?" Carson seemed always close at hand.

"They ain't stupid. They sent some of their warriors to the west to double back and see whether anyone was following." He shook his fist in the general direction of where the Apache were likely headed. Richards licked his finger and held it high. "Seems as though the wind is from the west, so it ain't likely they'd hear or smell us." He raised his spyglass. "Can't see them yet."

"What are we going to do, Captain? They going to spring a trap?"

Richards ignored Carson's pestering with questions. "Johnson! You, Carson here, and the rest of your patrol dismount, hide out alongside that Apache track, get your horses to lay down, and ready those Sharps rifles. When they come into sight, we'll take off, and y'all shoot the hell out of them when they chase after us." It was simple enough. With the devastating power of the Sharps, any Apache hit would likely be a dead Apache.

The Rangers didn't have to wait but about fifteen minutes before Richards spotted an Apache, then two, then about a half dozen. "Let's ride, Rangers!" Richards whooped, waved his hat, and led his decoys east at a gallop.

The Apache fell for the trap, likely thinking the White men were stupid. They jammed their heels into their pony's sides and took off after the Texas Rangers. Moments later, they'd ridden into a deadly hail of bullets. The 50-caliber slugs devastated the Apache and their ponies. None survived. The Apache hadn't even fired a shot.

Richards brought his men to a halt and doubled back to assess the damage. No Rangers were harmed, though a bullet from a Sharps had put a hole clean through Carson's hat.

"All right, men, gather 'round." The company joined up with Richards. "The other Apache likely heard the shooting and will send warriors back this way to check on their brothers. We're gonna give them something to mess with their heads." He pointed west. "Let's head that way, then we'll turn south, and surprise the main body of Apache. It's gonna be a hard ride, Rangers." He scanned the company. He was met with looks of determination. They were flush with confidence from their initial victory and ready to follow Bol Richards just about anywhere. "Follow me!" Richards headed west at a canter.

About two miles out, the captain turned southward. He figured that by the time the Apache scouts had found the scene of the recent skirmish, he'd be on top of the remaining warriors. He rode a bit further and turned eastward.

Sure enough, he so surprised the Apache that his Texas Rangers were on top of the savages and firing revolvers at close range before the Indians knew what hit them. The Rangers delivered all sorts of whooping and hollering that further added to the confusion among the Apache. When the dust of the melee had settled, only a cloud of gun smoke hung in the air, and the groans of a couple of dying Apache could be heard, Richards took stock of his situation. Two Rangers had been wounded but not seriously. All told, ten Apache lay dead or dying. All the stolen goods were accounted for. He spotted two Apache that had been sent to the previous battle scene, but they lit out when they realized the Rangers had won.

"What about those two, Captain?" Another question from Walker Carson.

"Let them go. They can tell their brothers that there's hell to pay if they mess around with Texans on the Nueces Strip."

Richards got his Rangers to organize the wagons and pack horses stolen by the Apache and assigned four men to take the goods back to Norias. "Let them know the price the Apache paid." And he turned the company to continue the ride south to Brownsville. They still had a date with Juan Cheno Cortina.

"Bernice…Agatha…howdy. How are my favorite ladies in Nuecestown?" Luke had ridden in early from Heaven's Gate and decided to stop at the boarding house first to offer greetings and then to benefit from the ladies' hospitality.

"Why, Luke Dunn, howdy indeed. Come on in and enjoy some coffee." The ladies had just finished serving breakfast to a couple of guests at their boarding house. "Tell us about Elisa and the children."

They spent the next hour chatting or more accurately gossiping, before Luke had to depart to visit a few other folks around the town. Before leaving, he reminded them, "Y'all please do watch out for Mr. Thorpe. We think he may have some ill intentions toward Miss Scarlett." The seriousness of his expression spoke volumes about the gravity of the threat.

Luke spent the remainder of the morning riding about Nuecestown alerting the folks to be sure to let him know when Horatio Thorpe arrived. He pretty much was of a mind that Thorpe had enjoyed Bernice and Agatha's hospitality at their boarding house back when he'd retrieved his son's body and would likely stop there before heading into Corpus Christi. Luke figured him for a creature of habit.

His final stop before heading back to Heaven's Gate was at Doc Andrew's place. It just so happened that Pastor Rucker was visiting with Doc at the time. The door opened as Luke reached to knock.

"Why, Captain Dunn, great to see you on this fine December morning." Rucker was in exceptionally good spirits. His sons would be visiting over the upcoming Yuletide season, both on leave from the West Point Military Academy. "What brings you to Nuecestown?"

"Horace, Doc, good to see y'all." Luke was sounding ever more like a Texan and less Irish-Texan. "I'm alerting the good folks about the expected visit of a man named Horatio Thorpe."

Rucker's eyebrows went up. "He simply won't give up, will he? Seems about as evil as they come."

Doc understood the dynamic and appreciated Rucker's sentiments. After all, Rucker had helped bring down Thorpe's Indian agency fraud ring. He'd been a US Army colonel under General Truax, who'd been Thorpe's right-hand-man in stealing from forts and Indian agencies throughout Texas and then selling the goods overseas through Thorpe's shipping company. "We'll keep our eyes peeled for sure, Luke. What's that lyin' swindler want around here?"

"He mainly harbors some sort of obsession toward Scarlett Rose, but I've got a feeling he wants a piece of my hide for killing his son, not to mention the other ne'er-do-wells he sent to kill me."

Rucker shook his head and nervously cracked his fingers. "I better not see him first." At Luke's advice, he wore a sidearm. He absentmindedly stroked the butt of the revolver. It had become a necessity for men of the cloth on the Nueces Strip.

"Now, Pastor, I don't want folks taking the law into their own hands. It's my job to rein in this sorry excuse for manhood. Rip Ford asked me to bring Thorpe to justice, and I aim to do exactly that."

"You can count on us, Luke."

Luke appreciated that Rucker had helped Doc maintain sobriety after many years of being the town drunk. "I know I can depend on you both." He fully valued these two men.

Rucker had saved Luke's life by shooting the man Thorpe had hired to kill him and then rode off to fetch Doc who tended that grievous wound Luke received from the would-be killer. It was hard to believe that nearly two years had passed since that terrible night. Elisa had feared she'd lost him. Luke fully trusted Doc and Rucker to do the right thing as concerned Thorpe.

Thorpe drew the small slip of paper from his vest pocket, fumbling with it a moment as the carriage jostled along. The little paper represented a little secret. He'd found it in Gascon's pocket. Frankly, he was surprised that no one else had found it. He permitted himself a self-satisfied sigh and a bit of a smile. Written on the well-worn paper scrap was the precise address of Scarlett Rose's seamstress business in Corpus Christi.

Now, he figured that the folks in Nuecestown might remember him from his visit a few months back to retrieve his son Gascon's body. He also felt that word of his travels would likely arrive ahead of him. There was no point in unnecessarily alerting the folks in the little ferry town, as he rightly thought it made more sense to sneak into Corpus Christi unannounced and under cover of darkness.

They were but two miles from the Nuecestown ferry crossing, when Thorpe called out. "Crane, pull up here!"

The driver brought the carriage to a halt. "Yes, sir, Mr. Thorpe. Is there a problem, sir?"

"I'm going the rest of the way by horseback. You camp here until I return. I might be a day or two, so don't go getting impatient. The other half of your pay awaits you in Austin, Crane."

Thorpe proceeded to unhitch the horse from the back of

the carriage, saddle him up, and mount. After several days behind the carriage, the horse likely had mixed feelings at being ridden, especially by a man of Thorpe's ample size.

Crane watched, suppressing a bit of a laugh as the horse indeed seemed to protest Thorpe's weight. "Do you want the rifle, Mr. Thorpe?"

"No, I won't be needing it just yet." Thorpe turned and rode off.

Instead of turning south to the ferry landing to cross the Nueces River, he headed eastward until he reached the north shore of Nueces Bay. Taking the ferry, after all, would have required him to ride through Nuecestown. A few miles farther on, he took advantage of another secret he carried with him. He'd done some inquiring in San Antonio and learned about an oyster shell reef that separated Nueces Bay from Corpus Christi Bay. For years, it had been a secret pathway for horse-thieving Comanche and other tribes to avoid going the longer route around the bay. He found it quickly enough and headed confidently across to Corpus Christi. Once on the south shore, he found a place to rest while waiting for the sun to set.

As nightfall approached, Thorpe headed toward the city. He rode past the house where Scarlett rented a second-floor apartment. He could see oil lamp light flickering from the windows. There was an outside stairway that led up to the entrance. He thought it wise to wait a couple of hours, as he recalled she had a daughter. It'd be best if the little girl were asleep.

He hitched his horse and took up a post across the street from where he could watch the windows of her place. He kept an eye on passersby, especially being on guard for the sheriff.

Finally, the light was extinguished in one of the rooms. It was like a signal. He looked up the street both ways, crossed over, and tiptoed up the stairway. He reached the landing. He knew that knocking at this hour wouldn't work. She'd be half scared to death. Neither would it do to break the door down. It was for this moment that he'd saved his final secret, his ultimate trick.

Thorpe pulled a whistle-like instrument from his pocket. He put it to his lips and blew into it, gently at first. The damn thing sounded just like a kitten in distress. What woman could resist a kitten in distress?

He heard rustling noises inside. He blew again.

The door lock turned, and Scarlett opened the door just enough to peek out at the landing.

Thorpe lunged forward, grasped her, placed his hand over her mouth, and forced his way into the apartment. "Be quiet. Make a sound, and I'll kill you and your daughter." His meaty hand pressed hard against her. "You gonna be quiet?"

She tried to nod yes as her panic-filled eyes peeked above the massive hand held over most of her face.

Thorpe slowly lifted his hand from her mouth but held her around the waist in a bear hug-like grip. "You remember Laredo, you whoring bitch?" He sneered the words out.

Scarlett stiffened at the sound. She knew now who this was. But fear was quickly giving way to cold calculation. How could she escape this dilemma? She tried to calm down. "Yes...yes, I remember." The man was nearly twice her size but she recalled that his manhood was undersized.

Thorpe tore at her nightgown while forcing her back onto a table. In a heartbeat, she was nearly naked and lying with her legs forced apart, giving him full access to her vulnerability. He still held her tightly, as he unfastened his trousers.

Scarlett's eyes darted about looking for a weapon.

"You look at me, you whore bitch," Thorpe snarled. He pressed his lips hard against her mouth, forcing her lips to part. He drove his now-erect penis into her, thrusting again and again. It took him but a moment, and he was finished.

For Scarlett, it brought back ugly memories of her life back in Laredo. Only now she felt even more defiled.

Thorpe smiled one of those sick, smirky, self-satisfied smiles that one might imagine a rapist giving his victim. Thorpe had waited a long time for this moment, and he was determined to have her in the future any time he wanted her. He grabbed her dress and wiped himself before refastening his trousers.

Scarlett couldn't maintain eye contact with him. She turned her head. "What…what do you want with me?"

"Why, Scarlett, my dear, we're going to do a bit of traveling. Put your nightgown back on, sit, and listen." He backed off of her. He pulled a large wad of money from his pocket. It was quite clearly a lot of money, more than she could ever hope to see in years of being a seamstress. He placed it on the table with nary a blink of his lecherous eyes.

She repeated her question. "What do you want of me?"

"I'm a widower now, Miss Scarlett. My son has purchased my Magnolia plantation, so I intend to purchase land and build a new life. My intention is for you and your daughter to come live with me."

Scarlett was perplexed at how this beast of a man could so quickly separate a violent rape from sharing his dream of taking her somewhere far away as his live-in mistress. "You actually expect me to do what you're asking?"

The way she responded didn't rightly make sense to a man used to always having his way. He looked her over from head to toe, his eyes pausing at her still-heaving breasts. She was as beautiful as he'd remembered her.

"Damn, Scarlett. Do you understand what I'm offering? All you'll need to do is keep my cock happy, and you can otherwise do as you will."

Her mind was roiling over ways that she might escape from this lunatic. She had the old Colt revolver in her desk drawer, but getting to it was chancy at best. She prayed that little Margaret wouldn't awaken.

"Now, I'm going to leave for now. You gather a couple of things you'll be needing, and I'll buy whatever else you need when we get to Austin. I'll be back first thing in the morning. You be ready to travel. Don't be doing anything foolish that might not end well for you and your little girl." He punctuated his threat with a villainous sneer.

Scarlett nodded and forced herself to offer just a hint of a fetching smile. She had to reassure the man were she to have any prayer for escape.

Thorpe tipped his hat and stepped from her apartment. He paused at the landing, a self-satisfied smile on his face. "Yes," he thought to himself, "she was worth waiting for." He thought about forcing himself on her again, but decided she'd be worth the waiting until morning.

The pause on the landing was costly. She'd reached her desk drawer. The bullet from Scarlett's Colt revolver ripped through the door and tore on into Thorpe's arm. "Stay away, you son of a bitch!" She screamed it as loudly as she could. You'd have thought all of Corpus Christi would have been awakened.

Thorpe staggered both from the force of the 44-caliber slug and the sudden pain. He tumbled down the stairway.

Scarlett stepped onto the landing and aimed the Colt down at him.

Thorpe was gasping for air. "You damned bitch."

She fired again, but missed.

Thorpe got up and staggered his way to the horse

hitched across the street. He managed to mount despite the excruciating pain in his arm.

Scarlett got off one more shot, missing again just as Sheriff Bill Meaney came running.

"Scarlett, what's happened? Are you all right?" He looked up at her from the street.

She was leaning against the railing with the revolver dangling at her side. "He…he raped me, Sheriff." She pointed at the now fast-escaping Thorpe. The momentary stillness was broken by a crying child inside Scarlett's apartment.

"Do you know who did it?"

"What are you just standing there for? Go after him, Sheriff!"

"Damn, Scarlett, do you know who I'm gonna be chasing?"

"Thorpe. Horatio Thorpe." She sat or, more accurately, crumpled on the top step of the stairway. "Please get him. I think I wounded him." She felt so tired, so violated.

"We won't find him in the dark, Scarlett. We'll chase him down first thing in the morning. He won't get far, especially if it's a bad wound." Meaney tried to be sympathetic. There really wasn't much he could do. He recalled Thorpe from when he had retrieved his son's body, so he knew what the man looked like. "You want I should get you some help, Scarlett?"

She shook her head. "No…thanks, Sheriff. I need to tend to Margaret." She got up and went back inside. She prayed that the smarmy son of a bitch hadn't made her pregnant. That would be the very worst. She sat on Margaret's bed and soon succumbed to exhaustion as she wondered whether she'd ever outlive her sordid past. She had to put this behind her once and for all.

Luke had gotten up early to head into Corpus Christi. He intended to warn Sheriff Meaney to be on the lookout for Horatio Thorpe and to alert Scarlett of the man's apparent intentions. He had no idea that Thorpe had taken a shortcut and already wreaked his havoc.

He pulled up in front of the sheriff's office to find Meaney especially well-armed, with a saddled horse ready to ride. He had his deputy with him. "Bill, what's going on?"

"Horatio Thorpe was here last night. He raped Scarlett, then escaped. She thinks she wounded him, and the blood on the stairway to her place confirms that."

Luke was deeply affected. He felt as though he'd failed Scarlett. It didn't matter that he couldn't have known of Thorpe's devious plan. It was terribly disconcerting to his lawman's way of thinking. "Mind if I join you?"

Meaney nodded. "Could always use an extra gun, Luke."

For a while, they were able to follow a blood trail. Thorpe had bled for about a mile before he'd stopped and striven to stem the flow of blood. They even found a place where he'd apparently rested. His horse's tracks went up to the shore and into Corpus Christi Bay. "Looks like he knew about the shell road, Bill. We'd best be careful. We could be easy targets for a man lying in ambush on the opposite shore."

"If we go around Nueces Bay, he'll surely escape, Luke."

"If it's a choice between careful and stupid, Bill, I much prefer careful. No point one of us getting killed."

"What do you suggest?"

"I'm thinking that we set your deputy here with the

Sharps rifle to keep a lookout. You and I will go the long way around."

Meaney knew that Luke made perfect sense. "We'd better hustle." He turned to the deputy. "You heard Captain Dunn, Smithy. Keep your eyes out for a big man with a gunshot wound trying to come back across the shell road."

Luke and Meaney rode west at a gallop. They hoped Thorpe had lost enough blood to be weakened and have to stop frequently to rest.

★★

Thorpe pulled up to the carriage by the roadside where he'd left it the day before. His hired hand Crane was sleeping in the shade underneath. At the sound of Thorpe's approach, the man roused from his slumber. "Mr. Thorpe?"

Thorpe dismounted and leaned against the carriage wheel.

"Damn, Mr. Thorpe! What the hell happened?" He helped Thorpe to sit in the shade. "Whew! You got tore up pretty good."

"I've got some liniment in the small case inside. Get that for me, Crane."

"Who done this, Mr. Thorpe?"

Too many questions. "None of your business. It's enough that I got shot…bushwhacked, if you must know." There was no way he was going to admit to having been shot by a woman. That was far too embarrassing for his perverted sense of manhood.

Crane did a fairly decent job of bandaging Thorpe's arm. The bullet had torn the forearm up quite a bit and had gone through without breaking any bones. How it missed the man's torso was anyone's guess. Likely as not, Thorpe wouldn't have walked away from that.

Despite the loss of blood, Thorpe was able to keep his wits about him. He'd never been shot before and found it a decidedly unappealing experience. He began to have serious second thoughts about spiriting away the Laredo whore, much less chasing after Luke Dunn.

"What are we going to do, Mr. Thorpe?" It was a reasonable question given the circumstances.

"I'm thinking, Crane. I'm thinking on it." He figured it was a fair bet that the sheriff had been alerted and would be chasing him. He thought about setting an ambush, but wasn't inclined to place himself at risk. Getting shot once was more than enough.

On the other hand, he thought back to the violence he'd wreaked on Scarlett. It had been exciting for him. Despite being weakened by his wound, it created an image in his mind's eye that served to arouse him. He simply had to have her again. He looked over at Crane, who still wore a what-do-we-do-next expression. Kidnapping Scarlett would have to wait. The sheriff and possibly that damnable Texas Ranger were surely on his trail.

"We're going to live to fight another day, Mr. Crane. Get the team ready. We're heading back to San Antonio."

Luke was grateful for the lack of rain and the road north of the Nuecestown ferry landing. There'd been a couple of folks passing through that morning, but he quickly found the horse with a deeper hoof print. The poor beast was carrying a mighty heavy load. "Looks as though we've picked up our man's trail, Bill. At the pace he was riding, the horse is sure to need rest." The implication was that it likely wouldn't take long to catch up with Thorpe.

About two miles up the road from the ferry, the horse

track ended. They'd come upon the spot where Thorpe's carriage had been waiting. They found a place by the roadside where someone had rested in the grass. There were traces of blood. "Damn, Luke. Looks like Thorpe had help."

"I'm guessing from the wheel ruts that it's a carriage. Looks like they tethered the horse to the back. No telling how far ahead they are by now with that danged contraption."

"You up to giving chase, Luke?"

Luke thought about what Scarlett might think if they returned empty-handed. Logic held that Thorpe had at least one hired hand with the carriage, and they didn't know the nature of that threat. It could be two or three men for all they knew. "Not sure we'll get another opportunity like this, Bill. He can't be too far ahead. How about you and your deputy here? You up to it?"

Meaney considered that they'd be moving out of his jurisdiction as sheriff. It felt a little lame to use that as an excuse, but it was legitimate.

Luke had a sense for the machinations of the sheriff's thinking. "No pressure, Bill. I understand. You have to do what's legal." He avoided referring to doing right as opposed to legal. "If it makes a difference, I'm going after him."

FIVE
OBSESSED

THE CARRIAGE WAS STILL a few miles from San Patricio when Thorpe had Crane pull over under the shade of a few trees alongside the river. He stepped from the carriage and stood for a moment, looking thoughtfully back up the road from whence they'd come. He couldn't let loose of the image of Scarlett, not to mention lascivious thoughts of how she felt under him. He was so close, yet so far.

"Crane, you take this carriage back to Austin. Here's a note to give to my man Samuel for the balance of your pay."

"You going out on your own, Mr. Thorpe?"

"Don't really have a choice." Thorpe knew he wasn't far from the tiny hamlet of Beeville, where he could recuperate in hiding and plan his next move. He handed Crane a second note. "Give this to Samuel as well. He'll pass it along to my son."

Thorpe unhitched the horse. He looked up the road again and then looked down at ruts caused by the carriage. If anyone was tracking him, it'd be too easy. He decided to walk his horse among the grasses by the roadside before breaking northeast toward Beeville.

He was pleased with his decision to get rid of the suit and vest. After a couple of weeks on the journey from Austin, he'd actually lost just enough weight that it had begun to hang on him. He'd had the good sense to bring suspenders, and they served to keep his pants from falling down around his ankles. A blue cotton shirt, broad-brimmed hat, riding boots, and leather jacket completed his traveling garb. He felt fortunate that winters in the Corpus Christi region were fairly mild. Soon enough, he gave a nod to Crane and headed to Beeville. He actually felt pretty good considering the throbbing of his arm.

He knew that this entire business with the Laredo whore and the Texas Ranger was nothing short of idiotic. Even to his own mind, the obsession was so out of hand that he realized he was likely not playing with a full deck. It'd been years since he'd done this sort of thing—cat and mouse, the hunter and the hunted. He'd climbed into the proverbial saddle and now he had no choice but to ride. This was a far cry from his endeavors of the past few years, but he was warming up to spicing his life with some adventure. He'd tied himself up in Magnolia plantation, his shipping busi-ness, politics, and illicit activities for far too long. He'd been totally focused on business and his lustful pursuits to the exclusion of his family. He hadn't yet realized that each conquest was simply making him hungry for the next. The prizes served as ever-sparser meals for his appetites. The lines blurred as to who was conquering who. Would taking Scarlett for himself and giving the Ranger his comeuppance truly satisfy him?

★★

It took a couple of hours, but Luke managed to catch up with the carriage. He was now on his own, as he'd sent Meaney and his deputy back to Corpus Christi. He didn't envy the sheriff telling Scarlett they'd hadn't captured Thorpe. Given her state of mind, he'd be lucky not to get shot for what she'd view as ineptitude.

He spurred Big Horse on to pull alongside the carriage. "Hey, pull your rig over!" Luke flashed his Texas Ranger badge.

Crane brought the carriage to a halt. "Yes, sir. Can I help you?"

"I'm Texas Ranger Captain Luke Dunn. Who are you and where's Horatio Thorpe?" He gave the man a hard, I-mean-business look that would have melted ice.

Crane didn't figure to get afoul of a Ranger with the reputation of this one. There was no point in lying, as he'd get paid no matter the outcome. "My name's Crane. Mr. Thorpe rode off on his own a few miles back, Captain Dunn. He told me to get on back to Austin."

"Did he tell you where he was headed?"

"No sir. I'm thinkin' he hopes to get back to Corpus Christi. I think it's about a woman." Crane tried to look innocent.

"He's wounded," Luke said. "How badly?"

"That 44-caliber slug tore his forearm up a bit, but he's mostly as okay now as you might expect. But he won't be holdin' no gun in that hand for a while."

To Luke's thinking, how badly Thorpe was wounded would determine how long he'd lay low before going after Scarlett again. It sounded like his arm had been shredded a bit by Scarlett's shot. "You carrying any messages to deliver for him?"

Crane flinched. He wasn't anxious to give up the notes

Thorpe had entrusted him with. Then again, he wasn't the trustworthy sort.

"I'm asking one more time." The implied threat couldn't be missed.

Crane handed over the note intended for Thorpe's son.

Luke opened it, read it, and handed it back. "And the other note?"

"That's for me, so I can get paid by Mr. Thorpe's man in Austin."

There wasn't much else for Luke to do. "What direction was Mr. Thorpe headed?"

"He was headed east and a bit north. Didn't say to where, Captain."

Luke had a vague notion as to where Thorpe might hide out. If Thorpe's wound was as serious as Crane described, he'd likely have a few days to hunt him down. If by some chance Thorpe made it back to Corpus Christi, he'd likely use that shell road again. Luke turned back to find where Thorpe had left the road.

★★

Bol Richards led his company into Brownsville. They rode smartly in a column of twos, displaying the Texas flag and the company standard. Richards had decided to give the men a much-needed rest for one night before heading off to Fort Brown and reconnoitering the area to find signs of Juan Cortina. He knew the red-bearded Cortina had an outstanding arrest warrant for stealing a couple of cattle.

The men were instructed to be on their best behavior and report back to their encampment by midnight. After three weeks on the trail and having fought a passel of Apache, he could only hope the men would stay out of trouble. He didn't want to deal with the local sheriff, and he knew that Cortina's mother's hacienda wasn't far away. In fact, it was seven or eight miles west of Brownsville. He'd need his men refreshed and ready to take on whatever Cortina threw their way. The man pretty much went back and forth across the Rio Grande with impunity.

Just as Richards felt strong loyalty to Texas and all he had given of himself to help carve the Republic away from Mexico, Cortina saw Texas as part of Mexico and held to a passion to fan the flames of social unrest toward achieving annexation. This translated into a mixed bag of national loyalties among the Hispanic populations along the Texas side of the Rio Grande. Richards would have to deal with many Cortina sympathizers.

Accompanied by Walker Carson and two other Texas Ranger compatriots, Richards strode easy-like into the *Toro de Oro* saloon. "Look here, men." They walked past a gilded bull statue that guarded the entrance. "Must be the town's main attraction." Richards laughed. As much as anything, he was trying to relax his men. What lay ahead after Brownsville would be pretty stressful. The saloon was packed with all manner of folks from cowboys to merchants to gamblers to whores. There were at least three armed guards by Richards's count to ensure relative peace in the decidedly raucous environment. Richards especially noted that two of the guards had modified their Colt revolvers by removing the trigger mechanism. This enabled them to fire their guns swiftly by simply pulling back the hammer and releasing it in one motion. It gave them an edge and meant that these were serious gunmen. Richards nodded as he walked past them.

The Rangers managed to find a small unoccupied table. Carson noticed that patrons gave the Texas Rangers a wide berth as they walked through the saloon. It was as though some invisible shield surrounded them.

Richards wasn't up to waiting, so impatiently walked over to the bar and dropped a single gold coin on the counter. *"Tabernero…aquí."* He flashed his Texas Ranger star for emphasis. "My friends and I are thirsty."

"Si, señor." The bartender nodded to one of the women to serve the Rangers.

Soon enough, the four of them were quickly imbibing the fruits of Richards's inquiry. Once they realized that they might enjoy the company of relatively civilized Texas Rangers, a couple of the ladies came over to try to work their wiles.

Richards feigned disinterest. *"¿Hablas inglés?"* What they understood would determine what might be talked about.

"Un poco, señor." The young woman smiled blithely as though she hadn't a brain in her head. Her ample breasts seemed to pour from the top of her bodice and she sat so as to reveal as much leg as possible. Her dark raven black hair fell in curls across her shoulders. *"¿Quieres follarme, señor?"* She didn't mince words. She was all about the whoring business.

Richards nodded to her. "Men, I'll be back in a few minutes. See if you can stay out of trouble." He took a swig of whiskey, grabbed the whore by the arm, and headed for the stairway to the second floor.

Richards had nearly reached the stairway when two men moved to block his way. *"¡Los diablos tejanos!"* They both had their guns drawn. It didn't matter that they reeked of booze.

Flashes of San Jacinto sped through Richards's brain. The whore wrestled herself free of his grasp as she sought to be out of any line of fire. "You boys don't want to mess with me. Just lay those guns down easy-like." He prayed they understood enough English to comply.

The two Mexicans hesitated. This man they were

confronting was bold to say the least. *"Son los rinches de Texas."* In their inebriated state, the men were caught up in the atrocities some Rangers had perpetrated on the Mexicans in Texas. They had just cause to be angry, but they'd picked the wrong Ranger to challenge.

By this time, Carson and the others saw what was happening. Carson had a clear view of the two men. He slowly pulled his Colt from its holster and leveled it at them. The two were so focused on Richards that they didn't at first see one and soon three guns pointed their way.

The saloon keeper saw what was unfolding. He dared not do anything that might cause a trigger to be squeezed, otherwise he might have fired his own gun into the ceiling. *"¡Alto!* Stop!"

Richards took the cue. "You heard the barkeeper, boys. Back off!"

The Mexicans realized they were seriously outgunned. They grumbled something in Spanish about getting Richards later to save face, then holstered their revolvers and eased out the back door.

Richards smiled, nodded to his men, grabbed the whore by the arm, and proceeded up the stairs. It was almost as though nothing had happened.

Christmas at Heaven's Gate conjured up mixed feelings as engendered by the memories from a couple of years before, when the Mexican bandit Carlos Perez and his four men had been killed in a gunfight at Christmas dinner in nearby Nuecestown. Sheriff and erstwhile Scarlett Rose paramour George Whelan had died in the melee. Bernice and Agatha hadn't hosted their traditional community dinner since that tragic event. Fortuitously, Luke had arrived to render justice with his Colt revolvers, while with his dying breaths Sheriff Whelan had dispatched Perez.

Luke had decided to take a couple of days leave from his pursuit of Horatio Thorpe. After catching up with the carriage, he'd followed Thorpe's track to the Nueces River, but decided the man had too great a head start. Luke dared not miss Christmas. He rightly figured the wounded man wouldn't act until he was at least mostly healed from the gunshot wound. Now, Elisa was thrilled to have her man home for Christmas.

"You ready, Lisa?" Luke had pulled the wagon around with a pair of mules hitched.

Elisa loaded the wagon with the makings for Christmas dinner, including her ever-more-famous cornbread. Peter, John, and baby Andrea Ann were secured, Big Horse was tied to the back of the wagon just in case. Jaime and Julia joined them, and they headed off to surprise the folks in Nuecestown. It was time for a new beginning. "You did remind Doc and Pastor Rucker?"

Luke gave her an "of course I did" sort of look and smiled. Off they went with Luke singing some Irish tune and Jaime trying to harmonize in his Mexican accent.

Beeville was planning a quieter Yuletide celebration. Horatio Thorpe had found refuge with a local family from whom he rented a small cabin while recuperating. He was pleased that he had full use of his hand and was hopeful he'd be up to returning to his mission sooner rather than later.

The family from whom Thorpe was renting the cabin had asked no questions about how he was wounded and even shared the hospitality of their Christmas dinner.

Otherwise, they had kept their distance from Thorpe, who acted as though he much-preferred solitude.

"I deeply appreciated your hospitality, Mr. and Mrs. Brown. I wish I could reciprocate."

The Browns didn't let on how much they appreciated the rent money, as times had been lean for them of late with just enough drought to have reduced their crop harvest, which meant that their beeves were not quite so fattened up for market. "We were pleased for your company, Mr. Thorpe." Indeed, their two young children had enjoyed Thorpe regaling them about the big Magnolia plantation and the hustle and bustle of the state capital.

"Where might I find some recent news about what's happening in Austin? I expect y'all know that Sam Houston is governor now?"

Mr. Brown smiled understandingly. "Yep, we're sort of a dot on the map here in Beeville. You've got to go to Victoria or Corpus Christi for the latest news."

"I appreciate that. Thanks again for your hospitality." Thorpe was soon headed back to the cabin. It was getting near time to begin his nefarious trek to Corpus. Perhaps he could try a different tactic with Scarlett.

"The diocese is giving me hell, Bill. The murders of those priests weigh right heavily on them and their parishioners. There's even talk about stirring up vigilance committees."

"Yes, sir, Colonel Kinney, I understand." Sheriff Bill Meaney was none too happy getting chewed out by Kinney, especially at Christmas. "I've been inquiring. Some sick person out there has a grudge against priests and enough money to part with gold coin at each murder site. Luke Dunn is keeping an eye out for clues, too."

"It should be your top priority, Bill. We must get to the bottom of this. Afore you know it, some idiot will retaliate against a Protestant, and we'll have even bigger troubles."

"I've advised the diocese to have their priests travel armed and by twos at a minimum. The cowardly murderer out there might be less likely to take on someone that can fight back. I've urged pastors to do the same thing."

"What's the world coming to, Bill, when men of the cloth must fear for their lives?" It was a rhetorical question and pretty much summed up the situation. "Say, you heard what Governor Houston is fixin' to do?"

Meaney responded with a quizzical look. Given the conversation, he hadn't expected to hear about goings on in Austin.

"Well, your friend Bol Richards and that Texas Ranger company he's leading might be headed for some extra special duty. Houston has ordered up lots of weapons, and I've heard he has more than a thousand Rangers deployed under Rip Ford. Rumor has it, he has his sights set on annexing Mexico."

Meaney was incredulous. "Annex to the United States? I'll believe that when I see it with my own eyes, Colonel."

Kinney nodded. "We'll see. Meanwhile, find that damned priest killer, Bill."

SIX
POLITICS & RELIGION

CHRISTMAS IN NUECESTOWN had exceeded everyone's expectations. They'd never forget the past, but they'd put tragedy behind them and focused on hope for the future. Lives filled with dreams and promises were being carved out of the frontier that was the Nueces Strip.

Luke, Elisa, and the children were gathered around a long table with Doc and the Sanchez's. By now, Jaime and Julia Sanchez had been fully accepted into the community and held a status not enjoyed by many Mexicans.

Bernice slipped in and pulled over a chair near Luke and across from Doc. "Luke, have you heard about the priests? My God, men of the cloth, Luke! What's happening with this world?" She spoke in a hushed whisper so as not to arouse guests at the other two tables.

"Horror, indeed, Bernice. We're trying to find out who the killer is. Hopefully, we can keep it from happening again."

Bernice lowered her voice, shielded her mouth with her hand, and leaned in close to Luke. "I have heard rumors, Luke. Some fella named Seth." Bernice had ears into all manner of conversations and apparently had heard some-thing on a recent shopping trip to Corpus Christi with Agatha.

"Seth?"

"Shhh." She shushed him. "As I heard it, he's a cowboy with a grudge against Catholics. He was talking up how the only good priest was a dead priest."

"How come you didn't tell Sheriff Meaney, Bernice?"

"Couldn't find him. Anyway, I had the impression this Seth fella droves cattle for an outfit out toward San Diego." She sat back and folded here arms giving a sort of smug smile at having delivered important information

Luke was amazed at the sorts of scuttlebutt Bernice could pick up. He wished he could refine his own listening skills so well as hers. "I'll let Sheriff Meaney know. I'll likely see him in the next day or so. I'm hunting that Horatio Thorpe fellow from Austin. He's the one who seems to be obsessed with Scarlett. Sheriff Meaney and I nearly had him, but he got away in the dark. I'll be leaving in the morning to track him down."

"Is Scarlett all right?"

Luke smiled and gave a nod to Elisa who by this time had tuned into the conversation. "Scarlett is sort of like my beautiful wife as concerns knowing how to defend herself. She seriously wounded the scoundrel, but not until after he'd raped her."

Bernice was horrified that Scarlett had been attacked. "That poor girl! Will she ever shake her past?"

Elisa gave her a reassuring look. "She's still got hope for the future, Bernice. She's become resilient."

"Speaking of Scarlett, how come she's not here to celebrate?"

"Actually, she decided to remain in Corpus. She's likely praying at George Whelan's grave. I understand she's enjoying a fine Christmas dinner with some of my cousins." Luke tried to assure Bernice that Scarlett was just fine. "I know that Bill Meaney's deputy is keeping an eye on her in case Thorpe returns sooner than expected."

Their conversation was interrupted by Pastor Rucker, who stood as his sons entered the room. Stephen and Rex were in their full-dress West Point cadet uniforms. "Ladies and gentlemen, it's my honor and pleasure to introduce my sons, Stephen and Rex. As you can see, they are home on leave from the United States Military Academy." Indeed, the young men cut dashing figures in their uniforms, and Rucker was bust-a-button proud.

With sunset just a couple of hours off and his children getting restless, Luke realized it was time to head back to Heaven's Gate. He excused himself and walked over to where Rucker was seated with his wife and sons. "Well, Pastor, seems as though you'll be having a joyful Christmas."

"Thanks, Luke. Boys, you might recall this is Texas Ranger Captain Luke Dunn. I've had the honor of working with the captain. He's just about single-handedly brought justice to this region they call the Nueces Strip."

Rex and Stephen stood and shook Luke's hand. As the oldest, Stephen spoke up. "It's a pleasure and honor to meet you again, Captain."

"At ease, men. I hope you have a great visit here in Nuecestown with your folks. Your father here is a brave man whom I'd be proud to have by my side in any battle."

"Thanks, Luke." Rucker was almost blushing at Luke's compliment.

"Y'all have a happy Christmas." Luke nodded, gathered Elisa, the children, and the Sanchez's. They all bid good-byes to Bernice and Agatha and headed on back to the ranch.

Thorpe was appreciative of the anonymity that Beeville afforded him but frustrated at being out of touch with the world at large. He very much missed the power and accompanying influence he enjoyed back in Austin. He decided to head to Victoria for a couple days, get communications off to his son Edward as well as to his house slave Samuel, and figure out how he was going to get Scarlett out of Corpus Christi now that she and everyone else were on guard. Once he finished business in Victoria, he'd head back to Corpus. He bid farewell to the Browns, paying them a bonus to not reveal where he was headed.

His arm still had a long way to go to fully heal. An upside to his current lifestyle was that he was gradually shedding body weight. The big question lingering in his conscious mind remained how to lure Scarlett out. All else was subsumed by his obsession. He'd even ceased to worry so much about Luke, though the Ranger's killing of his son was a very raw emotional wound.

Belknap had parted ways with Three Toes and was making his way south back to the Nueces Strip. He'd begun to better understand the plight of the Comanche, but recognized that they were often their own worst enemies. He was appreciative of the chief's dilemma and effort to better understand the White man and inevitability of settlement of the frontier. The nature of that settlement was a lingering concern.

The captain had first been directed to take command of Fort McIntosh near Laredo, but along the way he received orders to take over at Fort Ringgold outside Rio Grande

City. While pleased to have his first command, he had begun to feel more at home dealing with Comanche rather than the Apache that hung around Fort Ringgold and points south. The Apache were free to roam both sides of the Rio Grande, while the bluecoats were restricted from pursuing hostile marauders into Mexico.

He'd heard that Fort Brown down near Brownsville had been reduced to a skeleton garrison as soldiers were being drawn from several southern forts to the northern plains to fight Indians. It had allowed men like Cheno Cortina to wreak havoc just north of the Rio Grande. He'd also learned of the expansion of the role of the Texas Rangers in keeping law and order and wondered whether he'd run into his old friend Luke Dunn.

"Father, there's talk at the military academy of armed revolt over slavery. We could even be called to put down any insurrections." Horace Rucker's oldest son Stephen expressed his concern over dinner. He and his younger brother Rex would have to return to New York the next day, and he was anxious to see where his father stood on the matter. "I find it distressing to even think of the possibility of shooting our own citizens."

"Stephen, we'd be duty bound to follow orders," Rex said. "It'd be treason to violate our oath."

"I'm not saying we wouldn't follow orders, Rex. It's just that there are political forces at work that could destroy the southern economy that's become so dependent on slave labor."

"The very word slave troubles me, brother. It not only doesn't seem right morally, but the economics are all wrong. Free people with vested interests work harder. Now the Congress is talking about slave states versus free states. Seems ludicrous, Stephen. It's simply not right."

"I'm not saying it's right or wrong, Rex. I have trouble with the prospect of martial law being declared, and we might have to use force against civilians."

"Are we talking about taking sides, Stephen? Would you refuse?"

"I hope that's a rhetorical question, Rex."

Rucker observed his sons' argument with ever-deepening concern. It would be too easy to throw something biblical into the conversation, and yet he felt as though he was seeing a modern version of Cain versus Abel, Jacob versus Esau, Joseph versus his brothers unfolding before his eyes. Would this issue of slavery divide families? Would it take birth rights? Would brother be set upon brother? Rucker wondered further where he'd stand on this matter. After all, he'd been a colonel in the US Army. Could he or would he take a stand as a pastor?

"Stephen…Rex…we're not going to solve this here at dinner. It's not something that can be ignored, but we must trust in the Almighty that all will go well." Rucker may have been right, but it almost sounded glib in the face of the potential emotion of the issue.

Stephen eased back in his chair and looked first at his father and then at Rex. He glanced ever so slightly toward his mother, who busied herself serving second helpings as if to ignore the gravity of the conversation. "What if…and I'm just postulating here…what if states were to leave the Union?"

"Are you suggesting secession, Stephen?" Rex was incredulous. "I can't imagine that ever happening. No. It can't happen…not ever."

Rucker picked up "the look" from his wife. She'd had enough of this conversation. She didn't want the last night of her boys' visit to be acrimonious. Rucker strove to end the argument. "I think you young men may have plenty to talk about on your journey back to New York. You should rest up for your travels." Rucker did his level best to end the debate and bring calm back to the dinner table.

Stephen wasn't to be so easily dissuaded. "Would you fight, Father?"

Rucker looked from his sons to his wife. "If called, I'd fight."

Mrs. Rucker raised her eyebrows ever so slightly.

"I've got to carry a gun anyway these days. There are folks out there that take none too kindly to clergy these days. Do you boys know that three priests from Corpus Christi have been murdered by some crazed person in the past month?"

"I didn't know, Father. I'm sorry." Stephen realized that his concern over the future of slavery, while a valid matter, paled for the moment in comparison to the clear and present danger his father faced. Indeed, Stephen and Rex Rucker would have plenty of time on their journey back to the academy to talk of the nation's future.

It was right early as Luke saddled Big Horse to ride into Corpus Christi. He had plenty on his mind, as he wondered what Thorpe might be up to, whether Sheriff Meaney would see fit to pursue the priest killer, and how Bol Richards was making out leading the company of Rangers. He'd heard a vague rumor about Richards's company defeating some Apache and recovering cattle. To his knowledge, all the Rangers were safe and sound…and now battle-tested. Luke walked Big Horse up from the barn to the house.

Elisa waited on the gallery. The sun was rising behind and to one side of her man, casting him in an eerie glowing sort of light. It seemed like some sort of heavenly sign to her way of thinking. She was justly proud and certainly as justly drawn to her husband. His broad muscular arms and shoulders pressed against the constraining leather bounds of his coat. She felt a warmth radiate through her body despite the crisp late December air. If he weren't leaving, she'd have him right then and there in front of the house.

"I should be back in a couple of days, Lisa."

No. He was leaving. He had a mission…a duty. There'd be no further dalliances for desires of the flesh…for now. "I love you, Lucas. *Vaya con Dios.*"

He kissed her, mounted the big gray stallion, and headed up the lane out of Heaven's Gate. At the top of a slight rise, he stopped, turned, and waved. He saw her return his wave and was on his way. Such was the life of a rancher husband who served as a Texas Ranger.

Luke wondered when and where he'd wind up encountering Thorpe. It wasn't a long ride into Corpus Christi, but at least he had time to think. He'd pretty much have to adapt to whatever tactics Thorpe was of a mind to employ. The obsession with Scarlett was certainly the man's weakness. Somehow, Luke needed to use to his advantage the man's manic attraction to her. He was hesitant to use her as bait for a trap, but that seemed a valid strategy. How to best set such a trap and lure Thorpe to it would be the challenge. Could obsession trump common sense? Could Luke get Thorpe to throw caution to the winds? He'd have to see whether Scarlett might be up for it.

He was only a mile or so from Sheriff Meaney's office, when he first noticed the buzzards circling high above the shore of Nueces Bay. He had been so intent on getting into Corpus that he hadn't noticed them earlier. He sighed at the delay and the possibilities the scavenging birds conjured in his mind. He turned toward whatever they were circling over. The fact that they were circling meant that it was possible whatever or whomever they were concerned about was still alive.

Luke reached the shoreline and headed east a bit to where he figured the birds' interests might be focused. Big Horse snorted. Something had his attention. Luke turned to his right and rode a few feet into the high grasses. "Damn," he half-whispered reflexively. A priest was lying nearly hidden between a couple of clumps of grass. Had it not been for the buzzards and Big Horse, he might never have been found.

Luke dismounted. The man was pale, semi-unconscious, and barely breathing. He was seriously wounded, and it hadn't happened that long ago. The cross hanging from his neck had been nearly smashed to nothingness by a bullet. As it was, the priest had a serious chest wound, had lost a lot of blood, and likely wouldn't survive a ride on horseback. Luke strove to revive him with cold water from his canteen. As he knelt beside the priest, he saw the glint of the gold twenty-dollar coin lying in the dust beside him.

"I'm sorry I can't help, father. Can you tell me what happened?" Luke tried to talk as distinctly and gently as possible. This was his first chance to possibly have a first-hand account, a witness.

The priest half-opened his eyes, blinking in the bright morning light. "I…I'm Fa…Father…Murphy."

"Do you know who did this, Father Murphy?"

"Forgive…forgive   sinners…bless…merci…ful."   The priest's voice weakened and trailed off.

"Father, do you know who shot you?"

"Black…black   horse…black…hat…"   The   priest   was fading fast.

Luke had heard priests give last rites over dying souls, but he couldn't for the life of him recall a lick of what they'd said. But Luke needed more. "A name, Father Murphy? Can you give me a name?"

The priest looked up at Luke through ever-cloudier eyes. Blood had now begun to trickle from the corner of his mouth. He coughed. "Se…Seth…R…" Father Murphy coughed, gasped with pain, and gave up his final breath.

"May God rest your soul, Father Murphy." Luke remained kneeling over the man for a few more moments, praying for the man's soul.

Luke now had a first name and what was apparently the first letter of a surname. It confirmed what Bernice had learned from local gossip. Whoever held that name was likely close at hand. At least, he knew that he and Sheriff Meaney would be looking for a man named Seth R who wore a black hat and rode a black horse. He wrapped the priest in a blanket, hoisted him behind his saddle, secured the body, and headed into Corpus Christi.

★★

Elisa had invited Jamie and Julia to join her and the children for dinner. With Luke away for a night or two, she sought a bit of company.

Jaime had continued to be an asset to Heaven's Gate, especially with the prospect of Luke going off on special assignments. He had learned the ins and outs of handling livestock and become a *vaquero* of the first order. Having plenty of extended family around the region turned out to be a strong benefit in the spring for cattle branding and fall for round-ups to take the beeves to market. He was also quite adept at taming wild horses and, in fact, was seemingly able to simply talk most of the beasts into letting him ride them. While Jaime had been born of poor parents in South Texas, his wife Julia had grown up in Mexico proper from a moderately wealthy family. There was an economic caste system of sorts within the Mexican culture, so Jaime and Julia wound up eloping and escaping to Texas.

Living in Texas was a mixed bag for folks of Mexican descent. Some whites treated them as subhuman. When a Mexican was accused by an Anglo of a crime, there was often a missing component in the justice system: the trial by one's peers. Capture and punish was too often the case. Conversely, there were upstanding citizens like Luke and Elisa who treated Mexicans with respect and genuinely cared for their well-being.

Elisa was trying to perfect a recipe she'd come up with for chili. She would have nothing to do with beans in her chili, but she did have a secret ingredient. Served with her famous cornbread, her chili was to die for. In fact, it was hot enough from the peppers that it could send a diner to the doorstep of the Promised Land. She only eased back on the heat for Peter and John's share, as she was sensitive to their still young and relatively delicate stomachs.

"I'm delighted y'all could come share dinner with us. Luke's in Corpus Christi chasing after that man who attacked Scarlett Rose."

The dinner small talk went on to cover the weather and ranching and storage of food and feed for the winter. Jaime admired the fact that Luke had built a two-holer, an outdoor privy with two adjoining compartments. He'd promised Julia he'd do the same and joked that Luke dare not come up with a three-holer.

"We have some news, *Señora* Dunn." Jaime was always respectful of both his employer and his wife. It was also part of his charm and was reflected in the trust the Dunns placed in him.

Elisa looked quizzically at the couple. "News?"

Jaime grinned broadly and Julia blushed. "Julia is with child."

Everyone laughed. The Sanchez's already knew that Elisa was expecting, so now Heaven's Gate featured two pregnant women. "There must be something in the drinking water, Jaime." They laughed. "Congratulations to you and Julia." Elisa got up and walked over to the new cabinet that Luke had built for the kitchen. She returned with a yellow knitted baby blanket. "I was making this for just such an occasion." She handed it to Julia, who was overwhelmed with gratitude.

"Thank you, *Señora* Dunn. You are too kind."

Elisa served up some more coffee, and she and Julia cleared the table.

As they moved to seats that had been set before the fireplace, Jaime turned serious. He respected Elisa's opinions and had heard her express them on several occasions. He also respected her strength in defending herself and her family. He swallowed hard. "What do you think of the rumors that some states might leave the Union due to the slavery issue?"

It caught Elisa fully off guard. She knew Jaime to be an articulate, intelligent young man so wasn't surprised that he had been thinking about the slavery issue. It simply surprised her that he valued her opinion. In these times, women were discouraged from and often even abused for expressing opinions. "If you mean how do Luke and I feel about slavery, then rest assured that we think no one should be slave to another. Growing up in Ireland, Luke knows firsthand about indenturing and servitude and slavery. The British were quite harsh masters. I did hear that a man named Lord Wilberforce got the British government to abolish their slave trade."

"What if Texas were to leave, *Señora* Dunn?" Jaime pressed his case a bit further.

Elisa took a long sip of coffee. She saw Julia growing a little uncomfortable with her husband's questioning. "Leave the Union? We're Texans first, Jaime. As to what might happen…I'd rather worry about the spring growing season and giving my loving husband another child and living happily ever after." She hoped that would close the conversation.

Jaime looked at Julia, who raised one of her eyebrows slightly. It wasn't lost on him. "I appreciate that, *Señora* Dunn. We pray that all will end peacefully."

SEVEN
KING COTTON

SO FAR AS cultivated crops went, cotton was pretty much king in Texas. Antebellum-style plantations dotted the lush regions east of that famous 98th meridian. Slaves comprised a significant portion of the population, and even some of Luke's relatives weren't immune to the economic necessity of using slave labor to plant and harvest the cotton crop.

After depositing the dead priest's body with the local parish, Luke's next stop in Corpus Christi was to see Sheriff Bill Meaney and give him a heads-up as to what he'd learned about the murders and what he was thinking as to entrapping Horatio Thorpe.

He looked around just in case Thorpe might be lurking, dismounted, and hitched Big Horse to the rail in front of the jail. It was just cold enough that horses and men exhaled the telltale white breath vapors. Luke blew into his hands to warm them a bit. He looked up as Meaney came out to greet him. "Howdy, Bill, you ready to bring some more justice to Nueces County?"

Meaney put his finger to his hat and nodded. "Care for a cup of coffee first?"

Luke smiled. He was so anxious to get started that he'd skipped the niceties. "Pardon, Bill. Don't mind if I do." He figured to wrap his fingers around a hot coffee cup.

"So, what's got you so fired up, Luke?"

Luke took a long sip of coffee. It was hot, so he gasped a little. It was thick, too, as though it'd been sitting around for a couple of days. "Dang, Bill. I think I could stand a spoon up in this brew." He winked friendly-like then got serious. "For one thing, I just delivered another murdered priest to the parish. I found him near Nueces Bay about a mile or so out of town. He was barely alive, but didn't last long. I learned that his attacker wore a black hat, rode a black horse, and was named Seth. Last name began with an R, but the good father couldn't get the name out before he passed. Bernice back in Nuecestown heard a rumor that this Seth fellow is a drover out of the San Diego area. I'm thinking he might be in Corpus as we speak."

"We'd best go check out the local saloons, Luke. It's still early enough in the day that whoever it is might not be expecting the law to be hunting him and he'll be a tad more vulnerable. I expect you want to talk about Thorpe, too, but we can do that later."

"I think we ought to check the local livery first, Bill. There won't likely be too many black horses stabled around here."

"There are two stables, Luke. We should be able to cover them pretty quickly."

Luke and the sheriff mounted up and headed to the first stable near the edge of town.

"Clem, good morning." Meaney roused the stable boy.

"Can I help you, sheriff?"

"You have a black horse stabled here, son?"

Clem put his thumb to his chin as though in deep thought. He wasn't the brightest candle in Corpus Christi, but generally was a reliable source of information. "Matter of fact, Sheriff, we got two."

That immediately peaked Luke's interest. "Does one of the owners wear a black hat?"

Again, Clem dropped into deep thought. "Matter of fact, one of 'em did."

"Do you know where he went, Clem?" Meaney felt encouraged, so kept the questions flowing.

Again, the deep thought. "Well, Sheriff, this fella…he done rode out early and came back. Horse was lathered up quite a bit. Last I saw, he headed up the street toward the Longhorn Saloon. Seemed right nervous like."

"You've been very helpful, Clem." Luke handed the young man a small reward.

"Well, Luke, I'm thinking we ought to head up to the saloon. Seems like the guy's begun drinking sorta early. Maybe killing priests doesn't suit him so much as he'd like."

"Why don't you get your deputy, Bill, and have him watch the back door? I'll go down there and keep an eye on our murderer."

"Just don't go scaring him off, Luke. This Seth guy sees a big Texas Ranger come through the doorway, he just might get spooked."

"I'd like to capture the man without gunplay, Bill. Maybe I can talk to him and gain his trust."

"Up to you, Luke. I'll see you at the Longhorn in a few minutes."

★★

Seth Riker sat alone in a corner of the Longhorn Saloon. His back was to the wall, as he was just paranoid enough to not appreciate anyone approaching from behind. He'd hung his black hat on one of the back posts of the chair. For whatever reason, his Colt revolver lay on top of the table next to a half-empty bottle of cheap whiskey. He had a small knife in his hand and was industriously whittling on some object that was mostly hidden from sight. He wasn't an especially big man. He was still young but bore the gnarled hands, calluses, and rapidly leathering skin of someone much older. Droving cattle and working ranch hand duties could be right hard on a body. His nose was bent to one side just a tad, likely from some bar fight or possibly a kick from a calf or bronc.

Luke strode in purposefully and sidled up to the bar. He parted his coat to the barkeep just enough to show his Texas Ranger badge. "Just some water, thanks." The air was actually breathable at this hour, with just a hint of the sour aromas of booze, sweat, and urine. Fresh sawdust had been sprinkled on the floor, and that helped absorb lingering odors.

The barkeep was pleased to oblige.

"That young fellow in the corner…he been here long?"

"Seth? He's drunk down most of that bottle. Been here a couple of hours."

Luke acknowledged the information with an appreciative nod and walked easy-like over to the table where Seth was seated. "Mind if I join you?"

"Help yourself."

At least, Luke hadn't been told to go to hell. "My name is Luke. You from around these parts?" He was careful to keep his badge covered.

"Born here. Name's Seth."

"Whereabouts?"

"You ask a lot of questions. I don't even know you." Seth stopped whittling and placed the object he was carving on the table. He looked at his revolver but made no move to reach for it.

Luke saw that the young man was whittling a cross. "You mind pointing that Colt in another direction, Seth?"

Seth looked at Luke and used his forefinger to point the barrel away from the two of them. "No problem, Mr. Luke."

"You a religious man?"

"I go to church on occasion."

"You Catholic?"

A hint of red began to creep across Seth's face. He was none too happy with Luke's question. "Bunch of perverts."

Luke had touched a nerve. He'd have to proceed gently. "What do you mean?"

"None of your nosey business." The tone bordered on anger.

Just then, Sheriff Meaney walked into the Longhorn. He glanced over and saw that Luke had engaged a young man in the corner. He noted the black hat and assumed it must be Seth. The sheriff decided to stand over near the bar to avoid being threatening and to serve as backup in case Luke got into trouble.

"Damn. The local law has arrived." Seth was growing more uncomfortable.

Luke glanced over at Meaney and then back to Seth. "Hell, he's got no cause to bother you." He paused and looked hard at Seth. "Does he?"

Seth poured himself another glass of whiskey and gulped it down. He winced a little as its burn slid down his throat.

"You drinking to forget something, Seth?"

"Damned priests."

"They hurt you?"

"Sons of bitches raped my sisters." He started to get nervous. One eye twitched. "I gotta get outta here." He began to get up. As he did, he reached for the Colt on the table.

Luke was faster and swept it to the floor. The chair fell back as he stood. His six-foot-three-inch frame towered over the young man.

Seth froze, mostly from fear. He saw Luke's Texas Ranger badge. "I…I didn't want to kill them. I had to. They ruined my sisters' lives."

"Four of them? Four priests?"

"All of them."

Luke motioned for Sheriff Meaney to join them. Once the sheriff had come over, he turned to him. "Bill, this young man just confessed. I believe he's yours."

"Nice work, Luke."

"I'll see you in a bit, I've got to go see Scarlett."

In a few moments, Seth Riker was manacled and about to be marched off to the Corpus Christi jail.

"One more thing, Seth. What about the twenty-dollar gold pieces?" Luke had nearly forgotten.

"Damned priests treated my sisters like whores. I gave them sons of bitches a refund."

Meaney marched the young man off to jail.

Luke shook his head. Seth would surely hang for his crimes. But Luke was saddened by the extremes of brokenness that drove men like Seth to crime. Where had they lost their hope for justice and a better life? How did that happen to some and not others?

"How are you doing, Scarlett?" Luke sat easy-like in the

chair across from Scarlett and little Margaret. He stroked his mustache thoughtfully.

"Pretty fair, thanks to you and Elisa, Luke." She absent-mindedly tried to cover the residual yellow color of the bruise on her arm that she still wore from Horatio Thorpe's attack a couple of weeks back. Her fair skin bruised easily, and Thorpe had nearly broken her arm when he held her. She poured Luke a cup of coffee and another for herself. "You come to talk about that Thorpe fella?"

"Yes, yes, I have. He's said to be north of here around Beeville and Victoria. I expect he's healed up just enough to head back here, Scarlett."

"Dang bullet only wounded him. An inch over, and my worries would've been over."

"Our worries. Remember, he's looking to get me for killing his son."

"What do you propose we do, Luke?"

"I suspect the son of a..." Luke paused with deference to Margaret. "Um, son of a gun will come across using the shell road again. Part of me would like to hang out on the shoreline and cut him down."

"Something wrong with that, Luke?" Scarlett leaned toward him with earnestness as her arms stretched out and hands nearly grasped those of her Texas Ranger savior. She balled her hands into fists and slammed them on the table with enough force to make Luke's coffee cup jump. "Can you just rid the world of him?" Thorpe represented a final residual evil to the hard life that she'd led up to then. Memories of running away from home with her first man, a miscarriage, a riverboat affair, whoring in Laredo, escaping with her desperado lover, a child out of wedlock, and more swirled around in her brain.

"I know how just that would seem, Scarlett. But it wouldn't be right to bushwhack him. He's a lawbreaker, but he's mostly hired others to do his dirty work." He looked sympathetically at her. "No, that won't do. We've got to capture the man, try him, and let justice prevail."

Scarlett didn't like the answer but knew he was right. "So what do we do?"

"We need to lure him in, trap him so to speak, give him a false sense of security." He gave her an "are you ready for this" sort of look.

Scarlett sensed what was coming and interrupted. "You want me to be the bait in your trap." It was a no brainer.

"We need to get word to Thorpe that you'll meet him and go peaceably with him."

Scarlett fiddled nervously with the handle of her coffee cup. "How do you figure to do that?" She was all too well aware of the danger she'd be in. Thorpe raping her was still fresh in her consciousness. The memory disgusted her.

Luke proceeded to lay out a plan. "We'll leave a note for him here that you'll meet him in Nuecestown at Bernice and Agatha's boarding house. We'll drop Margaret off at Heaven's Gate to keep her out of danger. She'll likely enjoy Peter, John, and baby Andrea Ann anyway. The note will tell him you'll go with him on condition that he marry you. We'll have a wagon loaded with what will appear to be your household possessions, but I'll be lying in wait under cover to arrest him." Luke knew there was plenty of possibility for the plan to go wrong, but it seemed like the best way to avoid any bloodshed. If it worked precisely as he'd laid out, it'd likely qualify as a miracle.

"You think it might work?"

"We can never be sure, Scarlett." Luke took her hands to reassure her. "We care about you and will do all we can to protect you and Margaret."

"What if he senses it's a trap?"

"He's thrown caution to the winds, Scarlett. He's

obsessed. Thorpe will be like a mountain lion at the smell of blood, thinking only of having his prey." Luke gave her a reassuring look. "Now, let's write him a note so inviting that he can't resist."

Bill Meaney had sent a message to Colonel Kinney to inform him of the capture of the priest killer. With that off his mind and the killer secured in a jail cell, the sheriff decided to relax. He normally didn't drink much, but figured that an easy evening at the Longhorn Saloon wouldn't hurt. He was grateful that Luke had gotten the killer to surrender with no bloodshed, and he hoped they could get the man to trial sooner rather than later.

Meaney got himself washed up, put on a fresh shirt and vest, slicked back his graying hair, checked to be sure his guns were loaded, and headed to the Longhorn. As he walked up the street from the jail, his thoughts turned to his old friend Bol Richards. It'd been quite an experience when they'd fought together in the Texas War for Independence, and he was pleased that Richards had signed on with the Texas Rangers. Hopefully, they'd be able to put a whipping on Juan Cheno Cortina.

He knew that he must not stay out too late as he and his deputy needed to take turns keeping a watchful eye for the return of Horatio Thorpe. Luke had laid out the plan for him and he hoped and prayed it would work.

The sheriff strode purposefully through the double café doors of the Longhorn. It was not especially crowded this particular evening, and there didn't appear to be anyone looking to make trouble. It was unusually chilly outside, so many folks apparently decided not to venture out. In any case, the place didn't smell nearly so bad as it usually did.

As he sidled up to the bar, Meaney couldn't help but notice an animated conversation underway at one table. It was apparently over politics, as he picked up tidbits of the discussion. The slavery issue and its impact on Texas had gotten to be an ever-hotter topic, and one of the men seemed especially argumentative.

Meaney quaffed a jigger of whiskey, enjoying the feeling as it trickled down his throat and warmed his insides. He kept an eye on the five men arguing about slavery. The topic made him a bit uncomfortable, but his concern was more about ensuring that no one crossed the line and became violent over it.

One man with a loud voice and rather thick Irish brogue stood and leaned forward with both hands on the table. He was sort of in the faces of the others. "Damn it, lads! I've been raising cotton here since '53. I have a few field slaves." He looked around as though challenging the others. "It's an easy trip to get my bales to Corpus and then to markets in New Orleans and up the Mississippi. I make a fair living, but would lose money if not for the nigras. We simply can't tolerate having some politicians in Washington deciding our fate. Damn! Don't you see?"

So far as Meaney could tell, the other men appeared to be ranchers. Slavery wasn't an issue for cattlemen. The cotton farmer's pleas were lost on them.

"If there's violence over slavery, it'll spill onto your doorsteps for certain. You won't be able to avoid it. Cotton is king in east Texas and that's where the money comes from to run the state."

"Relax, John. There'll be no fightin' over slavery." One of the ranchers was trying to calm things down.

"You lads just don't get it. I know what it is to live under government oppressors." He looked from man to man.

"The British took ever more license with my Irish brethren. It's about our rights as free men."

That caught Meaney's attention. He'd long been thinking on figuring how someone could talk about free men and still be an owner of men...and women. "King cotton," he mumbled under his breath. He'd already been through one war of independence aiming to ensure the freedom of Texans. The country sure didn't need another. He wondered where Texas would stand as a state?

Just then, the cotton farmer slammed the table. "It's about our way of life, damn it!"

Meaney eased on over to the table, pulling back his coat to reveal his badge. "Gentlemen, y'all represent the backbone of our fine city. We survive from the fruits of ranching and farming. It doesn't do to get too riled up over issues we likely can't control." His words seemed to have a calming effect.

The cotton farmer eased back into his chair and reverted to a brogue mixed with a smooth sing-song Texas twang. "You're right, Sheriff. No sense stirring hate and discontent here in Corpus Christi. But it's frustrating. If there's violence, likely not of our choosing, it could pit brother against brother and friend against friend." He sighed resignedly.

"Well, gentlemen, for now let's keep our city a peaceful place to live."

Everyone nodded.

The sheriff's control of the situation had caught the eyes of one of the ladies. It had been a slow night for her, and she'd been watching him intently. As Meaney eased back over to the bar, Clara walked across the room and stood beside him. "You don't get here very often, Sheriff. My name is Clara." She looked up into his eyes, as though that were the measure of the soul of a man. He'd already impressed her by his calming of the men who'd been arguing.

Meaney shifted uncomfortably. Women, especially White women, made him nervous. He felt as though Anglo women had not-so-hidden agendas designed to change their men. He'd been married once to a Cherokee woman, much as his idol Sam Houston had been. She had been his first love. Meaney appreciated her for her open honesty and culturally embedded desire to serve her husband. Aleka had died within the year from yellow fever. The sheriff hadn't touched a woman since. It had been nearly four years. Something about Clara, despite her obvious profession, attracted him. Maybe he sensed a certain absence of guile in her, an honesty about who she was. It was not unlike what he found in his Cherokee love.

"What you thinking, Sheriff?"

"I'd like to ask what a woman like you is doing in a place like this, Clara, but I expect that's obvious." He touched her arm.

"Not always so obvious, Sheriff." She felt a warmth course through her at his touch. She knew nothing of this man, but something in her yearned to know more.

"You can call me Bill, Clara." He tilted his head questioningly. "Not so obvious?"

"I'd say let's get out of here, Bill, but I get the feeling you just might like to get acquainted in a different sort of way than most of the men who visit the Longhorn." She brought herself a little closer, took his arm, and led him to an out-of-the-way table.

Meaney second-guessed himself. What on earth was a lawman doing even thinking about courting a whore? It was a moral contradiction. And yet, he couldn't deny what seemed to be a mutual attraction.

★★

"I can't thank you enough, Elisa." Scarlett was deeply appreciative of Elisa taking in her daughter Margaret for a couple of days while she and Luke went off to Nuecestown to set the trap for Thorpe.

Elisa lifted Margaret onto her lap and turned back to Scarlett. "It's so risky. I pray you're doing the right thing."

Soon enough, Luke had brought the wagon around, and he and Scarlett headed off. Luke had Big Horse tied to the back and would be sure to stable the big stallion at the livery in Nuecestown so as not to give away their trap.

"Are Bernice and Agatha expecting us?" Scarlett asked Luke.

"No, but they'll go along with our plan. In fact. I'm sure they'll relish helping bring Horatio Thorpe's threat to an end."

Luke helped Scarlett into the wagon and then turned to Elisa. "Pray we can bring this nightmare to an end, Lisa."

"Will you get Pastor Rucker to help?"

"With his history of having been tainted by Thorpe's escapades, I'm sure he'll be enthused enough to help." Luke appreciated Rucker having turned against Thorpe to help him bring to an end the racket in defrauding the government that the Austin powerbroker had been running. As reward for his helping Luke, the pastor had been allowed to retire as a colonel. Rucker was especially pleased that both of his sons retained preferential admittance to the US Military Academy at West Point.

EIGHT
SPRINGING A TRAP!

A BANK of clouds drifted across and blocked the light of the moon. Under cover of the darkness, Horatio Thorpe managed to cautiously work his way across the shell road on Nueces Bay and ride on into Corpus Christi. He was determined to be a lot more cautious on this venture into the city. He was duly chagrined that a city of fewer than three hundred people could be such a challenge to him finding his way through its dim-lit streets undetected. After all, it was like some backwoods, hick village compared to thriving hubs like Austin, San Antonio, and Galveston. He figured Colonel Kinney still had a long way to go.

He wended his way slowly, watching out for any people that might be worrisome until he found himself looking up the stairway to Scarlett's apartment. He shuddered at the memory of her shooting him, but it was compensated by the thought of how it had felt to have had his way with her. The rape still excited him. There was enough chill in the January air that he kept his heavy coat wrapped tightly against the cold. His coat was black and he'd acquired a black horse. The combination made him not so easy for anyone to see him sneaking into Corpus Christi.

Thorpe hitched the horse, peered into the shadows to his left and right, and climbed up the stairs. He'd already observed that there was no light from inside. At the top of the stairway, he found an envelope stuffed between door and jam. In the dim light, he made out his name. This certainly piqued his curiosity. He broke the seal and pulled out her note, but it was far too dark to read there on the landing. It was obvious that Scarlett wasn't around. He needed to seek enough light to find out what she'd written in her note. As fate would have it, the bank of cloud cover hiding the moon parted and cast just enough light that he was able to read her note.

His obsessed brain devoured her every word of her professed willingness to go away with him. Her invitation to meet in Nuecestown appealed, given that he was plenty familiar with the town as a result of spending a night there at Bernice and Agatha's boarding house. From her tone, he had no reason to suspect anything was amiss. His common sense as a planter, politician, and businessman was tossed aside. He became aroused at the thought of a future of possessing her body every day and every night at his pleasure. He smiled at the prospect of indulging his lusts and looked down appreciatively at the pressing bulge in the front of his trousers.

As much as Thorpe was excruciatingly excited to connect with his Laredo whore, he decided discretion demanded he wait until morning light. He didn't want to foolishly fall into some trap. The situation demanded caution.

To make matters a bit more uncomfortable for Thorpe, a cold misty rain set in around midnight. He wrapped himself in his bedroll and took shelter under the stairway to

Scarlett's place. With his still ample girth, the bedroll barely afforded him protection from the elements, and the temperature dropped to near freezing.

From up the street, Sheriff Meaney kept a watch from the warm confines of the Corpus Christi jail. He'd been watching Thorpe's activities despite the darkness. It perversely amused him to see Thorpe's discomfort. He was in an especially good frame of mind after having spent several hours getting to know Clara. He'd begun to think of wresting her from her whoring ways. It made his present vigilance of Thorpe a bit ironic. Here Meaney, a common man, was falling for a local prostitute, yet he had cast their positions in life in a realistic perspective. The wealthy Horatio Thorpe, on the other hand, was nearly psychotic over a whore he'd been obsessively pursuing for several years. Thorpe slept outside in a bitterly cold rain. Being comfortably seated in front of a wood stove seemed quite just to Meaney.

Just before sunup, Meaney saw that Thorpe had roused and was preparing to continue his pursuit of Scarlett. The rain had stopped, and the landscape was covered with a patina of ice. The sheriff saddled up and headed to Nuecestown to let Luke know that Thorpe appeared to be taking the bait. With the advantage of being more familiar with the road to Nuecestown, Meaney had a couple of hours head start.

Sleeping in the damp cold on a hard, wooden landing did no favors to Thorpe's body. He'd lost some weight in his dogged pursuit of Scarlett but was still far from svelte. He was still recovering from the wound she'd inflicted. His horse had been at the hitching post through the night, and the poor beast was soaking wet and shivering with cold. By necessity, he led the horse to the livery stable. A serviceable mount was essential, so he wound up trading for another.

The stable boy was offended by Thorpe's treatment of the horse, but money has a way of soothing such matters.

Once on the road, Thorpe made slow progress toward Nuecestown. Ice had melted enough to create muddy conditions. He was deadly curious about what Scarlett might have in mind. He even boldly dreamed that they'd have a first night together at the boarding house. Despite the chill, he was warmed by repeatedly fondling and reading the love note she'd written to him.

Sheriff Meaney arrived in Nuecestown and awakened Luke, who'd spent the night at the jailhouse freezing despite a small wood stove. Luke was anxious to get the blood recirculating in his cold-stiffened limbs. At least he'd stayed dry. The two of them just needed to put finishing touches on their trap. The prey was willingly approaching as the lure of fulfilling his sexual obsession drew him in.

Horatio Thorpe rode cautiously into Nuecestown around mid-morning. He'd had a chance to dry out, but the dampness lingered and he appreciated the sun breaking the January morning chill. The horse was a bit slow, as it sought to accommodate its heavy rider. Horses tended to develop relationships with their riders, and this steed was nervously uncertain of Thorpe. Some would call him skittish. In any case, it contributed to a slow ride from Corpus Christi.

Thorpe's later arrival had bought Luke more time to set the trap. "We mustn't let him suspect a thing, Scarlett. An inadvertent glance at where I'm lying in the back of the wagon could give us away." If at all possible, they wanted to take Thorpe alive. Giving away the trap could lead to gunplay.

Scarlett had let her hair down and brushed it out in

wavy curls laying fetchingly across her shoulders. She'd found a blouse that exposed her shoulders and revealed an alluring view above the gentle curves of her ample breasts. A warm wool blanket temporarily hid her assets and kept off the chill while they awaited the arrival of their prey. Thorpe wouldn't be able to take his eyes from her. The only thing preventing him from raping her again right then and there would be their very public meeting place. The wagon was parked in front of the boarding house, and they'd be clearly visible from the windows. "I'm ready, Luke. God help us if we fail."

"Don't even think of failure, Scarlett. We'll surely bring this nightmare to a close." Luke looked up the street to the livery stable where Sheriff Meaney had hidden with his rifle at the ready and a direct line of sight to the wagon.

Nuecestown was normally a quiet sleepy place, so the sound of Thorpe's horse's hooves on the ground as it turned from ice to mud couldn't be missed. Thorpe was almost tempted to urge his mount into a canter as he entered the town and saw Scarlett with her beautiful long red curls waiting for him in the wagon seat. He stroked at the pocket where he'd secreted her note. At about a hundred yards away, he stopped and scanned the scene. Nothing seemed unusual. Other than sounds from within the general store and the clucking of a few chickens, all seemed at peace. He saw no threats. His overwhelming passion for Scarlett likely contributed to his willingness to accept what he saw before him as safe. He urged his horse into a slow walk.

Scarlett looked over her shoulder at him and smiled as lovingly as she could muster. She let the blanket partially drop. Her skin fairly glowed, though that could have been attributed in part to the chill still very much in the air.

Thorpe felt no chill. He was fully aroused, and it took all

he could muster to restrain himself. He rode up beside the wagon. "Miss Scarlett Rose, good morning, my love." He strove to be as gentlemanly as possible. He didn't even think of himself as the man who but a couple of weeks before had raped this woman and then suffered a gunshot wound at her hands. He was so into himself that the mere thought of being sensitive to her feelings escaped him. This was almost a business deal for Thorpe. "I've had the pleasure of your note and generous invitation, Miss Scarlett."

"I do forgive your ardor of nights past, Horatio. I expect it so excited me that I lost my head and shot you." She batted her eyes just a little and pursed her lips with just a touch of sauciness.

Incredibly, her reasoning and response worked for Thorpe. He was totally taken in. He dismounted and came even closer to her. "May I join you?"

"By all means, love. But are we ready to travel?" Scarlett didn't want Thorpe to be too distracted from her offer to accompany him.

With his bulk, Thorpe grunted just a bit as he climbed up into the wagon. "When we get to San Patricio, I'll engage a carriage, my sweet." He moved closer to her.

She felt the suffocating sensation of his bulk, and it brought back memories, bad memories. She had to stick to the script. "Are you going to kiss me with that pistol butt sticking in my ribs?" She drew close, letting him sample the sweetness of her perfume.

Thorpe gently pulled the Colt from his holster and laid it on the floor under the wagon seat. "Is that better, my love?"

Scarlett stood up, faced Thorpe, and leaned over enough to nearly fully expose her breasts as she held her breath and gave him a light kiss.

The scent of her perfume was now overwhelming.

Thorpe was fully mesmerized and didn't even sense that Luke had moved behind him within mere inches. His eyes bulged in surprise, as he felt the cold muzzle of one of Luke's Colt Navy revolvers nestled in the nape of his neck. "Horatio Thorpe, you are under arrest for rape and conspiracy to commit murder."

Thorpe froze—he dared not move a muscle. He murmured under his breath, "You son of a bitch Ranger." The look he gave Scarlett could have instantly melted all the ice at the North Pole. The flames of hell couldn't have been hotter. "You goddamned whore bitch!" he snarled.

"Put your hands behind you, Mr. Thorpe."

He complied and felt the near-freezing steel of the manacles clasped around his wrists.

Scarlett dropped her head in her hands and sobbed as tears of relief flowed. It was a cathartic release not lost on Luke. The trap had worked, the prey had been captured, and no blood had been shed.

Sheriff Meaney walked up from his back-up position at the stable. "Mr. Thorpe, welcome to Nuecestown and Nueces County, Texas. I'm pleased to offer you lodging across the street at our fine jail." He and Luke helped Thorpe down from the wagon. Given the man's size, it was a load, to say the least.

By this time, Nuecestown had fully awakened. Luke quickly became aware of how many folks had apparently been observing the goings-on behind the perceived safety of windows and doors. The dozen folks that emerged formed a crowd by town standards. Pastor Rucker gave Scarlett a handkerchief and helped her down from the wagon. He was rather helpless in the face of her emotions. Bernice and Agatha had emerged from the boarding house and relieved Rucker of the still-sobbing young woman.

Scarlett dropped the handkerchief from her eyes long

enough to watch as Thorpe was half-dragged, half-pushed off to the jail. The relief was overwhelming, but it wouldn't be full until punishment was exacted on Thorpe. The hangman's noose would be too good for him, but it was likely he'd wind up in some prison if his wealth and power didn't get him off altogether. The question lingered as to how justice would ultimately be served.

With Thorpe ensconced in a jail cell, Luke quickly returned to the scene. The crowd had dispersed about as quickly as it had formed. There'd be talk in the gossip mill for months to come. Rucker was waiting by the wagon. "Thanks for comforting Scarlett, Pastor. We'll be heading back to Heaven's Gate shortly."

"I heard about how you captured that priest killer in Corpus Christi, Luke. Seems as though you've managed to avoid gunplay lately. It sure puts minds at ease to know there won't be bullets flying around. I expect it won't always be this way, but I admire you for it."

"Keep in mind that Thorpe didn't have much choice, Pastor. My gun was sticking in the back of his neck. It was by the grace of God that he wisely chose to surrender." Luke stroked his mustache, as he often did when deep in thought. "I'd have pulled the trigger if he hadn't surrendered."

Rucker half-smiled. "He was the victim of his own lust. Sin just doesn't pay, does it, Luke?"

"Did the ladies take Scarlett inside?" It was almost a rhetorical question. Luke nodded to Rucker and entered the boarding house.

It was a place filled with memories for Scarlett. Already brimming with emotion, it was almost too much. She'd given birth to Margaret here and had lost the man who fathered her daughter and become her suitor. Sheriff George Whelan would always have a place in her heart. By the time Luke entered, she'd pretty much had time to compose herself. "Luke, thank God your trap worked. Thank you."

"You ready to head back to Heaven's Gate? I expect your daughter will be looking to hug her mother."

They thanked Bernice and Agatha and headed to the wagon. "I'll be coming back to help Sheriff Meaney transfer Thorpe to the Corpus Christi jail. Thorpe still has his wealth, and we don't want to take chances that he's got folks on his payroll that might try to spring him. The Corpus jail is more secure."

Scarlett sighed. "It won't be over 'til he's punished, will it?"

"Afraid that's the way it is, Scarlett. Keep praying that justice will prevail. Meanwhile, the perverse reprobate is our prisoner. He can't hurt you so long as we hold him."

Meaney ambled over from the jail. "See you in a couple of hours, Luke. I'll keep a close eye on him here."

Luke drew Meaney out of earshot of Scarlett. "Yeah, I'd be watchful, Bill. He was alone so far as we could tell. I'm more worried about days from now, when word gets out that Thorpe's our prisoner. Hopefully, Rip Ford can head off any trouble that stirs in Austin." He put his fingers aside his hat friendly-like to Meaney and headed back to the wagon. They'd stop off at the livery to fetch Big Horse before heading back to Heaven's Gate.

NINE
MEXICAN REVOLT?

"ER...BOL...I mean Captain Richards, where we heading now?"

Richards gave Walker Carson that look, the one that said to never ask that question. He sighed quite audibly. A smile reluctantly spread across his chiseled face with its three-day stubble of beard. "We're heading to Fort Brown, son. Now, fall back into the column, and keep your yap shut." He said it gently, so as not to sound as though he were scolding.

They'd ridden past and surveilled the hacienda of Cheno Cortina's mother outside Brownsville. There was no sign of the rebel, but that was no surprise. Word of a column of Texas Rangers approaching would have spread quickly in advance of their arrival. Likely, there had also been word of what Richards's company did to the Apache. Cortina was far from being anyone's fool. Discretion was in order.

Cortina was also concerned with Benito Juarez. The new president was diminutive of stature but enjoyed outsized power. He reluctantly suffered Cortina's harassment of the Texans north of the Rio Grande. Cortina, like Juarez, kept a close eye on politics in the United States. There were uneasy feelings as to what sorts of troubles might be brewing over the slavery and states' rights issues. Of course, Mexico had its own problems, a product of a culturally and economically diverse population. The days of the conquistadors were long gone, but the outcomes of their predations were still being felt. Indigenous Indians, French immigrants, and Anglos mixed under umbrellas of mostly Catholic but also pagan Indian rituals.

Having had a taste of combat with the Apache, Richards's Texas Rangers were itching for another fight. They soon pulled up before the gates to Fort Brown and discovered a skeleton garrison. It was debatable as to whether there were enough soldiers to defend the fort in the event of any significant attack. After conferring with—or, more-truthfully lamenting—the situation with the unfortunate lieutenant who'd been left in charge, Richards decided to move on to Fort Ringgold. He did learn that Cortina was in Mexico and headed west to stay out of the reach of the Texas Rangers. Cortina had no cause to fear the US Army, as soldiers were under orders to not follow his escapes into Mexico. Border violations would surely cause major international incidents.

Walker Carson was riding point with a fellow Ranger when a gunshot rang out and they heard the telltale whine of a bullet whiz past. The person who shot at them missed, but they couldn't count on that happening twice. Their first thought was to wheel their horses and make a beeline back to the column. Instead, Carson grabbed his Sharps and dove from the saddle to take cover in a nearby cypress grove. His companion followed his lead.

As he ran for cover, Carson chambered a round. He'd be ready come what may.

A second shot and a quick third ricocheted among the cedar branches barely over Carson's head. There was obviously more than one attacker.

Scanning the horizon, Carson spotted gun smoke at a couple of hundred yards out from their position. He had no idea yet who was shooting. It used to be that you could tell Indians from bandits by the use of bow and arrow versus gun. Now, Indians were just as likely to use rifles and pistols. He decided whoever was firing at them was either intentionally missing them or couldn't hit the broad side of a barn. In any case, he couldn't take any chances. A bullet through his hat brim quickly removed any suggestion of intentional missing.

By this time, Richards and the Texas Ranger company heard the gunfire and were headed Carson's way at a gallop. Richards was not about to miss out on a good fight.

The wisps of gun smoke quickly gave away the multiple locations of the attackers. They appeared to be dug in on both sides of the road the Texas Rangers were traveling on, aiming to unleash a devastating ambush. One of them had a nervous trigger finger and had fired too early for the Rangers to fully fall prey to their trap. From what Carson could see of the sources of gunfire, there could be as many as fifty or more attackers.

Carson and his fellow Ranger trusted that Richards had heard the shooting and would be on his way. They'd need to hold out for at least a couple of minutes, long enough to even up the sides a bit. Meanwhile, they returned fire aiming at the puffs of smoke. Judging from the occasional cry of a wounded attacker, they likely wounded or killed a couple. A 50-caliber bullet from a Sharps had a way of eliminating the shielding effect of clumps of grass or brush.

The Texas Ranger company stopped at a bend in the road to assess the situation before charging headlong into battle. Richards rode over toward a small hill that afforded a partial view of the ongoing attack. He couldn't see any of the attackers but like Carson could see the sources of gunfire. He judged that the attackers were spread over an arc of perhaps two hundred yards.

"Williams! Take ten Rangers and join Carson's defensive position. Spread out and make a lot of noise to make them think there's a larger force." He watched the Ranger peel off from the column with ten men. "The rest of you come with me. We're gonna get these bastards from behind." Crossfire be damned, he led the Rangers off to his left in what was to be a wide sweeping movement aimed at flanking the enemy. Richards was a bit more careful than in his youth, but he had a somewhat impulsive side that led to quick decisions. Mostly, his intuition worked, and this looked as though it would be one of those times.

Williams had quickly sidled up to Carson to let him know what was afoot. "Captain wants us to make lots of noise and get off as many rounds as we can. Whoever is out there needs to think we're big enough to be reckoned with." With that, the Rangers unleashed the first of several fusillades, all the while letting out yells that likely would have waked the dead.

With only a dozen Rangers, Richards understood that even coming at the enemy from behind was a huge risk. Surprise was essential. The battle had raged for better than ten minutes from the time Carson was ambushed. Richards spread his men behind the left flank of the enemy. By now, he could see that he was dealing with what appeared to be Apache with a handful of Anglo troublemakers mixed in. He figured to charge in full bore with a pistol in each hand, shooting as many Apache as possible and taking his line on a wheeling movement to gallop headlong into the remaining attackers. He counted on sowing maximum confusion toward inflicting heavy damage on the Apache and minimizing his own losses.

Carson saw Richards's line crest a rise a couple of hundred yards away and charge. As Indians stood to defend themselves against the surprise from their rear, Carson and his fellow Rangers could pick them off. It was certainly a doable range for their Sharps rifles.

The Apache line of dug-in attackers initially folded in on itself, trying to save their wounded and dying warriors as best they could.

As Richards continued his charge among the Apache, Carson was forced to hold fire to avoid killing fellow Rangers by way of friendly fire. Now, he took charge. "Rangers, let's go get 'em!" He led a foot charge toward the Apache.

By now the Apache were losing interest in the fight. Everywhere they turned there seemed to be a Texas Ranger pouring lead into them. Worse, they were cut off from escape by virtue of a couple Richards's enterprising Rangers having run off their horses. What had a few moments before seemed a perfect ground for an ambush had been turned into a killing field with Apache and their allies on the losing side. It was not a good day for the Apache.

A heavy haze of gun smoke hung over the area. After reaching the far-right flank of the enemy positions, Richards wheeled back. What he saw would be indelibly imprinted in his mind. Before him lay a path of blood with dead and dying Apache seemingly everywhere. He looked to his left and right. Of a dozen Rangers, ten still sat in their saddles with him. He'd lost two men versus countless Apache losses.

Carson and the other Rangers were already conducting mop-up operations, examining each enemy body for signs of life. He hated this duty, but they had no way to hold wounded prisoners. Several mortally wounded Apache were relieved of their misery as a mercy. A handful of live prisoners were being rounded up and tethered together. Two Anglos were among these prisoners. All told, there were eight captured men.

The Texas Ranger losses consisted of one dead and three wounded, though none of the three had serious wounds. They were a couple of horses short, so would track down some of the Apache mounts that had been scattered early in the battle. Carson and Williams brought the two Anglo prisoners over to where Richards had dismounted and was taking inventory of the scene. They forced the Anglos to their knees.

"Where you sons of bitches from?" It was almost a rhetorical question, as they reminded him of the rebel Texians who had fought with Mexico against Sam Houston. Richards was itching for an excuse to execute the traitors.

The Anglos stayed quiet. It seemed clear that they weren't inclined to talk. In fact, they had the temerity to sneer at Richards, and one of them spit at Carson who neatly dodged the poorly-aimed glob of spittle.

"Not talking, eh?" Richards gave them a hard look. "You boys have any idea who you're dealing with?"

They maintained their leering expressions while giving Richards a look that said they'd be uncooperative.

"I am Texas Ranger Captain Bol Richards. I fought at San Jacinto in 1836. I killed plenty of white treasonous bastards like you cowards. Now, I'll give you one more chance to answer my questions. Where are you from and who do you work for?"

Both men gave just a hint of fear when Richards

mentioned San Jacinto, the capstone battle of the Texas War for Independence. They remained silent, though by now there was a bit more trembling in their demeanor.

Richards drew his Colt and placed the muzzle behind the head of one of the men. He pulled the trigger. The explosion of bone and brain startled everyone. A horrified expression swept across Carson's face, but quickly disappeared

"Camargo. We're from Camargo. Cortina paid us to get some Apache together and attack ranches." The man's eyes had nearly burst from their sockets at the sight and the sound of his companion being executed and then seeing the gore spread on the ground before him.

"Untie him, Carson."

Carson was taken aback at Richards's order but complied.

"Okay, you damned bastard, you go back to Cortina and tell him that there's new law on the Nueces Strip and rivers of rebel bandit blood will flow on Texas soil." He kicked the man in the butt and sent him running on his way.

Carson shook his head admiringly.

"You like that, Walker?" Richards smiled broadly. "We'll let Cortina chew on this for a while." He scanned Carson head to toe. "You done damned good today, son. You made me proud."

"Thank you, Captain."

"Now, let's continue our ride to Fort Ringgold."

The dead Apache and turncoat Anglos were left to rot in the Texas sun. The wounded Texas Rangers were either mounted or, in the case of the dead Ranger, tied over a saddle. The few Apache prisoners were made to move at a trot in the midst of the column of riders, eating trail dust and walking in horse crap toward some indeterminate fate.

Richards was proud as a strutting peacock as concerned

the performance of his Texas Rangers in battle. Twice now, they'd aggressively carried the fight to the enemy and won overwhelmingly.

Captain Belknap rode slowly through the gate to Fort Ringgold. With the troops that accompanied him, he effectively doubled the size of the garrison. If Cortina had any designs on the fort, he'd at least encounter a respectable defensive force.

Belknap had barely had time to shake off the trail dust, when there was a clamoring at the gate. "Captain! Captain!" A guard waved animatedly. Approaching the fort was a column of Texas Rangers with half a dozen Apache prisoners in tow.

There was no time for formality. Belknap hadn't even had a chance to formally take command. He quick-walked to the gate just as Bol Richards rode up.

"Texas Ranger Captain Bol Richards at your service, Captain. We have a few hostiles for y'all." Richards smiled broadly, dismounted, and extended his hand to Belknap.

Belknap had heard about Rip Ford forming up several Texas Ranger companies, so this was no surprise to him. "Welcome, Captain. Captain Gordon Belknap here. Welcome to Fort Ringgold." He scanned the column. "I see you have some wounded men, Captain. We'll be pleased to help you as we can."

"I have a Ranger that gave his life fighting against the heathen Apache, sir. We'd like to give him an honorable burial."

"We'll help you with that. I'd be pleased for you to join me at dinner, Captain Richards. I'm sure we have much to discuss." Both his and Richards's men were exhausted, but

Belknap strove to be a considerate host to his visitors. "Captain Richards, I suggest you and your men will find comfortable accommodations up the road at Rio Grande City, though you're welcome to bivouac here for the night."

"Thanks. They've been through another San Saba."

"San Saba?"

Richards realized this was likely a piece of Texas history that no one had bothered to share with Belknap, much less teach at West Point. "Yes, Captain. Matter of some silver mines. Little skirmish back in '29, when a fella named Jim Bowie with only a dozen men fought and drove off a band of 120 Tawakoni hostiles. Son of a bitch was outnumbered ten to one…sort of fed Bowie's legend."

"This the man they named the knife after? Died at the Alamo, I heard."

"Yes, Captain, the same Jim Bowie. Now, my fight was every bit as one-sided, but I don't expect it to go down as part of any legend of Bol Richards." He laughed at his self-effacement.

"I look forward to our talk at dinner, Captain Richards."

They watched the Apache prisoners being led to the guard house.

A quite sobered Juan Cortina looked out across the Rio Grande and far out to the vast prairie that was Texas. He could see a couple of grazing longhorns, but no other sign of life. The water-logged Texian-Anglo dragged before him an hour ago had not brought welcome news. Moreover, the loss of dozens of Apaches over the past few days did not make it especially easy to recruit them to fight the Texans.

He'd sought to harass these new Texas Rangers, but it was becoming clear that making deadly forays north of the

Rio Grande was fast becoming a tall order. He'd have to come up with a new strategy and perhaps even put his Mexican loyalists to work.

Part of him wanted to kill the Anglo who'd brought the bad news, but it wouldn't do to be killing messengers... even ones that brought such news. He did learn that the Texas Rangers has skirted around his mother's ranch near Brownsville and appreciated them respectfully not disturbing her. Had he been there, it might have been a quite different matter.

Cortina knew he had a price on his head, owing to his having killed three Texans when he'd briefly occupied Brownsville back in September of 1859. His soldiers had even taken possession of nearby Fort Brown, though they failed to capture the munitions stored in the abandoned fort. Texans were rightly outraged at being so vulnerable, and it was this anger that contributed to the present situation whereby the powers that be in Austin funded companies of Texas Rangers under Rip Ford. Mexican troops had even crossed the border to defend the mostly Mexican-heritage citizens of Brownsville.

Cortina smiled at the irony of citizens having to be protected by Mexican troops on Texas soil. Texan vigilantes took to patrolling the streets of Brownsville at night. It was all part of Cortina's strategy to move the Mexican border north to the Nueces River. In any case, his prestige was enhanced, enabling his mostly unfettered rampaging throughout the southern Nueces Strip to steal livestock and terrorize settlers, both Anglo and Mexican. Cortina had to be mindful lest he run crossways with the *Federales* and upset *El Presidente*, Benito Juarez. In any case, Cortina was establishing his reputation as a champion of his people.

Meanwhile, Juarez was trying to consolidate his power as Mexican president while fending off incursions from the

French, Spanish, and English who were angered that he'd canceled Mexico's debts to them. In fact, it would only be a couple of years later, on May 5, 1862 (the real Cinco de Mayo), that General Ignacio Zaragoza fought off French forces near Puebla to stop their march from Veracruz to Mexico City. Zaragoza's defense brought him brief fame, but he wasn't to live much longer; he died in September, 1862 from typhoid fever. Juarez was under pressure from the United States to dethrone Emperor Maximillian, who Napoleon had installed. Maximillian was eventually captured in 1867 and executed on June 19 of that year.

Shortly after his arrival at Fort Ringgold, Richards received a dispatch directing him to join with other Texas Rangers at the hamlet of Rio Grande City. Rip Ford had already successfully engaged Cortina. The regular armyArmy troops that had been assigned to assist never participated in the fighting that had resulted in sixteen Rangers wounded and about sixty of Cortina's Mexicans killed. The rebel was none too happy.

Despite Ford's success and much to his chagrin, a Major Heintzelman had now been placed in command of his Texas Rangers. Ford's successor quickly earned the antipathy of citizens by taking their firewood and livestock with no compensation. It was enough to restore Ford to command, and it was in this situation that Richards arrived at Rio Grande City. The joint contingent of Texas Rangers headed southeast toward Brownsville, as they'd learned of Cortina setting up defenses.

Meanwhile, Cortina was at the Rio Grande trying to capture a steamboat owned by famed rancher Richard King's company. It was filled with valuable cargo that the

Mexicans dearly coveted. They were set to ambush the steamboat a couple of days ride from Brownsville, and that's where a battle was soon to rage.

Belknap by now had been directed to join, though he was under strict orders not to engage the enemy on Mexican soil. He wasn't happy leaving Fort Ringgold once again with a skeleton force. Ford and by extension Richards were under no such restriction. As Richards arrived, the steamboat had been swung around such that its cannon could be brought to bear on the Mexican forces dug in on the south bank of the river. Yelling wildly and loudly, and firing so effectively that the Mexicans could never hope to match them, the Texas Rangers charged into the Rio Grande right in the face of Cortina's forces.

Carson was right behind Richards as they charged through the water. Pistol and rifle fire were everywhere. "Stay close, Walker! Stay with me!" In no time at all, they were fighting at close quarters where the Sharps rifles were of no use. They relied on their Colt revolvers, firing and reloading as rapidly as possible.

"Captain, look!" Carson pointed to where Cortina's remaining mounted rebels, all sixty of them, were in headlong retreat. Unable to rally his men, Cortina was intent on breaking off the fight. A bullet whizzed through Carson's shirt, barely nicking his side. "Damn son of a bitch!" Carson returned fire, emptying his Colt at the Mexicans. As he reloaded, he saw Ford leading a headlong charge that continued the routing of Cortina's forces. Ford wasn't pulling up like the Mexicans probably expected, instead choosing to continue pursuit.

Richards decided not to follow Ford's lead. "Pull up, Carson." With the two of them drawn to a halt, the remainder of Richards's company pulled up behind. They continued to fire at the retreating Mexicans. The Sharps rifles were once again the effective weapon of choice.

Intense fire was directed at Cortina himself, but the rebel leader apparently led a charmed life. He took hits in his saddle and belt, but otherwise was unscathed. Carson had him sighted with the Sharps, but Cortina's horse turned just as the Ranger squeezed the trigger. There was no second chance.

Richards looked about the battlefield. Darkness was already enveloping the scene, and the dim light made accurate shooting difficult at best. Ford was last seen pursuing Cortina's forces. Some of the Texas Rangers had set fire to the *jacales* (huts) the Mexicans occupied. They wanted to be certain Cortina would not soon forget this day, though they'd be reprimanded later for stoking the fires of international politics.

Belknap watched the battle with frustration. Orders were orders, and he could not cross the Rio Grande. Meanwhile, the steamboat had run aground on a sandbar, and despite efforts to free it they'd have to wait for rising waters.

Richards crossed back into Texas to set a rear guard. He'd be ready to help Ford as necessary. Unbeknown to Richards, Ford and his nearly fifty Rangers were facing a mixed force of as many as eight hundred Mexican soldiers, of which Cortina's men comprised perhaps a quarter of the number. Ford was forced to negotiate his retreat back to Texas with assurance of protection of himself and the steamboat that by now had been freed from the sandbar. The Texas Rangers relished the idea of taking on the larger force, but decided that discretion might be the better part of valor.

"Looks like we're gonna have plenty of action ahead,

Walker. Son, you done good today." Richards smiled broadly. "You keep it up, and we're gonna turn you into a Ranger legend, boy." By his count, his young protégé had killed or wounded at least a half dozen Mexicans and likely scared off a bunch more. Once engaged, the kid didn't seem to understand fear.

Richards's Rangers wheeled their horses and made for higher ground to bivouac. Menacing clouds had begun to float in, and they didn't want to deal with a flooded Rio Grande.

"Tell me, Captain. Why are we Texas Rangers so successful, even against much bigger forces?"

Richards smiled. "We never warn them that we're coming. You catch them by surprise. They get scared real easy. A frightened man ain't much of a serious fighter, Walker."

Carson pondered that a moment or two. "Seems like the Army could learn a thing or two from that, Captain. In my observation, they seem to like ordered battle lines and give away their intentions." The young man whom Luke Dunn had taken a chance on months before up near San Diego was maturing. He was absorbing knowledge of strategy and tactics like a sponge. Richards's biggest challenge would be to keep him fully motivated.

"You know anything about that red-haired woman that was looking at me back in Corpus Christi?"

Richards was momentarily taken aback. He'd seen the little interaction, but hadn't thought all that much of it at the time. Apparently, it was weighing on Carson's mind. "I think she's friends with the Dunns. Don't fully know her story, Walker."

Carson crossed his arms purposefully. "I think I'll have to inquire when we get back to Corpus."

To Richards's thinking, women seemed to inspire men to do extraordinary things. He was pleased to see Carson find some purpose beyond whipping Mexican rebels.

TEN
STIRRINGS OF UNREST

THE BLAST from the muzzle of Luke's Colt Navy revolver echoed across the prairies surrounding Heaven's Gate. One by one, with each shot, a slat of wood set in the ground about fifty yards out was shattered. It was something he was driven by necessity and enjoyment to do from time to time, and the early winter evening with its dim lighting offered a bit of a challenge.

"You're already pretty good at that, Lucas." Elisa had been watching for several minutes, as he sent round after round into the targets.

"You know what they say, don't you, Lisa?"

She thought back to his words. "Don't just practice—practice perfect." It wasn't enough to aim and fire repeatedly. It wouldn't do to repeat bad technique. "When you're done practicing, you can come practice something else you're nearly perfect with." She caught his eye with a come-hither smile.

Luke holstered the Colt. He didn't have to be asked twice. Elisa's sexuality seemed to have increased with each pregnancy, and he had no problem with that. He unbuckled his gun belt as he approached the house and hung it on a hook just inside the front door. By the time he reached the bedroom, his manhood was ready to burst out of his trousers. He barely glanced at their children comfortably asleep in the adjoining bedroom.

Elisa drew him to her and pushed him onto his back. She pulled off his boots and pants. The rest didn't matter. She could feel shivers of ecstasy already running through her body. Her protruding belly made no matter as she wrapped herself around his erect member. Her hands stroked his well-muscled chest as he caressed her pregnancy-swollen breasts. The passion was beyond incredible as they sent each other into orgasmic heights. They were oblivious to all but themselves.

Finally, they collapsed with exhaustion, clutching each other tenderly. "You are amazing, Lucas Dunn." Indeed, he was every inch the man she'd dreamed of.

"And you…" He paused purposefully.

She looked expectantly up at him.

"…are beautiful."

Their post-coital tryst was soon shattered by a rapping at the door. Luke grabbed his trousers and boots. "Be right there," he shouted! He stole a lovingly wistful look at Elisa before heading to the front door.

"Bill?" Luke opened the door to Sheriff Meaney.

"Sorry to disturb your evening, Luke, but this couldn't wait."

"Well, what's got you so hot and bothered?"

"Brett Caulfield's been murdered!" Caulfield had been in the thick of the pro-slavery factions and had made a small fortune in the slave trade. He'd managed to maintain a fairly thriving business dealing with black merchantmen in Ghana who still thrived by capturing African natives and transporting them to the United States and the Caribbean.

Caulfield made regular runs to New Orleans, stopping at Galveston and other ports as he'd make his way back to Corpus Christi. Texas plantation owners would pay top dollar for good labor. Caulfield had even taken his profession a step further and got to breeding slaves to improve blood lines. To anti-slavery factions, he was a marked man. He'd even hired gunmen to act as security.

"Murdered? Why you telling me, Bill? Isn't this a Nueces County matter?"

"There's a lot of hate and discontent boiling in Corpus about the slave business, Luke. Something like this could have a widespread impact." He stroked his chin thoughtfully. "The ranchers around here don't give a damn about slavery—only a couple even need slaves—most ain't concerned with slaves. But the big farmers and some plantation folks depend on slaves to survive. It's an economic thing, Luke."

"I recognize that, Bill, but it's still a local matter. I'll help where I can…but that's likely the best I can do so far as jurisdiction." Luke shook his head. "Any idea who might have done it?" Jurisdiction or not, Luke couldn't suppress his curiosity.

"Horatio Thorpe is still sitting in my jail along with that cowboy who killed the priests. Thorpe actually has a few thoughts, but nothing specific enough to go on."

"Maybe I've missed out on the talk, Bill. Guess I don't hang out at the right places." He'd made a not-so-veiled reference to saloons. "I recall hearing a conversation or two, but I got the feeling most folks were more worried about the weather and their livestock than whether anyone owned slaves."

"It's getting a lot of attention in Washington, Lucas." Elisa had dressed and moved past Luke into the kitchen. "You want some coffee, Bill?"

"Thanks, Elisa, but I suppose I'll pass. It is getting late, and I'd best be getting back to Corpus."

"I'll let you know if I hear anything, Bill. I expect this is something we're going to be hearing more about."

As Meaney went on his way, Luke turned back to Elisa. "This civil unrest seems to be growing, Lisa." He drew her to him. The interruption had been inconvenient to say the least.

Elisa pressed her head against his chest. "Folks are getting right emotional about it, Lucas. There's plenty of strong feelings hereabouts. Most of our friends aren't inclined to stir the pot, but are fine with the way things are. Can't say as I cotton to the idea of any human being owned by another. It doesn't seem right, doesn't seem civilized, Lucas."

"Back in County Kildare, the British held us in near-slavery. They called it indenture, but it was slavery by any measure. Servants were regularly mistreated for even the smallest slight. When the famines came in the '40s, it made it even worse, and folks either rebelled or escaped or both. Seems I did both. Violence isn't the answer, but neither is doing nothing." He brought Elisa close to him. "I agree with you that owning another human isn't right, Lisa. It seems immoral. I'll follow the law so far as I'm obligated, but I can't compromise my moral principles."

Elisa hugged him tightly. "Let's go get warm under the bedcovers."

"What the hell did you think you were doing, Cal?"

"It was an accident, Zeke."

"You were supposed to scare the sonofabitch not kill him. That damned sheriff will be looking to track us down, and he's likely told that infernal Texas Ranger up in Nuecestown." Zeke Bose shook his full beard angrily, his eyes glaring as though they'd pop from his head. It was almost enough to shake the dried bread crumbs from his mangy scruff. The wild look in his eyes, coupled with the floppy hat, boots with hardly any soles remaining, and moth-eaten wool coat, completed a picture of a bombastic soul who was pouring heart and soul into fighting slavery. He looked more akin to a crazed troublemaker to the folks around Corpus Christi.

"Look, it's likely as not only the beginning, Zeke. Lots more blood's gonna be shed afore we get all them slaves freed." Cal Withers had already resigned himself to the eventuality of fighting over the slavery issue…maybe even war between states."

"You don't get it. Ain't hardly any slaves around these parts. The folks around here don't give a damn about slavery, just where they sell their horses and beeves. That slaver Caulfield didn't matter so much as a hoot to them." The last thing Bose needed was to stir the pot in Corpus Christi.

Rip Ford had to get himself back to Austin to strategize with Governor Houston. He'd dispatched most of the Texas Ranger companies under his command on missions to disrupt Cortina's activities along the Mexican border so far as possible. Richards and his company of Texas Rangers were to harass while avoiding any full-on, military-style engagement. Ford's strategy of deploying companies would serve to confuse and otherwise frustrate the Mexican troublemakers, not to mention any lurking Apache.

By now, Richards's Texas Ranger company had already engaged in three significant battles, and they were becoming a tad trail weary. Ford had pushed pretty hard, and Richards could fully appreciate that. He now had a company of battle-hardened men that would be hard to replace, yet he needed to seriously consider giving men leave and recruiting new blood into the company. He got to thinking that he might be able to do both by exchanging leave for recruiting.

By now, Richards had developed a solid working relationship with Walker Carson, and he sensed the young man's urge to get back to Corpus Christi to see the red-haired beauty who'd flirted with him. Certainly, Carson was incentivized. Richards lay back against his saddle, absorbing the warmth of the cooking fire. He scanned the faces of the men seated around him. "What do y'all think of some leave?"

Silence. Blank faces.

He caught Carson's eye. "What do you think, Walker?"

The men were deep in their personal thoughts as they sat around the cooking fire. They fully appreciated the warmth taking the damp chill out of the late winter air. They were all ears awaiting Carson's response.

"Kinda enjoying the fighting, Captain." Carson figured that's what Richards wanted to hear.

"Damn it, boy! What would you really like to do?"

Everyone around the fire perked up.

Carson looked around the fire circle. "I expect I could do a bit of recruiting back in Corpus, Captain." He smiled sheepishly.

That was more like it by Richards's reckoning. "Any of you men up to accepting my offer?"

"Will we still get paid, Captain?"

Well, that was a fair question by Richards's thinking. "Expect so, as long as you deliver recruits. I'd say two recruits for a month's paid leave." He figured he'd be lucky to see even one recruit from most of these frontier-tested veterans. They weren't known for running in large social circles, and most of their friends and acquaintances were already in Richards's company. "Now, not everyone can leave at once. Commander Ford would be none too happy with us if we let him down. I'd say it'd be fair if eight of you Rangers can take leave each month." He figured this would enable him to maintain an effective fighting force of at least 16.

"Where will the men we recruit rendezvous, Captain?"

Now, there was another good question. Richards's Texas Rangers would be patrolling an area 200 miles long by perhaps 30 miles wide. Could even be times that they'd be in Mexico. Communications were ponderously slow at best. He could feel their eyes boring intently upon him awaiting his answer. "Tell 'em to check in at Fort Ringgold. We'll be traveling through the fort regular like."

"Fair enough, Captain." There were a few minutes of pregnant quiet. "Er, Captain? How do we decide who takes leave first?"

"Come talk with me and give me good reasons. I'd say men with loved ones back home would carry most weight."

It was getting late, and the men grabbed bedrolls and began heading off to sack out under the stars. Fires were put out despite the chill March air and, soon enough, only the silhouettes of the horses under the moonlit sky and snoring of a few of the men gave any hint that a couple of dozen Texas Rangers were bedded down on the prairie. Richards posted sentries on two-hour shifts.

Belknap was bored nearly to tears. The daily routine of a relatively remote Army post like Fort Ringgold didn't lend itself to exciting diversions. There were occasional reports of Lipan Apache forays that they'd have to send patrols out to investigate. Usually, they were nothing more than someone hearing strange noises in the night, and now and then there'd be a legitimate theft of one or two head of livestock. Shootings were rare. It was hardly the romantic west described in dime-store tracts.

If Cortina's men were anywhere around, they seemed to travel a wide berth around Fort Ringgold. Occasionally, Belknap heard of disturbances in Rio Grande City, but those were the local sheriff's problem, and the Texas Rangers if and when they were around. He thought on the Rangers, calculating that there were perhaps nearly three hundred patrolling the border from Brownsville to *Piedras Negras*. He had to admit that the Rangers were tough *hombres* to a man.

Every couple of weeks, Captain Bol Richards would ride through and check with him. There'd occasionally be a new Ranger recruit awaiting them.

Walker Carson rode easy-like through the outskirts of Corpus Christi. He'd matured quite a bit during the past couple of months of fighting Apache savages and Mexican bandits. His experience had been far more militaristic than law enforcement. In any case, his mind was wrapped around a new mission. Where might he find that red-haired beauty who had flirted with him at the Texas Ranger parade? He'd have to do some detective work. He didn't even know her name. Of course, in a population of not quite 300 citizens, he expected that finding a pretty red-haired single woman ought not be too difficult.

It was mid-morning when he pulled up in front of the Corpus Christi jail. He rather hoped Sheriff Meaney would be around. Dismounting and hitching his horse, Carson strode up to the door and knocked loudly.

"Damn. Who the hell is it? Yur gonna wake the dead with that banging!"

Carson tried to turn the door latch, but it was locked. "It's Texas Ranger Walker Carson, Sheriff."

"Give me a minute, Carson." There was scuffling inside followed by the bang of a rear door being slammed shut. A moment later, the door opened and an unshaven, disheveled Sheriff Bill Meaney peered out at Carson through sleep-deprived eyes.

Out of the corner of his eye, Carson briefly caught sight of Clara trying to sneak off undetected. He smiled. Meaney obviously was going to be sympathetic to his quest for the red-haired woman. "Sorry to disturb you, Sheriff."

"Shucks, Walker. Come on in. Sorry to seem so riled up."

Upon entering, Carson noticed a drape hanging in front of the otherwise open jail cells. He guessed it was Meaney's attempt at a modesty screen. The jail wasn't all that big, and both cells were occupied. "I see you still have your prisoners."

"Yeah, we're waiting for a trial for Thorpe, though his lawyers up in Austin are trying to get him sent up there. Damned system. The other cell holds one of the town drunks…still sleeping it off from the sound of him. That fella Seth who killed the priests got hung a couple of weeks ago." Meaney scratched the itchy stubble on his chin. "So, how's Texas Rangering goin' for you?"

"You grow up real fast out there, Sheriff." Carson knew of Meaney's experience during the Texas War for Independence and the Mexican American War. "We whipped bands of Lipan Apache a couple of times and joined Rip Ford to engage that Mexican rebel, Juan Cortina. Chased the son of a bitch deep into Mexico. 'Course, the army was no help to us there. They aren't allowed to cross the Rio Grande."

"So, what brings you here, son? Gather you're on leave."

"Yeah, Sheriff. I'll be headin' back in a couple of weeks." He shifted a couple of times from one foot to the other.

"You got a woman on your mind, don't you, son?"

Was it so obvious? Carson gave an uncharacteristic "aw shucks" sort of expression. "Just afore we left a few weeks back, there was this right pretty red-haired woman smiling at me. She seemed to be taking a shine to me. You know where I might find her?"

Now, Meaney couldn't help but laugh. It was enough to wake Thorpe and even the drunk. Of course, Meaney was quite sensitive to Thorpe's obsession with the woman Carson was inquiring about. "Step outside a moment, Walker." He wisely figured it best not to be within earshot of Thorpe.

"You know her, Sheriff?"

Meaney had finally contained his mirth. "Yep, you could say that, son. Actually, you're about 100 yards from her right now." Meaney glanced up the street. Scarlett was just stepping away from the stairway leading up to her apartment. He nodded in Scarlett's direction. "That who yur talkin' about, Walker?"

Carson's head swiveled so fast he nearly sprained his neck. His knees immediately grew weak. "Er...yes. Yes. That's her, Sheriff."

"Well, what are you waiting for?" Meaney nudged Carson a bit. "Oh, and you should be aware that she's very good friends with Texas Ranger Captain Dunn and his wife. Anything you do had best be honorable."

Carson stepped away, offering a weak thank you as he pondered his next move. He grabbed the reins of his horse and began to walk toward Scarlett. He was perhaps 15 feet or so from her when she heard him and turned around to face him. Carson nearly tripped over his own feet. "My God," he thought, "she's beautiful."

"Are you following me, sir?" Then she recognized him.

What could he say? There was a momentary disconnect between his voice and brain. "Er…yes, ma'am. Yes, I was…er…am seeking to make your acquaintance. I remembered you from the Texas Rangers parade a few weeks ago, and…well…I had to come back and find you."

Scarlett was flattered. "Why, I'm touched that you remembered. As I recall, you were riding a very spirited horse and controlled him quite well."

Carson fell into the "aw shucks" expression again. He was nothing if not humble. "Yes. By the way, my name is Walker…Walker Carson."

"I know."

He looked up inquisitively. "You know?"

"I do have friends in high places, Mr. Texas Ranger Walker Carson." She smiled a bit of a winsome smile. "My name is Scarlett Rose. I am very pleased to meet you."

"Is there someplace we could set a spell and get acquainted, Miss Rose?"

Set a spell was a far cry from a room with a bed. It was a rather refreshing situation for Scarlett. "There's a place up the way with a nice gallery that looks onto the gulf. I've got a little time before I need to deliver some sewing to a customer."

"Please, lead the way, Miss Rose."

It wasn't all that far, and they were soon sitting on straw chairs enjoying coffee and a slight warming breeze wafting in from the sea. "You can call me Scarlett, Mr. Carson. I'd be taking no offense." She was quickly getting comfortable enough with this man that she'd also begun to think about full disclosure. At some point, she'd need to tell him about Margaret.

Bill Meaney stood for a few moments, smiling as he watched Carson go off to meet the potential object of his affections. He turned to re-enter the jail only to be looking down the steely-blue barrel of a Colt revolver.

"Just back up real-easy-like, Sheriff."

A second man leading three horses emerged from around the side of the jail. He was heavily armed and obviously meant business with what he was up to. "We're gonna borrow your prisoner, Sheriff. Hope you won't mind." Both men wore bandannas over their faces.

Meaney wasn't armed and had been taken completely off guard. He felt utterly helpless. The streets of Corpus Christi were surprisingly empty for this time of day. Of course, he'd forgotten about the battleship that had been scheduled to arrive that morning. Most folks would be down at the wharf to see it.

The man with the pistol grabbed the manacles hanging inside near the rifle rack. "If you'd be so kind as to wrap your arms around that hitching post, we'd be much obliged." Soon enough, Meaney was secured to the rail. A crack on the noggin with the butt of the Colt was meant to ensure that the sheriff wouldn't be shouting any alarms for a while.

Horatio Thorpe was brought out, blinking as his eyes adapted to the bright morning sun. He looked at a groggy and half-conscious Meaney and smiled triumphantly. "No jail is going to hold me for long, Sheriff. Sorry to ruin your day." He'd obviously been listening to Meaney's early morning tryst with Clara. "Give my best to Captain Dunn."

He fully relished his own sarcasm even as it was totally lost on Meaney. Thorpe was stiff from the cramped cell, but was able to mount one of the horses and ride out of Corpus Christi.

"Damn, Sheriff. What happened?" The youngster who tended the livery stable had just happened by.

Meaney gave the boy a look that would have melted steel. "The key to these damned things is in my desk drawer." It was a command, not a plea.

He was soon free of the manacles and softened a bit. "Thanks, Johnny, for getting me loose of these goldarned things." Once freed, Meaney knew he had to get word to Luke that Thorpe had been sprung.

"Sheriff, there's been a killing." Turned out the boy was on a mission of his own.

The words fell like lamp oil on a roaring fire. Meaney was already filled with seething anger over Thorpe having been freed. He didn't need a murder to add to his woes.

Undeterred, Johnny continued. "Some fella named Zeke Bose was strung up from a gallery rafter last night at the Smith's place. There was a note."

"A note?" Meaney was listening while he busied himself cleaning up toward being reasonably presentable for heading to Heaven's Gate and hopefully catching up with Luke.

"Yeah. Appears this hanging was revenge. This guy was accused of killing some slaver named Caulfield."

That got Meaney's attention. One murder solved—another to be solved. This slavery business was causing too much unrest for his liking.

"Bill? Where you headed?" Luke had arrived just as Sheriff Meaney was about to mount up.

"Damn, Luke, I was just fixin' to head out to your place. Thorpe's been sprung!"

An expression of concern spread swiftly across Luke's face. "How the…?"

"Couple of Thorpe's armed thugs caught me off guard."

"I didn't pass anyone on my ride this morning, Bill. Where do you think they were headed?"

"Well, I don't expect they'd have taken the time to look for Scarlett despite the son of a bitch's obsession. And I doubt they'd be riding in plain sight for a while, so no surprise that you wouldn't have seen them." Of a sudden, Meaney's eyes grew wide. "They just might look for you, Luke. Thorpe was angry about you puttin' him in jail and all, especially with you using Scarlett as bait. That, coupled with you having killed his son, could work a man into a lather."

"Elisa!" It hit Luke that she could be in danger if Thorpe was heading to Heaven's Gate. "Come on, Bill!"

The stable boy was standing to one side still listening to the dialogue. "But what about…?"

"Vigilante murder can wait, boy." Meaney sprung into the saddle, and he and Luke were off at a gallop.

"Scarlett, it's been a pleasure making your acquaintance. As I mentioned, I have a couple of more weeks of leave from the Texas Rangers, and I'd sure like to see you again." They were enjoying the stroll from the docks. Carson's horse dutifully followed behind.

"Why, that would be right nice, Walker Carson." There was still much to share with the young man, and she didn't want to deceive him into thinking her life had been all lily-pure and such. "Are you staying close by?"

"I've got a room at the boarding house up the street, Miss Scarlett. I'm gonna head up the road a piece to Nuecestown this afternoon to see Captain Dunn. Perhaps you could join me for dinner tomorrow evening."

"I'd love to, Walker."

They turned the corner onto her street in time to see Luke and Meaney riding off in a cloud of dust. Carson called out to the stable boy, "Hey, what's happening? Why are they in such an all-fired hurry?"

"Been an escape from the jail. They're chasing after the son of a bitch and the two men that sprung him."

Scarlett knew instantly that it had to be her nemesis, Horatio Thorpe, but she didn't say anything about her fears to Carson.

"Excuse me, Miss Scarlett, but I really must go help them." Carson mounted up, checked that his rifle and Colt revolvers were at the ready, and smiled down at Scarlett. He tipped his hat. "See you later, Miss Scarlett. The morning's been a pleasure." He spurred his pony toward Nuecestown.

ELEVEN
THORPE'S COMEUPPANCE?

THEY HAD STAYED clear of the Corpus Christi to San Antonio Road until they got close to Nuecestown. Thorpe rode as hard as he could to establish distance from the jail.

"Slow it down, men. Long as we've got that damned sheriff tied to the hitching rail, we've got time. I've got a little business to tend to." He halted them in front of the gate to Heaven's Gate ranch. "I don't know if the Texas Ranger is home, but I figure to give the bastard something he won't soon forget."

They began to walk the horses up the dirt trail to the ranch house. "This Ranger gutted my business dealings, frustrated my every attempt to hunt him down, including killing my son Gascon, and has kept me from the best damned whore in Texas."

Thorpe's two henchmen were listening raptly. "Whatcha plannin', Mr. Thorpe?" They were already feeling right cocky at having so easily sprung Thorpe from the jail.

"As I understand it, there's a cabin where Dunn's *vaquero* lives with his wife, and then there's the main ranch house. I figure it'll be best to sneak up behind the barn and see how many stalls are empty. If there are missing horses, that will mean the women are vulnerable."

"Um…boss, why are you going after this Ranger? You can live well near any place you choose." The implication was why should Thorpe take this risk?

Thorpe didn't answer.

They walked the horses the 100 yards or so to the barn. It was clear that horses had been saddled and ridden out that morning, especially as there were fresh hoof prints leading away.

"Let's get whoever's in that cabin, boys."

Crouching low, they snuck onto the gallery along the front of the cabin. They passed the new post that replaced the one a bullet from Elisa's Sharps rifle had shattered months earlier against Thorpe's hired gun, Roy Biggs. They two men leaned into the door and totally surprised poor Julia. She was gagged and tied up in record time. "You stay here and be quiet and we'll do you no harm."

Julia wasn't impressed with their sincerity and feared for Elisa. Would Jaime or Luke get back to Heaven's Gate in time?

"Okay, let's get on up to the house." Thorpe's expression was about as diabolical as he was capable of. He planned to show the Ranger not to mess with Horatio Thorpe.

Elisa thought she heard some noise outside, but it was windy and she paid it no mind. She thought it was likely a loose shutter or barn door.

Thorpe and his men had left their horses tethered behind the barn and ditched their spurs so they could move about stealthily. Soon enough, they were huddled near the back door to the house. One of Thorpe's men gently tried the latch. It was unlocked. As they prepared to storm inside, there was a bit of a commotion as Elisa came out, intending to use the privy behind the house. She was distractedly looking back at the fussing children as the men stepped toward her. They grabbed her by both arms and, struggle as she might, there was no escape from their vice-like grasps.

Elisa twisted, turned, clawed, and bit like a mother bear protecting her young. "Who…what?" A pistol butt aside her head ended further struggle.

"Come on…quick now!" Thorpe commanded. "Take her around front and tie her between the gallery posts."

Soon, Elisa was effectively spread-eagled between two of the posts on the gallery across the front of the house. A rocking chair was in the way, and Thorpe smashed that into the ground.

She began to come to. "Who…Who are you?" She could feel the warm trickle of blood run down her cheek from being struck by the pistol butt.

"Doesn't matter none, Mrs. Dunn. Your Texas Ranger captain husband is gonna pay for killing my son and ruining my business."

Despite the throbbing pain on the side of her head, Elisa was quick to put two and two together. "You…you're Thorpe! Horatio Thorpe!" She began to shout loudly enough that Thorpe had one of his men tie a bandanna over her mouth. Best she could do now were muffled gasps.

By the grace of God, Thorpe and his men as yet hadn't noticed little Peter and John staring out the front window.

"You are gonna pay Dunn's price, you little prairie bitch." With that, Thorpe ripped off most of her dress, leaving her pretty much naked in the cool late winter air. Her being cold didn't really matter much with what they had in mind.

Thorpe drew his knife. It was a big knife, one of those styles they called a Bowie knife after the hero of the Alamo.

Elisa twisted and pulled at her bonds. She could feel the ropes cutting into her wrists and ankles. Her eyes grew wide as her attacker placed the tip of the blade at her breastbone.

Thorpe looked down at her swelling belly. "Pregnant, are we?" There was a blood lust in his eyes. He saw revenge…revenge on Dunn…revenge on Scarlett. He pushed the tip of the knife into her fragile whiteness, barely breaking the skin. She tried to scream through the gag. Pain and fear coursed through her. He ran the blade down the front of her body from breastbone to groin. A rivulet of blood began to trickle from the long wound. "You damned bitch. I'll teach your damned Texas Ranger not to mess with a Thorpe." He stood back to admire his work. "Damn, but you bleed good, bitch."

By now, Thorpe's henchmen were standing back with some combination of horror and mesmerized curiosity. How evil could this man get?

Elisa twisted and pulled at the ropes in her struggle to break free.

Thorpe smiled. He was deep into the heat of the moment. "Watch this, boys. I'm gonna show you how we break one of these bitches for our brothels." The words were in a half-growl delivered with an arrogant sneer. This clearly wasn't to be his first rape. He unbuttoned his trousers and let them fall to his knees.

She could see his member, swollen and stuck out from under his roll of belly fat. Elisa twisted to try to clamp her knees together as best she could.

"You ain't never had anything like this, bitch." He reached behind her head and grabbed her hair, forcing her head up and pressing his lips against hers, bandanna and all. She could feel the ugliness of his nakedness against her sweating, bleeding body. She tried to shake her head side to side pleadingly. Finally, he tore the gag from her and pressed his lips hard on her mouth. He stuck his tongue in and she clamped down on it…hard!

Thorpe pulled away with the pain. "Damn! She's bit through my tongue." Blood flowed from his mouth. "Damn you!" He slapped her across the face and took out his knife again. "I'll teach you, you bitch."

Elisa pulled back from the knife so far as the ropes would allow. The vulnerability of her nakedness was less an issue now, as she glanced to one side and saw Peter and John crying and staring out the window.

Thorpe waved the knife back and forth in front of her. "What do the Comanche do?" he snarled out. "I hear they do some nasty tortures to women afore they kill them." The eyes of Thorpe and his men were riveted on Elisa as she kept fighting to tear herself free. "Damn, woman. I like a spirited squaw. Lookee here how it turns me on" He pointed down to his crotch. He glanced at his men. She spit in his face. "Y'all can take a turn after me." He moved to her again, this time holding the knife just under her throat. With his free hand he tried to get his prick aligned with her. She peed on his hand and on his boots. "Bitch!"

She could feel it against her as she strove again to bring her knees together…to no avail. His girth and her diminutive size would have made it awkward for him in the best of circumstances. For now, she was only able to make rape as difficult as possible.

He pushed and probed, making grunts like a bull in full rut. "Cam, hold her still, dammit!"

The man dutifully wrapped his arms around her in a nearly vain attempt to stop her squirming. With Elisa's near-nakedness, Thorpe's erection and probing, and his hands touching her skin, the thug was fully aroused with the lustful intensity of the moment.

"Pull the damn bitch's legs apart!" Thorpe poked the tip of the knife into Elisa's neck just enough to bring pain and more blood. It was enough of a cut that she momentarily lost focus on holding her legs as close together as she could.

Again, Thorpe's hired man tried to hold her legs apart. "Bitch is strong, boss." At last, he succeeded.

Thorpe stepped back and smiled. She could see his tongue, half- bitten through, as blood trickled from the corner of his mouth. He pulled back to get a better view of his engorged penis. He began to move in close again.

Meanwhile, Luke and Meaney had ridden undetected up to where Thorpe had left the horses behind the barn. Luke dismounted, slid the Sharps from its scabbard, and peered around the corner of the barn. His eyes grew wide with anger.

Of a sudden, Thorpe's head exploded in a shower of bone, brains, and blood. His body was hurled backward with what had been most of his head strewn across the ground. The split second of surreal silence was followed right quickly by the cannon-like report of a Sharps rifle. The Bowie knife went flying. Thorpe's men dove for cover. Too late. A second bullet burrowed through the torso of one of them. The other man let loose of Elisa and began to run, but only covered a few steps before being brought down. Luke would have kept shooting the dead men if it would have mattered at all. Dead was dead.

Luke Dunn remained calm in his anger. He took a deep breath and slowly exhaled. "Stay here, Bill." He didn't want the sheriff to see his wife strung up so exposed and vulnerable.

Luke absolutely had to get to her and pronto. He mounted Big Horse and galloped up to the house, grabbing the bedroll from behind his saddle as he dismounted. "Lisa…Lisa, I'm here." He unsheathed his own Bowie knife and cut her bonds, and then wrapped the blanket around her and drew her tightly to him. "It's over, sweetheart. It's over." His eyes dared not look at the blood covering her for fear that the sanctuary of his arms would turn to white rage at the men he'd already killed.

She buried her face in his chest and sobbed great heaving sobs. They stood tightly holding each other. Of a sudden, she pulled away and pounded on his chest. "Lucas Dunn, you almost didn't come in time…you almost didn't get here to save me." She broke into sobs and embraced him again.

Meaney finally saw fit to ride on up. "Holy…! You got 'em all, Luke!" Not one of the three men had a breath left in their foul bodies.

"Bill, go down to the cabin and see if Julia is okay."

Just then, another voice broke the near-silence. "Whoa, y'all! Is everything all right?" Walker Carson had near broken his horse trying to arrive in time to help. He was out of breath, and the pony was well-lathered.

Luke looked up from Elisa. "Thanks for coming, son. How 'bout riding into Nuecestown in a hurry to fetch Doc? Elisa's cut up pretty bad." By now, Luke was gently carrying her back into the house.

As if on cue, Jaime rode up from an afternoon of checking longhorns. He'd heard the boom of gunshots. He quickly saw that Luke had Elisa cared for and headed down to the cabin to check that Julia was all right.

Luke carried Elisa over to the settee near the fireplace,

grabbing some cloth to staunch her bleeding. "You're going to be all right, Lisa, sweetheart. I'm here for you." But he knew that the pain of this sort of attack wasn't just physical. He'd witnessed Scarlett's trauma, and she'd been a whore, after all. He'd sit and hold Elisa until Doc arrived.

Peter and John toddled over to be sure their mother was safe. "Mama okay?" Luke nodded and tried to give them a reassuring smile. Andrea Ann had been quiet throughout the ordeal but would need tending to soon enough.

Doc arrived. He tried not to look at the bodies strewn askew in front of the house.

By this time, Julia had assured Jaime that the danger was passed and had come up from the cabin to help tend to Elisa. She peeked in the front door, and Luke spotted her. "You okay, Julia?"

"Yes, *Señor* Dunn. I'm okay. Jaime is *muy trastornado...* very upset." She smiled nervously.

"Rightly so, Julia. I'm glad you're safe. You go be with Jaime." Luke carried Elisa into the bedroom so she could more easily be tended to by Doc.

An hour later, Doc emerged. "Her wounds will heal up just fine, Luke. Looked worse than they were. It's gonna take a lot of love and patience from you for her mind to heal. But she's always had a strong fighting spirit. Likely as not that saved her...bought her enough time that you could take action."

"Did he...?"

"Nope. You got here in the nick of time, Luke."

Luke felt a certain guilt at wondering, but he needed to know. He walked out onto the gallery with Doc. Meaney, Carson, and a now-calm Jaime joined them. They surveyed the bloodied bodies lying around them. It wasn't a pretty sight,

"Damn, Captain Dunn, ain't never seen anyone so good

with a Sharps." Carson was amazed at Luke's masterful marksmanship.

Luke turned to Meaney. "I expect Scarlett's gonna be relieved, Bill."

Carson looked at them inquisitively. "Why?"

Luke saw a helpless look on Meaney's face. "She'll have to tell you about it, Walker. Seems this Thorpe pervert had designs on her…sort of an obsession."

Carson looked baffled. In his mind, he'd apparently gotten a hankering for a woman of mystery. "Do I wait for her to open that door, Captain Dunn?"

"Likely for the best, son. I can tell you that her experience with Thorpe was far from a pleasant one." He recognized that the conversation needed to shift, as it was already uncomfortable. "Can we ever hope to understand men like Horatio Thorpe?" He shook his head and stroked his mustache thoughtfully. "The man had money, power, influence, just about anything he wanted, yet turned against the law. It was like sport for him. Hell, he even sacrificed one of his sons."

"Couldn't have been right in his head, Luke." Meaney looked down at Thorpe's body lying in the dust. Half of Thorpe's head was gone. "They say some science folk are studying brains of criminals. Dang, Luke, but you didn't leave them anything to study." He laughed, then quickly contained himself. It had been an inappropriate joke of the moment but a relief all the same. He guffawed. "Er…sorry about that."

Jaime surveyed the three bodies. "*Señor* Dunn, what are we to do with these bodies? I don't think our women will like seeing them." He shrugged. "Just saying. And they are already starting to smell." He forced a smile.

"Sheriff Meaney, I'm happy to loan you our wagon. I expect you have some paperwork to get done. I'm not sure who Thorpe's friends are, but they should get a burial."

"Thorpe can surely afford a box, Luke." Doc noted that a few gold coins had fallen from the man's pocket.

"Ought to be space here in the Nuecestown Cemetery, Bill. I'll let Rip Ford know about this, but I'd be beholden if you'd take care of notifying Thorpe's next of kin. I hear tell he has a surviving son, and they might want to bury the man at a family plot, though Lord knows he doesn't seem to deserve it."

About this time, Pastor Rucker rode up. "Hey, y'all, what's been going on?" He dismounted, tipped his hat to the assembled group, and looked at the large body lying in a grotesque twisted position with its brains spilled out. "Holy…! Damn, Luke. That's…that's Horatio Thorpe." Relief flooded Rucker's face, as he saw it as the closing of a chapter in his past that he longed to forget. "God bless you, Luke Dunn."

"Good to see you, too, Pastor." Luke smiled warmly. "Yes, the Thorpe saga does seem about finished."

Carson looked around questioningly. He was oblivious to the history of what evils Horatio Thorpe had wrought upon Texas. He shrugged. "If y'all don't need me, I'll be getting on back to Corpus."

"Stop on back in a day or two, Walker. Likely we'll be able to chat a bit. I've got to look after Elisa and get back to some ranch duties."

Jaime had gone down and hitched the mules to the wagon. Together they loaded the bodies for the trek to the cemetery. "We'll build a box for the big one, *Señor* Dunn. We may have enough wood." He hid a smile. It took three men to hoist Thorpe onto the wagon. He was truly dead weight.

"Thanks to everyone for your help. I'd best go see to my

wife." Luke turned to go inside the house, then paused. "Doc? Anything special I need to know?"

"She'll be right tender for a few days, Luke, but will heal up pretty much good as new. I don't think they hurt the baby, thank God." He smiled at Luke. "She's a spirited young woman and should recover quickly, Luke. She's handled Comanche and bandits, but keep in mind that this time it was personal. It'll take all your love to heal the wounds to her mind." Doc sought to emphasize to Luke what he might face.

Luke went inside. Julia had put the children to bed, and Elisa was asleep. She surely was exhausted. Luke climbed into the bed beside her. He looked at the wounds on her wrists rubbed raw by straining on her bonds. She was mostly under a blanket, but he knew her ankles shared the same bruises and abrasions. A dressing covered her chest and abdomen. She seemed to be sleeping peacefully. Luke gently placed his arm around her shoulder.

"No! Get away!" Elisa awakened with a start and thrashed about reflexively. Wild-eyed, she quickly took stock of her surroundings before realizing it was Luke. He wore an expression of total dismay. "Oh, Lucas...my love... I'm so sorry." She moved her head to his shoulder.

★★

Sheriff Meaney pulled the buckboard up at the Corpus Christi jail long about dusk. To say it had been a long and eventful day would be a gross understatement. He thought about getting together with Clara, figuring it might relax him. The jail was awfully quiet, what with no current residents in its cells. Carson had ridden into Corpus with him, but had gone on to the boarding house to get some shuteye.

Meaney hitched his horse and walked the short distance

up the street to Scarlett's place. He looked forward to bringing Scarlett some peace of mind.

Scarlett answered his soft knock. "Why, Sheriff Meaney, what brings you here?"

"Miss Scarlett, ma'am, I guess you know that Horatio Thorpe was sprung from our jail this morning."

She gasped.

"Fear not," Meaney told her. "Captain Dunn and I pursued him, and Luke disposed of Mr. Thorpe and his two henchmen. They've taken residence in the Nuecestown Cemetery."

"Thank you so much, Sheriff." Scarlett looked visibly relieved. "I saw Mr. Carson ride out. Was he involved?"

"He arrived just after Captain Dunn fired his Sharps for the third time, Scarlett. In case you're wondering, Mr. Carson knows nothing of your history but what you may have told him, as we didn't feel it was our place to tell him of your dealings with Thorpe."

"I deeply appreciate that, Sheriff. I expect I will have to share that with him. Is there anything else I should know?"

"Well, yes, ma'am, there is. Mrs. Dunn…Elisa…was attacked by Thorpe and was injured. You might want to pay her a visit. Doc says she'll be fine, but you never know."

"What about her baby?"

"Doc expects no problem with her pregnancy." Meaney smiled with relief at having gotten this necessary duty done. "I'll be on my way now, Miss Scarlett. I think I'll go look for my friend Clara."

Scarlett smiled. "You like her, don't you, Bill Meaney?"

Meaney blushed just a tad, then turned and descended the stairway.

Scarlett realized she'd have to be straight with Walker Carson about her odyssey into prostitution and crime. Of course, unbeknown to her, he had his own story of indiscretions to share, having left his father at a young age and gotten past a brief flirtation with crime in the form of a botched bank robbery. A common bond was that Luke Dunn had influenced each of them in a positive way. Both had overcome life trials—it was often a way of life on the Texas frontier.

Morning brought a sunny day and a touch of just enough humidity to remind the fine citizens of Corpus Christi of the months of hot temperatures to come.

For Sheriff Bill Meaney, the morning brought a new mystery. Zeke Bose was not dead. The hanging had been staged. Cal Withers and his co-conspirator Bose were on the run.

"Dang!" he thought. He was figuring to have a day or two to spend courting Clara. She sure had taken a shine to him, and the feelings were mutual.

TWELVE
WAR LURKS?

WHAT GOES through a mind when it's made up? Not much apparently. Luke sat in the rocker on the gallery thinking on how the world was getting more complicated every day. From what he read in the newspaper from Corpus Christi, it seemed as though folks were taking hard positions on the slavery issue. A lot of minds had been hard-wired one way or the other. Some people felt that there could yet be bloodshed.

Elisa slipped in beside him, and the boys were playing at her feet while little Andrea Ann napped. It had been nearly a week since Thorpe's horrific attack. She was healing well, and the nightmares had stopped after the first couple of days. "What are you thinking on, Lucas?" She desperately wanted to ask him whether he planned to continue working for Rip Ford. She knew that for him to be comfortable with that decision, it would have to come from his heart. She knew too that the attack still weighed heavily on him. He'd never intended for her to be at such risk. He thanked God every day that he'd fired the Sharps accurately under tremendous pressure. It was done and would gradually go away, but the potential for conflict over slavery was building.

"There's a lot of strong feelings about slavery, Lisa. I spoke with Sheriff Meaney the other day, and he said those men who murdered the slaver staged a fake suicide and then high-tailed it out of town. There's lots of talk in the local saloons. Folks get liquored up and get crazy."

Elisa nodded and laid her head on his shoulder. "You thinking there could be more violence?"

"Feel it in my bones. I recall a similar feeling back in Ireland just before there'd be an uprising against the British. Folks here are getting tired of the politics of slave state versus free. The newspapers I've seen are pushing hard to bend public opinion in support of slavery and even to leave the Union. There's a strong push for secession. I'm sure Governor Houston has his plate full dealing with the issue."

"I pray it doesn't come to more violence, Lucas." She looked off toward the horizon. "I was pleased that Scarlett came to visit yesterday. It was nice to see her with that young Texas Ranger, Walker Carson. Seems like a nice man."

"Yep, he's got a lot of potential, Lisa. Scarlett will do well to hang on to him, though I understand he'll be heading back to Rio Grande City in another week."

"She told me that they shared their pasts. Seems good not to be hiding anything. Turns out they both had some run-ins with the law."

Luke smiled. "Yes, indeed. But I saw some potential in the lad."

"Oh, you knew about Walker's attempt to rob a bank and hook up with Thorpe's man?" She smiled mischievously.

"You're seeming just a tad feisty, my sweet. You must be

feeling much better." Luke looked lovingly at her. "How about a ride into Nuecestown? I've a hankering to visit Bernice and Agatha."

"Captain Belknap, good to see you, sir." Bol Richards's Texas Rangers were on the road back to Fort Ringgold when they encountered Belknap. The men were roughly a half-day ride west of the fort. The company was tired, what might best be described as looking bedraggled. Several men were looking forward to taking some well-earned leave. A couple of Rangers sported non-life-threatening wounds from recent skirmishes: one with some of Cortina's rebels, and another with a small outlier band of Lipan Apache. Richards had lost two men: one killed and the other deserted. The deserter was hunted down and summarily executed.

The captain offered a courtesy salute. "Greetings, Captain Richards." Their horses faced each other nose to nose, so their conversation was pretty much private. "I was going crazy cooped up in the fort, so decided to lead a patrol. It's hotter than hell, isn't it?"

"Yep, Captain. Seems like there's enough water hanging in the air to float a boat."

"I gather you are headed to Fort Ringgold?"

"Yes, sir, if you have no problem with that. We'll bivouac over near Rio Grande City." Richards would have liked to have chatted more, but knew he needed to get his men some much-needed rest and see whether any new recruits had shown up.

"Sounds good to me, Captain. Your man Walker Carson returned with a couple of recruits. I'm thinking you'll be pleased."

"Much obliged, Captain Belknap." He paused to be sure he was out of earshot. "Y'all be careful about a day's ride west of here. A ranch was hit hard by a small band of Apache. The cowboys fought them off. We decided not to engage them, but you ought to be on guard. I'd keep your point rider within sight."

Belknap gave the Ranger another half-salute of respectful acknowledgment. "Appreciate the warning, Captain. Saints willing, I expect we'll see you in a few days." He was about to lead his men on past the Rangers when he paused. "One of these days, Richards, I'd like to hear about your time fighting for Texas independence."

Richards smiled and nodded. "Maybe when you get back from patrol, Captain." It wasn't something Richards talked about all that much. After all, he'd spent the past twenty years trying to get past his considerable resentment at Texas having joined the Union.

The wind rustled through the oak and juniper in harmony with the gurgling waters of the San Saba River and birds singing. Nature's symphony suited Three Toes, bringing peace to his mind as he prayed to the Great Spirit. A shriek like a wailing baby interrupted his ponderings. He listened up. It was unusual to hear a mountain lion in broad daylight. He had to wonder what had stirred it so. The memory of fighting off one of the beasts with his bare hands still lingered in the recesses of his mind, but he was far more curious than fearful. He felt a sort of kinship with the mountain lion, as it too was being pushed from its natural habitat. He would have to heighten his awareness of his surroundings, as he had no idea what might have stirred the lion.

The chief stood slowly and picked up his bow and quiver of arrows. He was on high alert, his eyes scanning the forest and his ears tuned to any unusual sounds. Quiet like a cat, he headed back to the camp.

Cactus Flower and Bird Woman were busily at work. Cactus Flower welcomed him. "It is a beautiful day, Three Toes."

He looked about the camp. They had settled into this site nestled among the junipers, perhaps a bit too settled in. He accepted the juicy piece of roast venison that Bird Woman offered. He was ravenous,, but tempered his hunger enough to be scanning the woods as he devoured the sweet flavors of the deer's bounty.

"What is it?" asked Bird Woman.

"Nothing…or something." It was as much statement as question. He looked from her to Cactus Flower. His senses told him they were being stalked. He sighed. He nocked an arrow to his bow. "Stay here." The implication was to continue to work around their little camp.

Three Toes left the two squaws. He moved swiftly and silently in the direction from which he'd heard the mountain lion's wail. The rocky terrain served to further muffle his movements, and there was plenty of cover among the trees. In his buckskin attire, he was nearly invisible.

It first appeared in his peripheral vision. A lone rider was moving slowly along the trail. The man was an Indian, but Three Toes didn't recognize his regalia at first. He dug into the innermost recesses of his memory. Then, he remembered from his youth. This lone traveler was of the Southern Arapahoe Nation. The Arapahoe had pushed the Kiowas and his Comanche brothers south so were sworn enemies of the Penateka Comanche. He wondered why this warrior was traveling alone in this region.

With his bow at the ready and an arrow nocked in its

string, Three Toes stepped onto the trail in front of the Arapahoe. Naturally, the warrior stopped. He'd been totally surprised by the chief. The two locked eyes, cautiously studying each other.

Finally, the Arapahoe smiled. He raised his hand as a sign of peace. "Kicking Bear." This was apparently his name.

The chief could barely comprehend the language. He motioned for Kicking Bear to dismount. "Me Three Toes, war chief of Penateka Comanche." He wanted to establish the pecking order from the start.

The Arapahoe warrior dismounted. He was unarmed and seemed to want to avoid being any threat.

"Why travel Comanche lands?" Three Toes asked. Obviously, the warrior wasn't lost. Was he scouting new territory for his tribe?

"On quest."

That resonated with Three Toes. He knew that tribes other than Comanche practiced vision quests. What sort of quest had Kicking Bear undertaken? Could it be to kill a Comanche? It wasn't proper etiquette to ask what sort of quest was being undertaken. Three Toes's quest had been to learn more of the White man's ways through his friendship with Luke. Nevertheless, he wondered at this warrior's intentions. He saw several scalps on Kicking Bear's lance. Still, if he'd earned his name by kicking a bear, it meant that he was likely a warrior of some reputation.

Kicking Bear read the chief's questioning expression. "Kicking Bear come in peace."

For now, that was good enough for Three Toes. He debated as to just how friendly he ought to get, reminding himself that their tribes were sworn enemies. The chief returned his arrow to the quiver. "Kicking Bear hungry?"

Kicking Bear nodded. Hungry would be an understatement. His empty belly was sufficient reason to overlook any past hostilities.

They walked side by side to Three Toes's camp. Despite their language differences, they managed to keep up a truncated but sufficient dialogue to get better acquainted. They had both done battle with other tribes and certainly fought the White man. They had counted plenty of coup and collected many scalps. Were they to share a campfire, they'd likely never run out of tales to share.

Cactus Flower and Bird Woman were surprised to see Three Toes's companion. Neither had ever met an Arapahoe.

Kicking Bear acknowledged the two but didn't show much interest. He turned to Three Toes. "Kicking Bear hungry from travels." Just maybe his hunger was more than merely in his stomach.

The chief placed his arms around the two women in part to reinforce with the Arapahoe that they were his and his alone. Kicking Bear was to be a transient guest.

Young Laughing Crow emerged from behind the teepee. He held a squirrel by the tail. "Look what Laughing Crow kill!" he announced before becoming aware of the new guest.

Kicking Bear smiled at the youth. "You must be true with your arrows."

Three Toes wasn't sure he liked the way the Arapahoe smiled at the boy. He vaguely recalled an Arapahoe word for men who liked other men, and wondered whether Kicking Bear was what they called a *huxuxunó*. He decided to divert attention from Laughing Crow. "Let's eat."

During the meal, which included corn biscuits in addition to the venison, Three Toes and Kicking Bear shared stories of their adventures with their respective tribes. It turned out that Kicking Bear had struggled with his people dying from White man's diseases and an ever-greater scarcity of game. To add to their woes, the blue coats were causing the Arapahoe considerable distress.

As they grew tired and the women had begun to clean up, Kicking Bear stared hard at Three Toes. "Why wear White man's cross?"

"Gift from Texas Ranger's woman. Holds great power."

"Humph. Three Toes believe that?" The Arapahoe clearly doubted the chief's belief.

"Believe cross power save Three Toes from sure death by White man torture." He stroked the cross as though reassuring himself.

Kicking Bear shrugged. "So Three Toes says." He wasn't convinced. "Kicking Bear tired. Continue journey in morning." He smiled warmly at Laughing Crow.

Three Toes followed the women into the teepee, motioning to Laughing Crow to follow him. The young boy did as he was told. The chief whispered, "Stay away from Arapahoe."

The chief had a fitful night's sleep. Even a few moments in the middle of the night spent pleasuring himself with Cactus Flower did not seem to settle his soul. Much was on his mind.

Soon the bright rays of the sun were breaking through the vent at the top of the teepee. The Comanche chief stretched and looked around. Cactus Flower and Bird Woman were just beginning to stir. He suddenly jumped to his feet. Where was Laughing Crow?

Unsure of what to expect and filled with his suspicions, his innate senses of treating non-Comanche as enemies kicked in. He grabbed his bow and quiver and stepped from the teepee.

He heard muffled voices off in the woods. The Arapahoe's horse stood hobbled over an empty bedroll. Slowly and ever-so-silently, Three Toes moved toward the sounds. He nocked an arrow as he stalked.

The chief entered a small clearing. Kicking Bear was sitting cross-legged in front of Laughing Crow, and they were talking in near-whispers.

Kicking Bear did not look up. It was as though he felt Three Toes's presence. "Welcome Three Toes, chief of the Penateka Comanche. I have been listening to the boy. He may be ready for trials." The implication was that Laughing Crow was getting old enough and experienced enough to be recognized as a man. "But that is for Three Toes to decide. It is time for me to go. Kicking Bear grateful." The Arapahoe arose, nodded at Three Toes, and walked past the chief toward his pony. In moments, he'd gathered his belongings and was heading southward.

Three Toes wasn't sure what to make of Kicking Bear's behavior. He'd apparently misjudged the Arapahoe. He turned to Laughing Crow. "Let's eat. Talk more of manhood."

He hailed from what would soon enough be called Wyoming Territory. He'd found steady work on ranches up near the North Platte River not far from Fort Laramie. So it was that it had taken nearly three years for word to reach Jubal Strong that his cousin Bart had been killed in a fight with a Texas Ranger. In fact, Bart's brother Sam had run afoul of the law and gotten himself hung thanks to the same lawman.

Jubal didn't enjoy the strongest family ties in the world, as he'd always thought of his folks as dysfunctional. His own ma and pa had been killed by Sioux when he was a teen, and he had been raised by Bart and Sam's folks. He felt that younger cousin Bart especially didn't handle getting whupped on so well as he and Sam. Bart had what some called a wild streak. Jubal thought he was just mean. In any case, both he and Sam escaped but went vastly different directions with their lives. Bart escaped shortly after having taken vengeance on his pa for the beatings. Jubal had heard one tale back in '54 of Bart killing a man over a horse. Early on, he had no idea what had become of Sam but eventually learned about the conviction and hanging.

The area west of Fort Laramie near the Sweetwater River had been discovered a few years back by adventurers looking to find gold. Strong observed the miners and the greedy rabble that accompanied them, and found it unattractive. There was an honesty to working a ranch that the miners looking for quick riches would never know.

Jubal Strong felt obligated to find out what happened to his cousin Bart. He'd salted away enough money to take a few months to search for his cousin's remains and maybe find the Texas Ranger who'd hunted him down. There was just a hint of vengeance on his mind, though he was up to recognizing that justice might have been served.

Arguably the most difficult part of his departure was leaving his Cheyenne wife and their four children. He'd made sure that Woman Who Laughs and the children were well provided for in his absence. In a way, it also gave him good reason to return upon completion of his quest. He'd found great peace there in the hills near the North Platte.

Captain Belknap led a rather bedraggled patrol into Fort Ringgold. They'd been surprised by an Apache ambush despite having been on guard against attack. They'd lost their point man, and two soldiers were wounded as the patrol managed to escape what had initially looked like certain annihilation. Belknap desperately wanted to return in force to the site and teach the Apache a lesson, but he knew it would be futile. They'd be long gone. Worse yet, he'd caught a glimpse of some Mexicans embedded with the Apache. Apparently, Cheno Cortina was still up to his old tricks.

Richards was standing with Walker Carson just outside the gate as Belknap's patrol rode up. "Lookee there, Walker. The captain found himself a hornet nest," he offered in a low voice. He was tempted to add that it had happened despite his warning.

Belknap rode up and gave a tired half-salute. "Captain Richards, I thought your Texas Rangers had already cleared those heathen away from Rio Grande City. It sure doesn't seem like it, if what we ran into is any proof."

"Welcome back, Captain. Sorry for your misfortune." He scratched the stubble of beard on his chin. "The Apache do have a habit of ranging pretty dang far. If Cortina was stirring them up, he likely gave them good reason." Richards defined good reason as guns and probably liquor. "We engaged a couple of small Apache bands over the past couple of weeks, Captain. Seems they tend to run off after they lose a warrior or two. They're never up for any sustained fighting…sort of like the Comanche in that way. 'Course, they run across the Rio Grande, and that may be the difference."

Belknap gave him an inquisitive look. "The difference?"

"Yep. We chase them into Mexico and do a bit of clean up—you soldiers can't. They know they can escape from you but it's not so easy running from us Texas Rangers. Throw in a couple of Cortina's rebels like the bunch that ambushed you, and they likely as not get just a tad braver."

"I've got to let my men get cleaned up and tend to the wounded, Captain. Perhaps you'd join me at dinner this evening? Your fellow Ranger here would be most welcome." He nodded toward Carson.

"That'd be right good of you, Captain Belknap. It'd be our pleasure. We're planning to ride back out in the morning. Spent the past couple of days training some new recruits, and it's time they learned what Cortina is made of."

Belknap smiled, gave a somewhat smarter salute than before, and passed on through the gate.

THIRTEEN
SCARLETT VINDICATED

ELISA PASSED the steaming cup of coffee to Scarlett. She glanced at her twins Peter and John playing over near the fireplace with Scarlett's daughter Margaret. Luke had carved a few toy horses, and Margaret shared a doll that her mother had made for her.

At some future time, Scarlett would share with her daughter that the fabric used for the doll was from a shirt belonging to the little sprite's father who died protecting Scarlett. "I'm hopeful that this Walker Carson fella is all he seems to be, Elisa." She sipped the coffee slowly. Years of suffering false romances had nearly jaded Scarlett so far as trusting in relationships. "He says he wants to learn to speculate in livestock. I hear tell Luke has a cousin who's getting pretty good at that.

"Luke says Walker has come a long way from the scared boy he met on the road from San Diego. Some men simply take a bit longer to grow up, Scarlett." She placed a couple of slices of warm cornbread on the table. "From Luke's advice and what you say, he could very well be one you can trust." She prayed that Scarlett wouldn't do something foolish like have sex with Carson before he committed to her in marriage. There was a bit too much of that sort of thing on the Texas frontier where encounters between men and women were often brief at best. As cities like Corpus Christi grew and churches took root, she expected that practice might change for the better. Families, faith, and enduring business endeavors seemed to be the answer.

Scarlett gazed thoughtfully out the window at the vast reaches of Heaven's Gate. "Y'all have built a wonderful life here, Elisa. I hope those political rumblings about slavery are just rumblings. Folks can do crazy things when emotions run high." She thought back to her former nemesis, Horatio Thorpe, who'd run a plantation with more than a thousand slaves. She was relieved the man was dead, but that didn't do away with the slavery issue. "In a way, we're all slaves to something, but it's so different to be actually owned. I can't imagine what that must be like."

"Luke and I have talked about it," said Elisa. "Hopefully, it'll all be resolved peacefully."

"I've heard all sorts of talk in Corpus about what might happen if it all came to violence. Folks might be forced to take sides, what with emotions and all. There's lots of strong feelings one way or the other." She set her cup on the table.

Elisa nodded. She was about to respond when they heard the hoofbeats of a couple of horses pulling up. Luke and Jaime had ridden up from a long morning on the range chasing down stray longhorns. "They'll be wanting some coffee and lunch. I think Julia has the lunch covered, so let's get them some coffee."

Luke smiled as Elisa and Scarlett appeared on the gallery carrying cups of coffee. "Why, lookee here, the two most beautiful ladies in all of South Texas." He laughed heartily. He looked lovingly at Elisa. "Sure could use that coffee, sweetheart. It's dry out there. Used up our water today."

As the men dismounted, they saw Julia walking up the path with a basket filled with grub for the two tired cowboys. Luke motioned Jaime to the bench on the gallery then strode up the steps, planted a kiss on Elisa, and took a seat. "Grab a seat, Jaime. My, but it's great to see you so at peace, Miss Scarlett. If I were a betting man, I'd bet you've got some man on your heart." He laughed again.

Elisa enjoyed seeing such happiness. She was truly grateful for all she'd been given, though ever aware of what she'd lost. The frontier certainly had its way of taking and giving. Her physical wounds had fully healed, though she was still mentally getting over Thorpe's attack..

For Luke's part, he was enjoying the break from chasing lawbreakers. Arising each morning to tend to the chores around Heaven's Gate was far preferable, though he did have just a hint of an itch to get back to delivering justice on the Nueces Strip. He wondered whether the men who'd murdered the slaver were still anywhere around. He'd heard nothing from Rip Ford about whether he should tend to it, though it was likely more something under Sheriff Meaney's jurisdiction.

They sat and enjoyed Julia's cooking. Luke was mostly quiet through the meal. In one of his brief introspections, he caught sight of a tumbleweed rolling toward the grasses out on the prairie. Those darned things seemed to appear as if on cue when he pondered his life choice between rancher and lawman. Little did he know what might yet be in store for him. He looked down at the Texas Ranger badge stuffed in his shirt pocket and then lifted his gaze to take in Elisa and the children.

"You okay, Lucas?" Elisa put her hand gently on his arm.

"Just thinking how I love this life, Lisa, and how I love you."

His smile and the way he stroked his mustache made her feel just a tad weak-kneed. She looked at the gathered folks and hoped no one caught the signal they'd exchanged.

Scarlett saw the look. "I think Margaret and I had best be heading back to Corpus, Elisa. We've enjoyed our visit."

Julia tried to get Jaime's attention. She motioned that they ought to get back to the cabin.

It was nap time for Peter, John, and Andrea Ann. Luke took Elisa's hand, and they headed into the house.

"Looks like one more patrol, and we'll be heading back to Corpus Christi, Captain." Richards sipped the Mexican wine. The wine had just a bit of a bite and sweetness to it, unlike the French pretenders usually offered up north of the Nueces Strip. "I've heard rumor from Austin of concern over the slavery politics and even the possibility of insurrection."

Belknap raised his eyebrows. "Insurrection?"

"Not sayin' there would be, Captain, nor that I'd have any part of it. But emotions are running high. If the worst happened, we could be vulnerable to more than Juan Cortina and his rebels. Comanche...Apache...damn, western Texas could get to be a right riskier place. Also have heard the French are angry that Juarez stopped repaying Mexico's debts. Gonna be trouble down south."

"I really hadn't thought of anything beyond seeing more political wrangling, Bol."

Carson sat silently taking in the conversation. As the wine flowed, Richards and Belknap seemed to grow more comfortable. The dropping of references to military or Texas

Ranger rank was the first hint. "Captain, what was it like in Texas back in '36?"

"I can't speak for all that was going on, son. I recall a bunch of folks holed up in San Antonio at a place they called the Alamo. Guess a trio of near legendary men were there. Davy Crockett, the Tennessee backwoodsman and politician joined the scrap just a few days afore Santa Anna's troops were sighted marching up from Mexico. Jim Bowie was there sort of as a co-leader. Though his motives as a land huckster were debatable, his intentions were in the right place. The man in charge was a fella named Bill Travis, a lawyer with a heart for Texas independence. But Travis was deathly ill, so command pretty much fell to Bowie. Travis kept sending couriers out to Sam Houston asking for reinforcements, but Houston was familiar with Travis tending to exaggerate so failed to send men. In due course, the Alamo fell. All killed, of course. Along with Goliad, it became a rallying cry for independence."

Belknap and Carson were listening with rapt attention. The wine went untouched.

"So, what's my point? Personally, I found myself like so many others fully caught in the emotion of the moment. Even folks who simply yearned for a return to the Mexican constitution of 1824 found themselves in the grip of the movement for Texas independence. Hatred for Santa Anna ran strong. I'd traveled from the northern reaches of Texas and arrived in time to join the fight at San Jacinto. Emotionally, I could just as well have fought Santa Anna at the Alamo or Goliad. More than one Mexican ate my bullets."

"Then what?" Carson was fully in the grip of Richards's tale.

"Well, we gained our freedom...of sorts. The Republic had no money, was in debt, and waiting on the United States to come through on its promise of statehood.

Emotions had cooled by this time, and a lot of resentment—myself included—was felt toward the Union. And we still had to fend off Indians and Mexicans. I, for one, wanted Texas to remain independent...still do."

Belknap leaned forward and took a thoughtful sip of wine. "You're saying that the Texas War for Independence transcended common sense?"

"Oh, it made sense, Gordon. Folks had been yakking for months about peaceful solutions to Santa Anna's policies against Anglo settlement. It had gotten plenty nasty at times, including imposing military rule on Texas settlements. That Jim Bowie fella got himself in a Mexican hoosegow several times just for trying to buy and develop land. Things began to reach a boiling point, mostly by the ever-increasing number of incidents. It took emotion to make it all happen. Sam Houston saw the stirrings up of folks and seized the opportunity. It's kind of ironic...and maybe just...that we have Sam back in the saddle as governor just when another emotional political pot has begun to boil."

"You think there's going to be some sort of insurrection, don't you, Bol?" Belknap was fully intrigued by Richards's conjecturing.

"I've fought Mexicans and Indians, Gordon, but I sure hope to high heaven that I never have to fight fellow Texans or Americans, for that matter, over a political dispute that could be resolved peaceably. Emotions seem to make things take nasty turns." Richards thoughtfully swirled the wine in his goblet. "I can't say as I'd want to own another human being but, as I understand it, it seems to be a nasty part of mankind's story."

Carson was mesmerized by Richards's story. He hadn't yet been born when the Texas War for Independence was fought. He actually was one of the first true Texans birthed under the banner of the Republic of Texas. It gave him pause to wonder what he might do if he had to make a choice. But then, what might that choice be?

Three Toes stood face to face with Laughing Crow. The Arapahoe had been right. It was high time for the boy to become a man. The chief was unsurprisingly concerned that the normal rituals could not be observed on an appropriate scale because he and the boy were the only men in the camp. While he'd have to adapt given the circumstances, he was all too well aware that Laughing Crow's transition could not be put off. If something were to happen, it was important that the boy could fight and possibly die as a Penateka Comanche warrior.

Three Toes looked deeply into Laughing Crow's eyes. "We go on hunt." The boy knew what this meant. Tradition required that he kill a buffalo. It would be no easy task, especially with only he and the chief. Normally, several warriors and women would be involved in buffalo hunts. This indeed would be a strong test.

They returned to camp. Bird Woman knew what was afoot and was ready to present Laughing Crow with a bow and quiver of arrows. Three Toes gave the boy one of his lances. The chief selected the two strongest ponies from the half dozen they possessed. A third pony would be used to drag the dead buffalo back to their camp.

"We go find Laughing Crow a buffalo." Three Toes had seen a small herd of grazing buffalo a few days earlier, so felt confident they'd have a successful hunt.

For his part, Laughing Crow was beyond excited. He'd dreamed of this moment for many moons. "Laughing Crow ready."

Cactus Flower and Bird Woman offered reassuring nods. They could only hope the two would return safely. Normally, they would accompany the men, mostly to carve up the buffalo for meat and hide. That would not be the case this day.

★★

The Texas Rangers rode out at sunrise, heading east toward Edinburg. Richards had heard talk of Cortina stirring up more Apache in that area. For his part, Richards thought he'd pretty much cleaned the savages out of that region, but they'd apparently traveled south of the Rio Grande under the protection of Cortina. It seemed that every time they figured to have whipped the damned Apache, they'd come back.

"Will we chase them into Mexico, Captain?" Carson seemed to know what was on Richards's mind.

Richards winked. "What do you think, boy?" They rode on a piece. There were nearly twenty Rangers in the company, now, given the five new recruits added at Fort Ringgold. "So you done fallen in love with that red-head back in Corpus?"

Carson couldn't help a bit of a blush. "Lookin' that way, Captain."

Richards smiled knowingly and spurred his mount ahead.

About a days' ride from Fort Ringgold, the point rider came galloping back to the company. "Captain! Captain! Hostiles up ahead."

"Did they see you?"

"No, sir, Captain. They're breakin' camp, sir. Maybe a dozen or thereabouts. Looked like they're splittin' up some loot and celebrating while gettin' ready to leave. Couple women be strung up to a tree all naked like."

That last piece of information was important. It meant there'd be no wild charge into the midst of the Apache camp. "Carson, take six men and skirt around the left flank. I'm going to ride on in with the rest of the company with rifles ready. We'll see if we can get them to surrender." Richards smiled knowingly. "Of course, they won't. We'll have fire on them." He looked again at Carson. "Your job will be to protect the hostages."

Carson led his men as directed, downwind and out of sight of the Apache. Richards and the remaining Rangers formed up and began the ride toward the camp. As they appeared over a crest in the road, the Apache stopped their revelry.

Richards rode to within one hundred yards before the first sign of defense. Two Apache grabbed rifles. Richards didn't have to say a thing. The Rangers knew what to do. Two shots and two Apache were quickly dispatched. Most of the others began to run toward their ponies. One Apache ran over to one of the women with his knife raised high. He was cut down in Carson's crossfire. As many as eight of the savages mounted their ponies and tried to head south at a gallop. A hail of bullets took two more Apache from their mounts.

"Carson, see to the hostages," shouted Richards as he headed after the Apache in hot pursuit.

Soon enough the Rio Grande came into view. They splashed across not more than fifty yards behind the panicky Apache. More Texas Ranger gunfire, and another warrior dropped from his pony. Just as they were about to fully close the gap, the Rangers were brought to a halt. Opposite, perhaps a mere 100 yards out, was a company of Mexican dragoons.

Richards had to make a split-second decision: fight or flee. The dragoons were moving forward. The Rio Grande was a mere quarter mile away. "Oh, what the hell! Let's go get 'em, men!"

Whooping and hollering, Richards and his Texas Rangers charged headlong at the dragoons. The Mexicans initial confidence quickly wore thin. They broke and ran with a frenzied panic in the face of the Texans, dropping rifles, a few sabers, and lances in their haste. Richards was savvy enough not to pursue very long. Nobody had been shot except one more wounded Apache, but lots of Mexican dust had been kicked up. "Whoa! Hold up, men. We've shown them not to mess with Texas Rangers doin' their sworn duty. Let's get back to the camp." Richards led the men, still letting out occasional shouts and cheers, back across the Rio Grande. Adrenaline was running heavy.

Carson had untied the hostages and wrapped blankets around the two women to afford them a bit of modesty. Two men had been beaten and were in sorry shape, but they could ride on captured Apache ponies. The women had been raped, and that was horrible enough. The scene could have been far worse had the savages been Comanche. Richards was pleased with Carson's actions.

"Men, let's get these poor folks to Edinburg. After that, we're headin' to Corpus Christi." A muted cheer went up. It was still a long ride, and there was no guarantee that it would be peaceful.

Three Toes and Laughing Crow walked their ponies quietly through the grasses. The chief had shared with the young man instructions as to where to strike the buffalo with his arrow. He'd aim for the lungs and perform the follow-up kill with his lance. It wasn't quick for the animal, but it was a safe shot. The brain would have been the quickest kill, but such a target was small and surrounded by thick bone.

It didn't take all that long before a buffalo cow loomed before them. She had a calf with her. The two Comanche exchanged glances. A cow simply wouldn't do for their purposes.

Then, there it was: a magnificent buffalo bull. The beast had a thick shaggy mane, nasty set of horns, and was just a bit irritated at whatever was annoying his cow.

Three Toes nodded at Laughing Crow who deftly nocked an arrow and let fly. It was a perfect shot, deep into the bull's chest. The boy dug his heels into his pony's flanks and charged at the buffalo. The beast turned and ran no more than a hundred yards before crashing to its knees and rolling over stone dead. Laughing Crow plunged his lance in for good measure. The boy's kill was an amazing feat, even for an experienced hunter.

Three Toes was fully impressed. "Laughing Crow make good kill."

The two Comanche field-dressed the bull, tied rawhide ropes around it, and began pulling it back to the encampment where Cactus Flower and Bird Woman could carve it up, utilizing virtually every inch of the buffalo for food, shelter, clothing, and more.

Tradition was that the boy had to go on his own vision quest and then participate in an actual battle. But circumstances had changed for the Penateka Comanche. Three Toes wasn't so sure they'd be doing battle any time soon. He decided it would be sufficient to send the boy off to meditate for a couple of days in a modified quest. As to battle, there was a fair chance such an event would happen eventually.

Three Toes was determined to do some meditating

himself. They needed to expand their number, and it likely would make sense to move the camp.

Upon learning of his father Horatio's death, Edward Thorpe felt a mixture of relief and freedom. He was now the last remaining member of his immediate family. Father, mother, sister, and brother had met their respective fates in heaven or hell, depending on how they'd conducted their lives and met their ends.

Now, he felt an obligation to retrieve his father's body and inter it in the family plot at Magnolia. He heard that a Texas Ranger had shot and killed his father in the midst of his committing some heinous crime. Thus, he harbored no ill will toward the lawman who was merely doing his duty. Thorpe had no idea that Luke Dunn was the very same Ranger who had killed his brother Gascon and dismantled his father's fraudulent business interests. Even at that, Edward wasn't the sort of man who thought of revenge as a worthwhile endeavor. He saw vengeance as a personal, rather selfish, even self-centered, sort of undertaking. Edward Thorpe wasn't going to make it his life mission to hunt down Luke Dunn. He had, as they say, bigger fish to fry. What was done was done.

The threat presented by emotions overflowing over the issue of slavery was foremost in his mind. He had a large, very productive plantation to run. Like it or not, he had slaves, lots of slaves. His vast acreage produced cotton and tobacco for sale and enough vegetables to feed everyone who lived on Magnolia.

As to slavery, Thorpe was disinclined to hang out with the politicians in Austin. He found owning human beings decidedly immoral. He relished the diversion from running the plantation that traveling to Nuecestown would afford. Digging up his father's body and bringing it home was almost incidental.

Scarlett fondled the letter, holding it close to her breast. She'd never been sent a letter before. Her Texas Ranger was coming home. Likely as not, Walker Carson wouldn't be too far behind the postal service, assuming nothing delayed the company's ride northward from Edinburg. She prayed the worst they'd have to deal with would be the heat. It was mid-summer, and the temperatures on the Nueces Strip hovered around sizzling.

It seemed that she'd lived a lifetime in a mere five years. She had run away, endured a miscarriage, fallen into prostitution, robbed a bank, killed a man, suffered a rape and resulting motherhood, and survived an obsessive-compulsive monster. Through it all, she'd endured. She'd overcome an outsized set of odds against her surviving on the rough-and-tumble Texas frontier. Her prospects for what seemed like a normal future seemed within her grasp. In effect, she was close to being vindicated for her blind faith in life. She longed for her man to return—she longed for a new beginning.

FOURTEEN
MISSION ACCOMPLISHED

JUBAL STRONG WAS in no hurry. He felt that it was his family obligation to learn how his cousin met his end. He wasn't exactly what you'd call enthusiastic, but duty was duty. Leaving his family and ranching duties even for a few months was not something he especially liked. It'd likely be well into winter by the time he returned from his travels, and the winter snows and winds of Wyoming could make for a tough existence, much less travel. In a word, he was reluctant. Just the travel from Laramie to Laredo was going to take more than a month, even as he was taking the fewest possible stops for rest.

The rancher he worked for had gifted him with a fine mount and loaned him a pack mule. He'd already spent better than a week on the trail through some of the most scenic and dangerous territory in the west. Aspen trees abounded and occasional rocky outcroppings offered spectacular views of the flora and fauna through which he traveled. Danger did lurk. He'd already seen what appeared to be a Lakota Sioux war party and had managed, by dint of his own stealth, to avoid it. Just the day before, he'd seen some Arapahoe and rightly figured he was getting ever closer to Comanche and Kiowa territory.

Strong carried a pretty fair arsenal with the hope that he'd not have to use it for other than occasional game. He had a trusty old Colt 1851 Navy revolver. It was a heavy piece at something like seven pounds, but could be reloaded right easily as necessary. He had a long rifle. It was a bit of a relic and took what could seem like forever to reload. When not bringing down man or beast with powder and ball, it could serve as a wickedly effective club. He rounded out his weaponry with a knife and hatchet. He'd downed a white-tailed doe a few days earlier, and he enjoyed snacking on venison while on his journey. It had been reassuring to know the long rifle still worked.

It might have seemed natural for Richards's company of Texas Rangers to feel over-confident as they began their ride back to Corpus Christi. Bol Richards was far too wise, far too experienced to let that happen. He broke up the travel routine with occasional tactical drills to ensure that they retained their fighting edge. His intuition, honed over the years of trekking across vast stretches of Texas fighting critters, Mexicans, and Indians told him this ride northward wasn't likely to be so peaceful as they hoped.

They maintained a good pace, covering about twenty miles a day. Richards had gotten used to young Carson riding with him at the front of the column. Despite being on alert for trouble, they invariably engaged in conversations whereby the older warrior was afforded the opportunity to share his wisdom.

Day five welcomed the Rangers with a drizzling rain. It made for uncomfortable travel as men and horses endured wetness that went to their very bones. It necessarily slowed them a bit.

The company was plugging along about two miles south of the Nueces County line near what was called the Salt Lagoon when the point man came riding toward the column at a full gallop. "Captain! Captain! I heard shooting up ahead!"

Damn, thought Richards, *who the hell would pick a day like this to stage an attack*? He pivoted to face the company. "Men, Jed here says he's heard gunfire. We're gonna ride far enough ahead to find out what the hell is going on." He turned to Carson. "Walker, take a half dozen men to ride ahead of us and see what you can find."

Carson immediately recruited the first six Texas Rangers from the column and led them out at a gallop. He figured to ride hard for perhaps half a mile before having to slow down to reconnoiter. Richards and the rest of the company followed, urging their mounts to a fast canter so as to not let too much distance open up between them and Carson.

It didn't take long for Carson and his Rangers to pick up the sounds of shooting along with barely audible whooping and hollering. They pulled up just as they crested a rise in the road. Not more than a half-mile out, they saw smoke rising from what appeared to be a ranch. He rightly figured that whoever was in the middle of causing the ruckus was pretty bold given how close they were to Nueces County and thence to Corpus Christi. He led his men forward at a trot until they could get a better view of what was going on.

Soon enough, what the Texas Rangers saw before them wasn't for the faint of heart. They'd happened upon an attack by something like thirty Apache on a ranch defended by what appeared to be no more than seven or eight folks.

Carson knew that Richards wasn't far behind, but figured time was of the essence. He had to act then and there. The Rangers drew their Colt revolvers and charged headlong into the battle. From their banshee-like yelling and throwing of plenty of lead, it seemed as though a huge army was descending on the ranch. The Apache paused from their attack and, as a couple of them fell from their ponies, they broke and high-tailed it. Carson and his Rangers came careening into the ranch yard in a maelstrom of mud, sweat, and gunfire. The Apache kept on riding away as the ranch defenders emerged with cheering and much arm waving.

Richards and the remainder of the Texas Ranger company arrived but a minute later with the outcome of the attack already settled. Richards featured a broad grin as rode on up to Carson, "Damn, Walker, damn, but you done right good, boy." He looked his protégé up and down. Aside from mud pretty much everywhere, he appeared unscathed.

Carson wasn't done. As he tipped his hat to Richards, he sent his six Rangers to pursue the Apache for a short distance to be certain they were not going to be doing any counterattacking. He finally took a deep breath. The entire skirmish had taken perhaps three minutes. Blessedly, the drizzle had come to a stop.

The Rangers began dismounting. Richards was especially concerned with how the defenders of the ranch had fared.

"Thank God y'all got here when ya did!" The apparent ranch owner or manager came forward with hand outstretched. He walked straight past Richards and grasped Carson's hand. For his part, Carson shrugged, blushed sheepishly, and looked over at Richards. The captain nodded his approval. "My name's Callahan, Pete Callahan. Them Apache, they come out of nowhere."

"Glad we could help, Mr. Callahan." Carson managed to sputter out a response. He glanced back at Richards. "This here's Captain Richards. We're part of his company of Texas Rangers."

Callahan looked disconcertedly at the captain and kept up his chatter. "Well, y'all done earned your keep today, son. Couple of my men were wounded, but it could've been a lot more serious."

Richards strode on over and shook Callahan's hand. "Glad we happened by, Mr. Callahan. Is this your spread?"

Callahan hesitated. "Er, yes, yes, it is, Captain."

Something wasn't quite adding up for the captain. "Mind if we look around to be sure them savages are gone?"

"Oh, they're all gone all right, Captain." Callahan had become a bit too fidgety for Richards's liking. It was quickly becoming clear that he didn't want the captain snooping around.

Richards scanned the area. The men didn't look as though they'd been doing any ranch chores that day. None wore chaps. They weren't even muddied. Of the five, two had been wounded by the Apache. Their wounds didn't appear serious, so Richards wasn't especially concerned.

Meanwhile, Carson had ambled over to the barn and peered inside. "Captain, come look at this."

Callahan made a move for the revolver in his belt.

"Lookout, Captain!" Carson moved quickly and pulled his own Colt from its holster.

The warning was too late, as Callahan got off a shot that hit the distracted captain.

Carson's shot put an end to Callahan, and he reflexively pointed his gun at the remaining men. "Raise your hands.

Rangers, get their weapons." As the Rangers closed in, Carson ran over to Richards. It didn't look good. "Captain...damn, Captain." Richards was losing a lot of blood and growing paler by the moment. Carson kneeled down and cradled the grizzled old captain's head. He wasn't breathing. "Don't you go dying on me, Bol Richards." One of the Rangers came over and lifted Carson up. "He's gone, Walker. Nothing you can do." Indeed, Bol Richards had breathed his last. He who'd fought so many battles had met his final struggle. Worse, it had been an ignominious end, a cowardly murder. It wasn't befitting of so heroic a soul.

Despite fighting them back, a couple of tears traced their way down through the mud on Carson's cheeks. If only he'd fired his Colt a split second sooner. If only the captain hadn't been distracted by Carson's discovery in the barn. If only.

"Wilson, take a couple of men and untie the folks in the barn." It seemed natural for Walker Carson to take charge. "Davis, get the manacles on these men."

Carson began to take stock of the scene. The prisoners soon emerged from the barn. Apparently, the man who called himself Callahan was a bandit intent on stealing whatever was of value from the ranch, including rustling the livestock. His larceny had been interrupted by the Apache.

The ranch owner was guardedly elated. He was exhausted, as his emotions had run from fear of the bandits to helplessness as the Apache attacked to not knowing who had run off the savages. Two women emerged along with another man and a couple of *vaqueros*. By this time, the Rangers had also opened the ranch house and freed a handful of children. "Sir, my name is Walker Carson. We're Texas Rangers, sir. Y'all are all right now."

"My name is Bland Wright, Captain. Thank God y'all got here when you did."

"I'm not the captain, sir, but I expect I'm in charge. That bandit shot and killed Captain Richards." Carson pointed to Callahan's inert form lying face down in a mud puddle. Richards had already been carried over to dry ground under the gallery roof of the ranch house. "We run off the Apache, sir." For the first time, Carson noticed three dead Apache.

"We're sorry for your loss, Mr. Carson."

Carson looked around the area surrounding the ranch house. The resident folks seemed to be okay. The women were hugging the children and ever grateful at the good fortune that brought the Texas Rangers in the nick of time. "We'd best be getting on to Corpus, Mr. Wright. We've got to turn in the prisoners and see to proper burial of our captain. We'll let the folks up there know what happened here. They'd best be on their guard."

"I don't think the Corpus Christi jail will handle so many prisoners, Mr. Carson."

Carson sighed and mounted up. "Thanks for the advice, Mr. Wright. If y'all don't mind, we'll leave the Apache to your disposal." He stood tall in the saddle. Richards's body had been wrapped in a blanket, draped over the saddle of his horse, and tied in place. They decided to leave the bandits' horses for the Wright family, leaving the bandits to walk the trek to Corpus Christi. "Let's move out, men."

Three Toes and Laughing Crow dragged the buffalo bull's carcass back to the encampment. Cactus Flower and Bird Woman quickly set about to carve the beast up so as to make use of every inch of its body.

"You have done well, Laughing Crow." The chief looked deeply into the young man's eyes. He broke away and pointed to a rocky outcropping about a mile away. "In the morning, you will go to that place and talk to the Great Spirit. You will do this for three days. Listen for what the Great Spirit tells you."

While Laughing Crow was on his vision quest, Three Toes would also be meditating to decide on the young man's warrior name.

The two men entered the teepee and shared a pipe for the next few hours, as the chief mesmerized Laughing Crow with tales from his life experiences he'd not told the young man before.

The next morning, Laughing Crow journeyed to the overlook the chief had directed him to. For his part, Three Toes told the women that he'd be gone for much of the day but would return before sunset. He took special notice of Cactus Flower. There was no question that she was with child. He smiled warmly at her as he departed. Perhaps there was yet hope for the Penateka Comanche.

The chief rode northwestward for a few miles before alighting from his pony and laying out a blanket. He had his own communing to undertake with the Great Spirit. He'd chosen a sheltered place on high ground with an excellent view of the trail below. The rocky terrain would make it very difficult for anyone to approach on horseback without being discovered, as hooves would make plenty of noise on the rocks.

He'd been sitting there no more than an hour when he heard a horse. The rider soon appeared. It was a White man with long blond hair. A pack mule was being led behind horse and rider. Three Toes picked up his bow and arrow. He looked to his pistol to be sure it was loaded. This was a tempting target. The hunter sized up his prey.

Three Toes moved from his perch in the clearing to the shelter of a nearby juniper. He nocked an arrow and watched the rider draw ever closer. The man's shirt gave the chief pause to reconsider. It had symbols that were not of the White man. He thought back to many years before. These were Cheyenne signs. The rider was indeed a White man, apparently connected with the tribe that was at various times both friend and enemy to the Comanche. He stood back behind the tree, letting the man pass within little more than a dozen feet of his hiding spot. It would have been an easy kill. The scalp would have been an impressive adornment to his lance.

Jubal Strong rode on. He would never know how close he'd come to his hair decorating a Comanche war lance.

Three Toes watched the man slowly fade off into the distance. He found himself asking why he'd chosen not to follow his instincts. Was he getting soft? Was he losing his Comanche heritage? Was the strong medicine of Ghost-Who-Rides influencing him? What was changing? He returned to his blanket to ponder these questions.

Walker Carson had become the *de facto* leader of this company of Texas Rangers. The men had actually taken a vote, and Carson emerged the clear winner. It was humbling for him. In his young mind, he was all too aware that filling Bol Richards's shoes was a tall order.

As to orders, they were still to return to Corpus Christi. Carson looked forward to seeing his new lady friend. The prisoners represented an unfortunate delay. The entire company was anxious to return home, and there were a few among them that were of a mind to save the time and inconvenience of a trial for the prisoners. Carson knew what was morally just, but he understood the men's impatience and resentment. To Carson's Rangers, the prisoners were dead men walking. It was likely a blessing for the prisoners that there were no trees on their path appropriate for hanging. Of course, there were other methods of execution, but Carson didn't figure his company to be up to tolerating any method resembling torture.

That evening, the Rangers bedded down on the open prairie. Thanks to the rains of the previous couple of days, they'd managed to replenish their all-important water supply and were in reasonably good spirits. Carson set up a rotation of pairs of sentries, both to guard the prisoners and to be on the lookout for hostiles. The full moon was a welcome harbinger of good weather ahead. All seemed well. Too well.

Gunshots!

"Captain! Captain!"

Carson had been rudely awakened just as the sun was peeking over the horizon. "Dang, what's the ruckus?"

"Sir, two prisoners have escaped!"

Despite the morning haze traipsing through his mind, Carson wondered how anyone manacled and under guard might possibly have managed to escape. By now, the entire company was awakened. Carson quickly noted that the remaining three prisoners were bug-eyed with fear.

By now, Carson had pretty much shaken out the cobwebs of a solid night's sleep. "How could that happen?" His question was to no single Ranger in particular. Silence. "In which direction did they escape?" More silence. "Well, by damn, men...I expect answers. Who was on sentry duty?"

Two Rangers stepped forward. "Show me your guns," Carson ordered.

The men knew what was coming. They reluctantly handed their Colts to Carson butt first. The cylinders were warm, and it wasn't from body heat.

"Where are the prisoners?" The two men motioned out toward the prairie. "Dead, aren't they?" They nodded affirmatively. On the one hand they knew what they'd done was wrong. On the other, they'd reflected the sentiments of many of their fellow Rangers. Carson eyeballed the men. They expected him to take action. There was no waffling on this matter. "Damn it! Wilson, arrest these two."

It was one of those moments that invited mutiny in any less disciplined a group. The Rangers knew that Carson was acting properly. The two Rangers had broken man's law and God's law. Justice must be served.

Carson shook his head in dismay. They were less than a half-day out of Corpus Christi.

Scarlett Rose was going about her successful seamstress business fully oblivious to the happenings to the south. Her new beau had been very much on her mind, as she prayed her life fortunes would be turning for the better.

She and daughter Margaret locked the apartment and left to deliver some garments she'd just repaired for a customer. The sun was blazing hot already, and it was only mid-morning. She was in great spirits, even dressing herself and Margaret in matching yellow dresses replete with parasols. They were out for a morning stroll every bit as much as making a customer delivery.

Scarlett heard a commotion coming toward her up the

main street. "Listen up, Margaret. Do you hear those shouts? Something pretty big must be going on."

There was cheering indeed. A line of horsemen appeared with one of the lead riders carrying the Texas flag. They began to draw close enough that Scarlett could begin to make out faces. "Margaret…Margaret, look who is out front." It was none other than Walker Carson sitting tall in the saddle. Scarlett's heart leaped to her throat. Her joy knew no bounds. He had returned. She ran toward the Rangers, pulling little Margaret behind her. The parasols nearly turned inside out.

"Walker! Walker!" There was no holding back.

Carson saw her running toward the Texas Ranger column. Momentarily perplexed, he brought the men to a halt. Scarlett had run right up to him. It was as though no one, no Rangers, no cheering bystanders existed. She grabbed his horse's reins. What could Carson do? Well, he leaned down from the saddle and kissed her. "I'm home, Scarlett. I've got some business to tend to, but I'll be by your place right quick as I can." He released her but didn't want to. The feelings that coursed through his body with her kiss were as nothing he'd ever experienced before. For her part, Scarlett stepped away with desperate reluctance. She so wanted to hold him, to have him right then and there.

Carson took a deep breath to gather his wits, shook off a slight blush, sat erectly, and motioned his men forward. The bystanders continued to offer up their huzzahs as the column made its way to the Corpus Christi jail where Sheriff Meaney awaited.

Meaney had heard the moving celebration and had a hunch what it might be about, so stood on the gallery in anticipation of seeing a company of Texas Rangers and the return of his friend, Bol Richards.

Walker Carson rode right on up to the front of the jail and tipped his hat. "Sheriff Meaney, I am pleased to deliver our prisoners for Nueces County justice." He knew Meaney was looking for Richards.

Two Rangers solemnly escorted Richards's horse up to the jail. The body was wrapped in blankets, but Meaney sensed all too well who was draped across the saddle. He stepped from the gallery and put his head against the blanket.

"He got shot breaking up a gang of rustlers, Sheriff. Nothing we could do to save him. He was about as brave a man as ever we served under. May God rest his soul."

The three prisoners were escorted into the jail and locked up along with the two Texas Rangers who had killed two of the prisoners. Despite only two cells, they wisely separated the bandits from the Rangers. "I'm deeply sorry, Sheriff. I know you and Bol went way back. He and I had become close friends in the past few months—at least, as close as Bol would let anyone get. He sort of took me under his wing and tried to teach me about as much as he could about life."

Meaney didn't seem quite ready to talk about Richards. "How'd y'all wind up with the prisoners?"

Carson glanced around at his company of Texas Rangers, still mounted in anticipation of his next order. "Hang on a second, Sheriff." He turned to his men. "Remember what we talked about, men. You are Texas Rangers. You need to make sure Texans stay proud of you." He gave them as commanding a sort of look that a young man could muster. "Go and shake out the trail dust. Be back here at the jail tomorrow at mid-morning."

It was as though the Corpus Christi atmosphere suddenly lightened for nearly twenty Texas Rangers. There was laughter and carrying on as the men dismounted and carried on with the bystanders, including friends and family for some. Carson already had his next step figured. Scarlett would have to wait just a tad longer.

"Let's walk up to the church, Bill." They led their horses up the street, including Richards's mount with the body still draped over the saddle. "I expect the good father will help us out."

Meaney kicked at the dust as they walked slowly. "So what happened?"

Carson explained it in as much detail as he could recall, ending with Richards's death. "It was like an ambush right there in front of us all. The snake got off his shot before we could react. I killed the son of a bitch, but not until he'd shot Bol."

It was obvious to Meaney that Carson was carrying a ton of guilt for not having reacted faster to the threat against Richards. "Walker, you can't beat yourself up over this sort of thing. Bol lived a full life. Dodged a lot of edgy encounters. Likely as not, he coulda been killed at least a dozen times. Taking on challenges was in his blood. He thrived on it. This just happened to be his time." Meaney stopped walking and faced Carson. "Look at you, son. You've got a lot going for you. Your men elected you as their captain. That says a lot...and it says they don't blame you for Bol's death. Hell, you likely saved a bunch of them from getting shot."

Carson forced a smile. Meaney was making perfect sense. "Thanks, Sheriff. You're right."

"When we're done here and you've had time to spend with your sweetheart, go out to Heaven's Gate and visit with Captain Dunn. He'll sure as shootin' tell you what I just told you."

They soon enough finished their business with the parish priest, freeing young Carson to go visit Scarlett. For

Sheriff Meaney's part, he had some paperwork to do before getting together with Clara. "Before you go, Carson, you'll need to come by in the morning and write a report about those two Rangers. Dang, but they were stupid."

Carson nodded, grabbed the reins of his horse, and wasted no further time heading to Scarlett's place.

FIFTEEN

FRUIT FALLS FAR FROM TREE?

EDWARD THORPE FELT as though he was leading a circus of which he was the ringmaster. He rode out in front of the little caravan comprised of two wagons, two pack mules, and a pair of armed outriders. The teamsters served as cooks and were responsible for setting up and breaking down their campsites as they traveled. They'd also be the crew that would dig up Horatio Thorpe's remains. The first wagon was similar to a carriage and could double as shelter in case of inclement weather and sleeping quarters as necessary. The second wagon hauled supplies for the trip to Nuecestown and a casket that would house his father's moldering body on the return trip.

He still resented having to go fetch his father's body. Common sense might have dictated simply sending a couple of Magnolia employees with his father's slaves, but folks would talk. Thorpe didn't especially appreciate gossip. Besides, his mother always quoted the Good Book, and it advised to always honor your father and mother. In this case, honoring the father was rather hypocritical so far as Thorpe was concerned.

At this time of increasing emotional and political turmoil about state sovereignty and slavery, he yearned to be in Austin tending to the distasteful task of influencing legislators and back at Magnolia supervising his interests. He was none too happy at a personal level about having inherited slave labor, but the economics made it a necessity if he was to compete in the markets for cotton and tobacco. Even were he to switch to less labor-intensive farming, it would take years to transition out of slave operations. For the present, slave labor seemed to be the way it was to be. He recalled from his school studies that a fellow named Adam Smith had written that slave labor made no sense morally or economically. Paid labor was incentivized to work harder, to work more productively. Given what he'd learned, Thorpe was committed to gradually divesting himself of slave labor and radically changing the economics of the plantation industry.

It took a bit more than two weeks to make the journey from Magnolia to Nuecestown. The late spring weather had cooperated, so the caravan had not found it necessary to deal with wagons mired in mud or the time-consuming task of drying out rain-soaked equipment. The caravan finally pulled into Nuecestown.

Thorpe knocked on the front door of the jail. There was no answer. "Hello! Anyone here?"

"Say, mister. Sheriff's gone down to Corpus Christi." Bernice had heard the commotion and stuck her head out the front door of her boarding house to learn what was going on.

"Is he coming back?"

"Who wants to know?"

Thorpe was a little agitated and letting it cloud his judgment. He'd assumed that Meaney would have received his letter and would be waiting. Clearly, he had no concept of the vastness of Nueces County that Sheriff Bill Meaney was responsible for. He took a deep breath. "Sorry, ma'am. My name is Edward Thorpe, and I'm looking to claim my father's body from the cemetery here."

Having met the father and his youngest son Gascon, it was natural for Bernice to assume that the proverbial fruit wouldn't fall far from the tree. She took a deep breath herself. "He may be back up here today, Mr. Thorpe. You're welcome to wait here or you might try to catch up with him in Corpus."

Thorpe knew there'd surely be some sort of official paperwork, so it wasn't a matter of simply driving out into the cemetery and digging up his father. "I appreciate that, ma'am. How far to Corpus?"

"Only about ten miles." Bernice tried to encourage Thorpe to seek out the sheriff. It would give her time to let Luke know that Thorpe was in town. "It's an easy ride, Mr. Thorpe."

"Much obliged." Thorpe tipped his hat to Bernice. He turned to his caravan. "Men, you set up camp down yonder." He pointed to a clearing just outside of town. "Thanks again, ma'am."

"Name's Bernice. You should have no trouble finding Sheriff Meaney."

Thorpe spurred his horse eastward toward Corpus Christi. He hoped to get there and back with the sheriff, or at least with permission to dig up his father's body by sunset.

Bernice reacted quickly after Thorpe rode out of sight, getting Dan to ride out to Heaven's Gate to let Luke know that Thorpe was in town to claim his father's body. Dan operated the local livery and smithy operations, but was always pleased to be of service to the likes of Bernice and Agatha, and he deeply admired Luke. He wasted no time high-tailing it to the Dunn spread.

"Thanks, Dan. I appreciate you coming out here and letting me know." Luke handed him a couple of coins. He knew that Dan was sparking a young lady whose folks had a small spread just north of Nuecestown, and just about every bit of money he could earn would be going toward buying a place of his own.

"Did Bernice say anything about how the man acted?"

"No, sir, Captain Dunn. She said that other than being annoyed at the sheriff not being there, he was pretty even-tempered."

Luke thanked Dan again and went inside to let Elisa know. "Lisa, I'm going to head into town later on. I've gotten word that Horatio Thorpe's son has come to claim his father's remains."

Luke's words brought a flashback moment for Elisa. She felt a chill, as she recalled the cold touch of Horatio Thorpe's knife to her skin, the cut down the front of her chest, and the sweaty heat of his large body pressing against her in his attempted rape. As safe reality in the form of Luke stood before her, the memory was as quickly gone. "Must you?" It was a rhetorical question. It was Luke's duty to be certain the days of the Thorpe family's lawbreaking were finished.

Luke gently pulled her to him and wrapped his arms around her. "Not to worry, Lisa. We do need to be sure this matter is fully closed. I don't expect trouble, but I'll be ready if there is any."

The warmth of Luke's body coursed through her. In his well-muscled arms, she felt secure. She could feel him becoming aroused.

His hands caressed her belly, ever growing with the life within her. Her breasts were swollen in anticipation of the birth that would be happening by summer's end.

"I think it's a boy, Luke. Feel how he kicks."

Luke flashed a broad smile. "Could be another feisty girl like you." He stroked her long golden red locks and pressed his lips to hers. He broke away and looked deeply into her eyes as though seeking to touch her very soul. "You are a beautiful woman, Lisa Corrigan Dunn."

Andrea Ann was napping and the boys playing peacefully. Chores could wait, travel to Corpus Christi could wait. The bedroom beckoned.

Three Toes was waiting. He tried to appear as though he wasn't concerned, but Cactus Flower and Bird Woman knew. They could barely suppress giggles as they anticipated Laughing Crow's return.

The young Comanche finally returned from his vigil. Under normal circumstances, there would be a ceremonial fire, gifts would be heaped upon the initiate, and he'd be given his warrior name. In addition to the hunt, Laughing Crow would have accompanied warriors in battle. Well, there was no battle to be fought, but the young man had killed a buffalo. And with but a single arrow. That was strong medicine.

The chief had meditated with the Great Spirit at great length as to the proper warrior name for the young man. There were no warriors to gather at the ceremonial fire, so the women would have to do. They'd dance and present gifts. Laughing Crow would be too nervous and excited to feel short-changed.

And so, as the sun set on the western horizon, the ceremonial fire in the little Comanche encampment blazed brightly. Cactus Flower kept a beat on a hand drum as they all proceeded to dance around the fire in their very best buckskins adorned with colorful feathers and beads. They drank an agave-based beverage laced with just enough peyote to bring them to a near trance-like state.

Three Toes sensed that the time was right and stretched out his arms to stop the drumming and chanting. He let the silence hang in the air for what seemed like forever. "Laughing Crow. Stand before me."

Laughing Crow did as he was told. He'd anticipated this moment. The adrenaline rush fully replaced any high brought on by the peyote.

The chief measured his words. "Laughing Crow has fulfilled obligations set by our ancestors. He has slain buffalo and spoken with Great Spirit." Three Toes was never known for long speeches, and this was no exception. The Comanche language was rather limited in any case. He already felt as though he'd said too much but continued nevertheless. "Laughing Crow rode his pony at mighty buffalo and a single arrow found its mark." The women were very impressed, it was unheard of to kill a buffalo with a single arrow. Three Toes placed his hands on the young man's shoulders and looked deeply into his eyes. "Forever you are to be called One Arrow." There, it was done. The new initiate had his warrior name.

One Arrow thought that was the end, but the chief still held his shoulders fast in an iron grip. He dared not pull away.

The chief dropped one hand. From the wampum bag at his side, he drew out a necklace of bone beads. He placed it over One Arrow's head. From its center hung a carved wooden cross similar to the metal cross Elisa Dunn had gifted to him. "One Arrow, wear this. It is powerful medicine." With that, Cactus Flower and Bird Women bestowed their own gifts on the new warrior.

One Arrow had wondered at the cross from the day they'd first encountered Three Toes. He'd never had the temerity to ask the Penateka Comanche chief about it. He made a note in his mind to ask, but this was neither time nor place.

They were all exhausted, full of food and drink, and soon overtaken by sleep.

Knowing that Thorpe was headed to Corpus Christi to find Sheriff Meaney, Luke felt that it made best sense to head that way himself. Might as well venture to get acquainted. He eased Big Horse along at a brisk walk, and the big gray stallion responded with satisfied snorts and whinnies at being on the road again with Luke.

The countryside was fairly flat with gently rolling terrain that didn't much obstruct line of sight. It was no surprise to Luke that he found himself perhaps a half-mile behind a rider he presumed to be Edward Thorpe. He figured that to be a sufficient distance and, as far as he could tell, the man was clueless as to Luke following him.

Luke figured he'd arrive at the Corpus Christi jail a convenient few minutes after Thorpe. He recalled that Meaney still had the prisoners Carson had deposited so, if he was with Clara, the sheriff's rendezvous wouldn't be at the jail.

Thorpe pulled up in front of the jail, dismounted, and threw the reins over the hitching rail. He was about to climb the step leading to the front door.

"May I help you?" It was the deep voice of Sheriff Bill Meaney.

The voice startled Thorpe. He turned and found himself face-to-face with the sheriff. "Er…yes. Are you the sheriff?" He saw the badge, so it was a rather rhetorical question.

"I am Sheriff Meaney. And you are?"

"My name is Edward Thorpe, and I've come to retrieve my father's remains from the Nuecestown Cemetery."

"Sorry for your loss, Mr. Thorpe. The necessary paperwork is back in Nuecestown. If you'll give me a few moments to secure the jail, I'd be pleased to accompany you back to the town."

"Is there any way I can meet this Texas Ranger Captain Luke Dunn?"

Meaney wasn't sure how he should react. The man didn't appear to have violence in mind. He had no sidearm and Meaney judged that this man had likely never even fired the rifle in the scabbard alongside his saddle. "Well…" As he was about to respond, Luke rode up. "Speaking of Captain Dunn, here he is."

Luke rode up and dismounted.

Thorpe didn't come close to sharing his father's height or bulk and now found himself looking up at what must have seemed like a giant.

"Captain, this here's Mister Edward Thorpe, come to fetch his father's remains."

Luke extended his hand. "Pleased to meet you, Mr. Thorpe. Sorry for your loss."

Thorpe at least appreciated that these men seemed sincerely respectful at the loss of his father. "Is there someplace we could talk?"

"Honestly, Mr. Thorpe, there's not much to say. I suggest

that if we hope to get to Nuecestown before dark, we'd best talk while traveling."

Thorpe nodded, and the three men were soon riding out to Nuecestown.

They'd ridden along in silence until they cleared the Corpus Christi city limits, and then Thorpe opened the conversation. "So, how did my father die, Captain?"

Luke thoughtfully stroked his mustache as he rode. He measured his words but rightly figured there was no point in making nice. "He'd bound my wife and was attempting to rape her when I shot him." The truth was delivered bluntly.

Thorpe nodded. "Is your wife okay?"

Luke appreciated the question, as it raised Thorpe's stature in his eyes. "She's pretty much okay now, thanks." He didn't figure details were necessary.

"And my father? Did he suffer?"

Luke thought about what a slug from a .50-caliber Sharps rifle did to anything it hit. "He pretty much passed instantly, Mr. Thorpe. I was forced to kill his two hired thugs, as they resisted arrest. Killing them wasn't my first choice, but then, I didn't really have a choice."

"What about my brother Gascon?" Thorpe knew that his father had sent his younger brother to take the Laredo whore and kill Luke.

They were actually riding near the spot where Gascon tried to ambush Luke. "See that motte of live oak over yonder? Your brother was setting an ambush for me. The sun reflected from his spyglass and gave away his position. He had his rifle at the ready when I had to shoot him. Shame. The young man had so much life ahead."

Thorpe appreciated Luke's candor. He was learning that mayhem was all too common to this part of the Texas frontier. "You Irish, Captain Dunn?"

Luke's first reaction was to say he was Texan, but he held off. It sounded as though Thorpe sought to change the subject. "County Kildare, Mr. Thorpe."

"You've got a just a hint of brogue mixed with your Texas twang, Captain. Why did you leave?"

Luke found this interesting.

Meaney for his part was all ears.

"Got caught up in the rebellion against the British. Wasn't safe to stay. I've a few cousins here around Corpus Christi, so this seemed like the place to be. What about you, Mr. Thorpe?"

"English ancestors. My apologies if my people didn't treat your countrymen well in Ireland." Thorpe flashed a hint of a smile. "My family immigrated from Nottingham back in the 1770s to raise cotton and tobacco in South Carolina. My father moved us to Texas when his folks died of the fever. I helped with the plantation he'd named Magnolia as I grew up, but got sent off to school back east. There, I met with some financial fortune. I recently learned that my father was fearful of the stirrings about ending slavery, so was planning to sell his plantation with its thousand slaves. I was able to purchase Magnolia from him and am trying to make a go of it."

Luke didn't quite know what to make of Thorpe. The man seemed honestly to hold no ill will against Luke. So far as Luke could tell, the man wasn't an especially big admirer of his own father. "There's ever more talk around these parts about slavery. I can appreciate your father's concerns, though it was hard to figure why he turned to lawbreaking."

Thorpe's expression turned serious. "I've heard it said, Captain, that power corrupts and absolute power corrupts absolutely. My father was raised on the elixir of power. In addition to his huge plantation, he ran a successful international shipping company. He held sway with most of the legislators in Austin. He even held influence over kings and queens. His female slaves were under his control like personal concubines, plus he had his string of brothels. I heard that he'd even started defrauding the government. But he had what might be called tragic weaknesses."

Luke flashed him an inquisitive look.

"One was an obsessive nature. Another was hating to lose. A third was a compulsion to eat. And perhaps the worst was vengefulness. Combined, they kept him from being able to love. Guess you've seen the result, Captain."

"You seem to have known your father quite well, Mr. Thorpe." By now, they were nearly halfway to Nuecestown. "You say your father worried about the impact of ending slavery. So, why did you buy Magnolia?"

"I appreciate the sincerity of your question, Captain Dunn. To be honest, I foresee bloody conflict hanging on the nation's horizon. My father felt that the folks opposed to slavery were poisoning people's minds about it, and such talk would stir emotions to the boiling point. I do see some sort of showdown coming about slavery."

"But why did you purchase Magnolia?"

"I think there's going to be a lot of value in the land, and there's plenty of profit to be made selling it off piece by piece. I'm also turning to less labor-intensive crops. The result is that I've already freed more than a hundred of my father's...and now...my slaves. I just hope there'll be time to complete my efforts before any trouble starts. In fact, my plan is to pay them a wage, Captain."

Luke was impressed. Here was a man who was clearly adapting to the environment. It reminded him of something his cousin had said about longhorns. They were hardy beasts and withstood disease that infected other breeds, but they were lean so far as producing meat. The future would be in bulkier meat-producing beeves. "I think I understand, Mr. Thorpe. I do appreciate what you're trying to do. Once this matter of tending to your father's remains is cleared up, I'd take it right kindly to stay in touch."

Thorpe nodded affirmatively.

They made small talk for the remainder of the ride to Nuecestown.

SIXTEEN

BROTHER VERSUS BROTHER

TALK at the United States Military Academy at West Point up in New York was increasingly animated as politics crept into the educational bulwark of the military establishment. The long gray lines were experiencing unmilitary-like rifts as emotions ran ever higher concerning what slavery abolitionists were framing as a national issue, and what slavery advocates saw as a state sovereignty issue. The exploits and leanings of graduates like Robert E. Lee, Jefferson Davis, George Armstrong Custer, and William Tecumseh Sherman were being closely followed. Whether fighting Indians or Mexicans, they along with others were exerting strong influence over the Corps of Cadets.

Stephen and Rex Rucker were no exception to this influence. Their father, Horace Rucker, retired US Army Colonel and now pastor of a small church in Nuecestown, Texas, had mostly raised them in a strict military style. In fact, the Rucker household had been run at one time like a military command post. They'd caused their father no end of consternation during their recent holiday visit, as the cadets held positions on the opposite extremes of the issue of states' rights. Rucker feared that if any violence were to occur, he might find his sons fighting against each other.

Blessedly, the brothers were in different cadet companies lest they spend their nights arguing the finer points of military tactics and national politics. When they did get together, well…it could get right volatile.

"Rex, did you read the letter from father?"

"Sure, what's your point, Stephen?"

"What did you think about those abolitionists killing the slaver?" Rex squirmed just a bit at his brother's challenge. He'd made his point repeatedly that they were duty bound to follow the orders of the Army and country they'd committed their lives to. Their obligation had been established by virtue of being part of the Corps of Cadets. Stephen, on the other hand, felt that state sovereignty held sway over national loyalty.

"There's no excuse for that sort of violence, Stephen, and you know it. The abolitionists are making a moral issue out of it all."

"It's economics, not morality, Rex. The government is mired in indecision and compromises by admitting equal numbers of what they refer to as slave states and free states. It's insane, of course. The Constitution guarantees state sovereignty. It doesn't make moral distinction between slaves and free men."

"Are you suggesting that the nation should divide? That would weaken us terribly, Stephen." Rex raised his hands in disbelief.

"If Texas left the Union, I'd be hard-pressed not to go with my fellow Texans." Stephen had his hands on his hips, as though to more fully challenge his brother.

Rex shook his head in dismay.

About this time, a fellow cadet saw the increasingly

animated discussion and sauntered over to take in the dialogue. "Is there a problem here, Cadets?"

By his stripes, the brothers recognized the interloper as a corps sergeant. They couldn't turn him away.

"As I said, is there a problem?"

Wearing a slightly disdainful expression, Rex responded, "This is my brother, Cadet Stephen Rucker. We were discussing family business."

The cadet sergeant looked from one to the other. "I suggest that you return to your barracks, Cadets. It's late." He paused thoughtfully. "And the United States Army is your family now."

Luke was pleased to see Edward Thorpe's departing caravan cross at the Nuecestown ferry and head northward. There even seemed to be the beginnings of a friendship with Thorpe.

Meaney grabbed Luke's attention. "Luke, I've got to head back to Corpus and take care of the prisoners. Have you heard anything about those abolitionist fellas, Zeke Bose and Cal Withers?"

"Rip Ford gave me wide latitude on that, Bill. It's more a state and national issue than a local one. I must say, though, that with the murder occurring in Nueces County, I'll send them to you for safekeeping if I find them." Luke threw Meaney a wink.

"You'll need to watch your back, Luke."

Luke had gotten used to that. His success at bringing lawbreakers to justice had made him a target. "Anyone special?"

"Remember that Bad Bart Strong fella you brought to justice back in '56?" It was a rhetorical question, as Luke wouldn't soon forget his hunting Strong and the unusual and appropriate circumstance of the man's death by rattlesnake. "Well, his cousin Jubal finally heard about it. He lives up near Fort Laramie on the North Platte River and is headed our way. Not sure whether he's looking to uphold family honor, such as it seems, or just learn the circumstances and get closure. I wouldn't take any chances."

"Any idea where he might be?"

"Word had it he was in Laredo but lookin' for you. Should be heading east soon enough."

"I appreciate the warning, Bill." Luke stroked his mustache thoughtfully. It was enough of a habit that folks had come to expect something profound when he did it. "What did you think of that Thorpe fellow, Bill?"

"Well, he sure didn't seem to be like his father. I expect he's all right. What's on your mind?" Meaney knew by experience that there was often more to Luke's questions.

"He got me thinking about life at Heaven's Gate. I've heard that Richard King is looking to breed some cattle that produce more beef than longhorns. I like the idea, but it would demand more of my time."

"You thinking of quitting the Texas Rangers, Luke?"

"I've thought about it ever since Elisa had the twins, Bill. I just can't seem to lose this sense of bringing justice to this godforsaken Nueces Strip."

"It'd be a tremendous loss for Texas if you quit the Rangers, Luke. Then again, I heard from Colonel Kinney that there's a lot brewing up in Austin. Governor Sam is trying to hold the republic...er...state together. There's a bunch of folks running for president. From what I've heard and read, it's politics at their downright nastiest. They have that fella Lincoln from Illinois who wanted to send the slaves to Liberia, John Breckinridge from Kentucky fighting for states' rights, and then a couple of also-rans named Bell and Douglas. It's anybody's guess who'll win, Luke. With the Democrats splittin' the vote between Breckenridge and Douglas, the election will likely go to that Lincoln fella."

"Guess Elisa and I will have to get down to Corpus in a couple of weeks and vote. 'Course, it would happen just about the time she's ready to birth our fourth. You have any leanings, Bill?"

"Luke, it's a secret ballot." Meaney smiled. "Honestly, I won't know until I cast my ballot. The country is a mess over this slavery business, Luke. Emotions are riding high."

Scarlett Rose was by now head-over-heels taken with her Texas Ranger Walker Carson. They'd begun to talk about a future together. Carson thought they should consider expanding her seamstress business into a full haberdashery right there in the rapidly growing city of Corpus Christi. They saw it as truly representing new beginnings for the two of them. There was still the rather important detail of their relationship. Scarlett was ready to tie the knot, but Carson needed to take the initiative to ask her.

So it was that they found themselves on a warm summer evening sitting on a bench in front of her apartment. It had rained buckets that afternoon, so moisture hung heavily in the air. Humidity was a fact of life around these parts. The clouds had cleared, and stars were peeking out through the dewy haze. Scarlett had put Margaret to bed early so she and Carson could enjoy some time together.

"I like your idea for the haberdashery, Walker." She sidled up to him just a bit more. His nearness gave her a chill despite the humid heat. She felt just a hint of a surge run up her spine.

Carson wasn't happy with the stickiness of the night air, but having Scarlett so close next to him made it bearable. He could feel himself becoming aroused. "Er...Scarlett...do you think it'd be all right to walk over to the pier? I mean... can we leave Margaret alone here for a bit?"

Scarlett especially appreciated his understanding. Carson's thoughtfulness had an endearing quality about it. "Let me tell my landlady. She can listen for any trouble." She gave him a quick sweet kiss on the cheek and went to tend to arranging for Mary, Luke Dunn's cousin, to watch over little Margaret.

They strolled arm in arm down to the waterfront. Once at the pier, they were able to enjoy a light breeze coming in from the gulf. While the sea air had a cooling effect, Scarlett began to feel warmer at the proximity of Carson. Her hand rested gently on his arm, but it seemed to her as though her blood was about to start boiling. She was alternately hot and cold. "Hold me close, Walker." She sought his strong sheltering arm around her.

These feelings were all new to Carson, but he felt the natural urges welling up deep within him. "Scarlett..." He brought her to him and turned her so both his arms wrapped around her supple, yielding body. He brought his lips so close to hers as to just sense the passion she held within. The primal part of him wanted to touch the most intimate parts of her body. He could only imagine what the tender warmth of her naked body might feel like against his. He took a deep breath and pulled back just a little. "Scarlett...Scarlett, I love you."

Their lips melted together. Her hand went to the nape of his neck while her other hand pulled his body tightly against her. She so wanted to open herself to him, to take his manhood deep inside her. Her hands urgently wanted to explore him. Somehow through their kiss, she managed a quiet "I love you," tinged with a hint of passion. This was unlike anything she'd ever experienced. It certainly was nothing like the dandy who'd spirited her away from Richmond as a teen, or the riverboat gambler that knocked her up and forgot her, and certainly not like the disgusting bandit Carlos Perez, the adventurous outlaw Dirk Cavendish, or obsessive Horatio Thorpe. What she felt was far more than she had for Sheriff Whelan who'd raped her in a jail cell, fathered Margaret, and then died defending her. No, this was far different. She'd never before felt these sorts of feelings. These went to the very depths of her soul.

It was all Carson could do to hold back, to keep from possessing her right there on the pier. He had quickly figured out that they couldn't continue on this way. He'd dreamed of her ever since that moment when his Texas Ranger company had paraded on the streets of Corpus Christi, and he'd caught her laughing eyes. He mouthed the words silently then blurted it out. "Scarlett Rose, will you marry me?"

Tears flowed down Scarlett's cheeks. She buried her face in his chest and sobbed uncontrollably. Luke and Elisa had assured her that she'd have a good life. Was this the beginning?

Carson was dumbstruck. "What did I say? What did I do?" He was fully flummoxed, bewildered. He had no idea what tears of joy looked like.

She held him even tighter, if that were possible. "Yes, Walker Carson…yes…I'll marry you."

They stood together as the stars spread their shimmering facets as a diamond-like array before them.

★★

As the sun broke the horizon and morning dew settled on grass and leaf, Three Toes emerged from his teepee and took in the brisk autumn air. Cactus Flower had already arisen and stoked the cooking fire. She'd speared a couple of slices of venison and placed the spit over the flames. The chief was pleased and hungry.

A noise off to the north startled him. He strained to hear. It sounded like horses, but it was more. There were indeed voices. The hooves were unshod. The dialect was familiar. It was Comanche. Would it be anyone he knew?

He called softly over his shoulder. "Cactus Flower, Bird Woman, One Arrow…come out. We have visitors."

The three emerged, sleepy-eyed and immensely curious. "What is it, my chief?"

"Listen."

They heard it, too.

Three Toes sighted up the trail. Soon, a mounted warrior emerged followed by two more and two horse-drawn travois with squaws walking beside them. A trio of young children darted and danced around their mother's paths. The lead warrior paused upon seeing the chief, then proceeded toward the encampment.

The chief stepped toward the Comanche in greeting. "Me Three Toes, war chief of the Penateka Comanche. Welcome to our camp."

The travelers saw the venison that Cactus Flower had already begun cooking. Hunger was spread across their faces. Their journey had apparently been long and difficult. The warrior dismounted and approached Three Toes. "Me War Cloud. These my sons and wives. War Cloud passed through Camp Cooper. They say you come this way." He forced a smile while his eyes were obviously riveted to the now-sizzling venison.

Three Toes couldn't miss the Comanche's glance at the

venison. "You tired and hungry, War Cloud. Come and share our bounty."

Bird Woman had anticipated Three Toes's invitation so added more venison on the spit and stoked the flames higher. Cactus Flower prepared cornbread.

"Why you seek me?"

"Chiefs say you have strong medicine. Say you know White man ways."

Three Toes smiled inwardly. Perception didn't always match reality. He still found himself confused by White men and their strange culture. The White's idea of land ownership staggered his imagination. Their religions were confusing, monogamy inconceivable, and diseases frightening. Some, like Ghost-Who-Rides, were honorable, while others cheated. Most treated his people with disrespect, as less than human. "From where have you come?"

"We Kotsoteka, buffalo hunters. We Mow-way's people."

The chief knew of them. The Kotsoteka could usually be found a considerable way north near what the whites called the Canadian River in what would one day be called the Texas Panhandle. The Kotsoteka had been hit hard by Texas Ranger Rip Ford. War Cloud had traveled a long way.

"I have heard of Mow-way," Three Toes said. "He great chief. Why you leave?" The chief ushered his guests toward the fire as he spoke.

Bird Woman and Cactus Flower began to serve the meal with the help of the visiting Comanche wives. That gave War Cloud a moment to think. "Kiowa." He chewed thoughtfully. "Friend turned enemy."

Three Toes read that answer as indicative of a dispute having arisen. The chief also knew that the Comanche and Kiowa sometimes joined forces for raids. He looked quizzically at War Cloud. He expected more.

War Cloud exchanged looks with his sons. "Kiowa take women and run."

The implication was that War Cloud's sons' wives had been kidnapped. Three Toes shook his head. "Did you find them?"

"Kiowa head south. We caught them near Camp Cooper." War Cloud's face flushed with anger. "They kill women. They pay price."

Three Toes, One Arrow, and the chief's women paused at the thought of what likely became of the Kiowa. To say Comanche torture was brutal was a gross understatement. The Kiowa surely died slowly and painfully. Three Toes nodded respectfully. "Will you go back to Mow-way?"

"Mow-way headed further north. We wish to learn of Three Toes and Penatekas."

Three Toes considered this thoughtfully. The Kotsoteka warriors would increase their band to five, plus there would be more women to share in the work around their encampment. He was still of a mind to relocate, but he was willing to delay that and get better acquainted with War Cloud and his family. In any case, they surely would have good stories to share.

War Cloud's sons were of some concern, as they now had no wives. The chief was not about to share Cactus Flower or Bird Woman. Still, Three Toes determined that his small party need to join with other Comanche sooner rather than later.

Stephen Rucker stared at the letter in disbelief. It was from one of his friends from his teen years in Austin. He determined to share it with Rex at first opportunity. Perhaps it would bring his brother to his senses. He knew there'd be a few minutes after dinner when he might be able to talk.

As they sat at dinner, Stephen strove to catch his brother's attention. They finally made eye contact from across the dining hall, and Stephen made it obvious that they needed to talk.

"Damn, Rex, what's so all-fired important?" Rex had felt embarrassed among his tablemates.

Stephen produced the letter hidden inside his tunic. "Read this, Rex."

It was a brief letter, two pages of what seemed like chicken scratching and hard to read in the dim light. "Stephen! This…this is treason!"

It's what he had expected Rex to think. "I knew you'd see it that way, Rex, but can't you see what's happening?"

"I can, and it's dangerous. Your friend…he isn't mine… at least no longer…is forming a militia in case there's armed conflict over states' rights. As I read him, he thinks states dependent on slaves will secede. That'll be treason, Stephen. You need to stay away from the man." He shook his head. "And burn that letter. Don't be caught with it, brother."

Stephen shook his head. "You'll see, Rex. You'll see." He turned and headed back to his barracks.

SEVENTEEN
RUMBLINGS FROM AUSTIN

RIP FORD LEANED FORWARD in the ornate mahogany chair with its dark-green leather-covered seat. He was no stranger to the machinations of politics, though his heart and soul were in mustering and leading Texas Rangers to make the frontier safe for Texans. It wasn't so long ago that he'd led a virtual army of Rangers to tame the Comanche up on the Canadian and Red Rivers. Most of the tribes had at least for the present been confined to the Comancheria, that rough territory west of the 98th meridian. Ford still published his newspaper and was turning out articles that thinly disguised his sentiments on state sovereignty. If Texas ever took the bold step that rumors were being conjured up about, Ford would support secession and Texas independence. Texas had been an independent republic once before, and Texas could be a republic again.

Lincoln had won the presidency with a plurality of popular votes. Dominance in the Electoral College had put him over the top by a substantial margin. As expected, the Democratic vote had split between Breckenridge and Douglas. Already, South Carolina had held a state convention that voted to secede from the Union. It had thrown the lame duck administration of President Buchanan into chaos. Federal troops were already moving to consolidate their position in Charleston at Fort Sumter.

Governor Houston was certainly no stranger to politics. His sensitivity to the mood of the Texas citizenry enabled him to become the leader in the Texas War for Independence back in 1836. The first president of the Republic of Texas, elected to the US Senate upon statehood, and now the governor, he was fully tuned in to the rumblings of secession creeping through most of Texas. He was stone-cold sober, a significant feat of late. He knew Ford, along with John Coffee Hays, had just returned from engineering the clean-up of marauding Lipan Apache and most of Juan Cortina's Mexican troublemakers on the Nueces Strip and would soon be heading there again. "Rip, I'm afraid there's going to have to be a wholesale change to the role of the Texas Rangers. You know there's a push for a referendum on secession. You and I know, given the tenor of the times, it's highly likely to be overwhelmingly approved. I expect many who've served as Rangers will join the Texas militia that's sure to form. But we'll be in danger of leaving ourselves vulnerable to Comanche, Kiowa, and Apache predations as well as more trouble from that rascal, Cheno Cortina. That damned Mexican rebel makes a wild hog look cuddly."

Ford shook his head resignedly. He wasn't about to argue the points Houston made. "I understand, Governor. Guess I knew it was coming. I expect the Indians and Mexicans will figure it all out soon enough."

"I've heard about your man down in Corpus Christi."

"You mean Captain Dunn?"

"Yes, that's him. Seems an impressive young man, Rip." He leaned forward and lowered his voice so as to be out of earshot of any possible eavesdroppers. "I hear tell you've had him working alone on special assignments."

"Yes, Governor. Dunn is notorious for some natural sort of ability to deliver justice. Hell, he's even made friends with a Comanche chief. The savages respect Dunn…even call him Ghost-Who-Rides. He's a solid citizen, too. Has a ranch down near Nuecestown, and he's married with a passel of kids."

"Well, we're going to need an effective force of men like Dunn to combat those Indians and Mexicans, but they'll sort of be working in secret. We can't officially authorize Texas Rangers if hostilities break out. For one thing, we won't have the funds to pay them."

Rip absorbed the last phrase and thought hard on it. Texas had seemed to have always struggled financially. The Texas Rangers hadn't been paid for the past three months. He leaned back in the chair and tried to gauge where Houston was coming from. Secession was seeming to take on a life of its own. It was, as Houston was saying, inevitable. "I see the Rangers being disappointed as well as elated, Governor." He ran his fingers through his hair. "As to Luke Dunn, I expect we'll cross that bridge soon enough. I know he's been conflicted over staying on his ranch to raise his family versus bringing lawbreakers to justice. He seems to be exceptionally good at both."

"I'll leave it to you to deal with Dunn and any others you might have in mind. If hostilities do come, it could be a nasty business." Houston knew the words were a gross understatement the moment they left his lips. His dream of becoming president of the United States was apparently going to be overtaken by events beyond his control. He'd held out hope that he'd have been able to muster the resources to make war on Mexico and annex that nation to the United States. The plan fell through as troops, cannon, and funding were not forthcoming. Annexing Mexico would have enabled him to make a legitimate run for the presidency. His last hope would be that, if secession were to come, he could avoid joining any Confederacy and be re-elected as president of a Republic of Texas. "Say, Rip, you did vote back in November, didn't you?"

"Yeah, but it looks like my vote won't count for much. That Lincoln fella sure put a licking on my man John Breckenridge."

"I hear tell—and it's no secret—that Lincoln is a free-stater. I'm thinking it's going to fan the flames for more states seceding, Rip. This won't end with South Carolina. Texas is sure to follow."

"You could be right, Governor. If I have anything to say about it…well, you know where I stand."

"Lucas?" Elisa shook him awake. She was urgent but not panicky. "Lucas, it's time. Fetch Julia."

He sat bolt upright, smiled lovingly at her, pulled on his pants, grabbed his boots, and headed for the door. "Be back in a heartbeat, Lisa." He ran down to the cabin to get Julia, having the presence of mind along the way to stoke the hearth fire and hang a pot of water over it. He was becoming an old hand at this and knew they'd want warm water.

Luke was determined this time not to wait outside the room twiddling his thumbs with anxiety while Elisa delivered. He hustled to the cabin to arouse Julia and bring her up to the house to assist with delivery. Time was a blur. Jaime answered the door, but upon seeing the just-short-of-panic look in Luke's eyes, encouraged his wife to hurry up to the house to help Elisa.

Luke and Julia ran up the hill, into the house, and up the stairs to the bedroom. Elisa was seated semi-upright and already working at pushing the life that was struggling to emerge into the world from the secure warm confines of her womb. "Lucas!" She held her hand out to him. "Help me."

He gulped reflexively. He had no idea what he was about to face. Her grip was amazingly strong.

"Help me, Lucas…help me." She continued her pleadings.

What was he to do? He held her hand and wiped her sweating brow. "You can do this, Lisa." Words of encouragement seemed to be in order. She needed to hear those words from her husband's lips.

Julia was hovering between Elisa's legs. "I see *la cabeza, Señora* Dunn. I see the head."

Luke further encouraged her. "Push, Lisa. Push." He found himself feeling more love for her than he'd ever imagined. He'd had no idea what hard work delivering a child was. "That's it, love, just another push." She amazed him.

Julia was beginning to break into a smile. "*Señora* Dunn, it's a boy." She deftly tied and cut the umbilical cord, helped the newborn Dunn take his first lungful of air, swabbed him with a warm wet cloth amid his cries of protest, and wrapped him in a light blanket before placing the newborn in Elisa's arms.

Elisa was exhausted but incredibly happy. She looked up at Luke. "Why, Lucas Dunn, are those tears I see?"

"Can't help it, Lisa. You are so beautiful. It was all so beautiful." He'd never experienced anything to compare. He'd helped more than one cow birth a calf. He was a trail-hardened lawman and cowboy, but this human child-birthing business was totally different.

She placed his hand on the baby as it clung to her milk-laden breast. "I love you, Lucas." Her eyes said it all. "Are we giving this young man a name, dear husband?"

"How about Michael? Michael Dunn?" It was a common name throughout the Dunns of County Kildare.

"Michael, it is."

"I think I'm done here, *Señora* Dunn." Julia prepared to leave.

She smiled at Julia. "Thank you, Julia. Bring Jaime up later." Then she looked at her again. "Julia?"

Julia winced with her own first contraction. "I think it is my time, too, *Señora* Dunn." She staggered and then sat on the edge of the bed as her water broke.

"Luke, get Jaime!" Elisa had no time to enjoy her own joy. She found the energy to make space for Julia.

"You have no fresh scalps, mighty Chief." War Cloud good-naturedly ribbed Three Toes. The not-so-obvious implication was that they needed to find a battle to fight.

Three Toes thought on the warrior's comment. He had been very much caught up in his own vision quest and the making of decisions about the future of himself and his people. The Great Spirit had not sent him any clear message, though he felt compelled to move to a new location. "We will know when time for fresh scalps has come, War Cloud. When sun rises, we will begin journey to our next place." The chief hoped that, with any luck, they'd happen upon a worthy adventure along their travels.

War Cloud and his sons had decided to support the Penateka Comanche chief. He smiled at Three Toes, a smile with an edge to it. He dared not disrespect the chief, yet wondered what sort of medicine the Penateka Comanche was following. "Has the Great Spirit guided you...or the

White man's medicine?" He was staring at the cross on Three Toes's necklace.

"We head south." That was enough. The warrior's implication was ignored. The chief figured that three or four days of travel with travois and women and children would take them roughly a hundred miles to the south. This assumed there'd be no delays and a brisk pace could be maintained. Three Toes would pray to the Great Spirit and to the sun, moon, and stars for safe passage and a bountiful place to relocate his growing encampment. Several other Penateka Comanche had found their way to his encampment—thus his band had now grown to twelve, including seven warriors. He felt confident that they could defend themselves against attack and perhaps even initiate an attack themselves.

He'd be traveling upon lands that were more familiar to him. His hope was to reach what the White men called the Pedernales River and set up a new encampment. Hunting would be good and water plentiful. Perhaps there'd even be opportunities for more scalps, though hanging around Luke had him rethinking the practice. Counting coup and killing enemies seemed satisfaction enough, though he was chief and had to set the example for his warriors. He seriously doubted that the Kotsoteka Comanche warriors would refrain from taking scalps.

Sheriff Meaney had made a leisurely ride from Corpus Christi. That morning, he'd overseen the hanging of the three desperadoes who had delivered mayhem on the village of Norias back in southern Nueces County. The tougher duty by far, however, was having to release the two Texas Rangers who had been responsible for killing prisoners on the way to Corpus Christi. Seemed as though there was a tendency in the justice system to be just a bit slack when it came to convicting Texas Rangers of any lawbreaking, no matter how serious.

He pulled up in front of the Dunn house to the sounds of newborns screaming their little lungs out. He dismounted and hitched his horse. He shook his head at the thought of what Luke might be enduring and whether he'd get a full night's sleep for the foreseeable future. "Hey, Luke! Got news for you!"

Luke emerged looking understandably bedraggled. "Dang, Bill. You've missed all the action. Elisa gave us a new son, and our *vaquero* Jaime's wife delivered a girl." He forced a smile and shouted, "Noisy, ain't it?" Just then Luke's toddler daughter Andrea Ann joined the chorus.

Meaney nodded. He barely heard what Luke said. He felt as though he also had to just about shout to be heard over the newborns. "Noisy? Seems like, Luke. Say, I've got a message from Austin. Colonel Kinney passed it along." He passed the envelope to Luke, then turned to go.

"You don't get away that easy, Bill. Come and take a gander at Michael Dunn. Lisa would be hurt if you came by and didn't come in."

Meaney reluctantly climbed onto the gallery and cautiously walked through the front door. The babies were quieting a little, though the sounds tended to be amplified indoors.

Luke thrust baby Michael in front of Meaney. "Look at this boy, Bill. He's got my eyes."

"Yep, good-lookin' kid, Luke. Congratulations." He tipped his hat to Elisa who'd just come downstairs.

She was tired but managed one of her sweet smiles. "Must you run, Sheriff?"

Meaney thought fast. "Well, Clara is expecting me, and

we're gonna get together with Walker and Scarlett. Guess you heard they're gettin' hitched?"

Elisa decided to let him off the hook. "Go ahead on your way then, Bill Meaney. Come back and stay a little longer next time."

Meaney nodded with relief in Luke's direction, fled through the door, climbed into the saddle, and rode off as politely fast as he could.

Luke turned to Elisa. "Lisa, how's Julia and her baby?"

"Doing just fine, Lucas." She laughed. "You and Jaime might help her and the baby down to the cabin." She saw the envelope in Luke's hand. Envelopes generally meant Texas Ranger assignments. But there'd been enough excitement for one day. "Let's open that in the morning, Lucas."

He smiled and stuffed the envelope in his pocket.

War Cloud had been serving in the role of advanced scout, riding a half-mile ahead of Three Toes and the rest of their modest Comanche band. In addition to staying alert for rival tribes and Anglos, he was looking for a desirable place to set up camp for the night. As he scanned the trail ahead, he noticed a spiraling column of smoke slightly to the southwest and decided to investigate. As luck would have it, he soon found himself at the crest of a hill that gave him a view of the ground ahead, including a cabin, two wagons, and a corral with four horses and a couple of mules. He watched for a few minutes. Three men, a woman, and a girl child were the only visible inhabitants, though he understood that there could be one or two others off hunting or gathering harvest. He judged it unlikely there'd be more than one or two more people, given the number of horses.

He headed back to the trail at a gallop, and he quickly intersected with the rest of the Comanche party. He rode straight up to Three Toes. One Arrow and the other four warriors were immediately on alert. "My chief, I find food, horses ahead."

From the direction War Cloud had ridden, Three Toes recognized that what was likely a small farm or ranch was off their path. "How far? How many?"

"Close. Three men, woman, and child in cabin. Maybe couple more White men. Many horses."

Three Toes saw War Cloud's report as a sloppy mix of exaggeration, but could see that One Arrow and the other warriors were anxious for battle. One Arrow was especially excited at the prospect of his first battle. Three Toes directed the women to pull the travois and livestock under a nearby rock outcropping. The chief checked that his old Walker Colt revolver was loaded, and he readied his bow. Black warpaint was smeared in two broad bands across his face. "Comanche count coup."

War Cloud and the others didn't need to be asked twice. They were ready for battle.

Three Toes led his band toward the smoke. In but a few moments, Three Toes saw the cabin War Cloud had scouted out. Apparently, another couple had shown up since War Cloud had done his scouting. The chief smiled, as he knew precisely what to do. "War Cloud...block chimney." He pointed to the smoke curling up from the chimney. This was a critically important undertaking, as it entailed getting on the cabin roof undetected and stuffing a blanket into the chimney cap. It would force smoke back inside the cabin and drive the inhabitants out for air. The Comanche could easily pick them off as they emerged.

They waited while one of War Cloud's sons climbed stealthily onto the roof and blocked the chimney. Three Toes then led the others quickly to positions on either side of the only door.

Inside the cabin, there was confusion at first. "Caleb, go out and see what's wrong with that damned chimney."

Caleb dutifully stepped out, was surprised to feel the tap of Three Toes's lance, and then felt its point plunge deep into his chest. Death was mercifully quick. The chief had counted coup by touching the man, and then he killed him. He wasted no time depriving Caleb of his scalp and holding it high for all to see.

There was more noise from inside. Another man opened the door. "Caleb, what's hap—" He fell victim to an arrow from War Cloud.

Two men and two women remained in the cabin. They now realized they were under attack. The men hid the women and the child in a cubby hole built into the wall near the fireplace. They primed their weapons, which unfortunately only consisted of a couple of old Kentucky rifles, and grabbed their knives. The smoke inside the cabin had become overwhelming. They struggled for air. They had no idea how many savages they faced, but they knew they couldn't stay inside.

The remaining two men finally emerged ready for a fight. One of the rifles misfired and the other missed its target altogether. They found themselves face to face with seven fearsome-looking, well-armed Comanche.

Three Toes motioned them to fall on their faces. One Arrow and one of War Cloud's sons tied the men's hands behind them with wet rawhide. They were dragged to the corral and tied to fence posts. Their shirts were ripped off and pants dropped to their ankles.

The blanket was lifted from the chimney cap so smoke would clear from the cabin. War Cloud ventured in and quickly found the coughing women trying to hide in the cubby hole. They had taken in enough smoke to be nearly asphyxiated. He pushed the women out of the cabin. The child was perhaps seven or eight years old. War Cloud and Three Toes exchanged glances. War Cloud's shoved the little girl from the cabin, then his club split open her head, and evoked screams of horror from the women despite their smoke-induced breathing struggles.

The women were quickly stripped and tied up near the men. Three Toes nodded, and the warriors went to work viciously raping the women before the helpless gazes of the men. One man was yelling the loudest, so War Cloud went over and put a knife to his throat. His hot breath fell full on the White man's face. A quick thrust upward would kill the man, but that wasn't the Comanche's plan. He stepped back, grabbed the man's hair and scalped him while he was very much still alive. Blood poured from the man's head. The pain made him scream in agony. War Cloud wasn't finished. The Comanche custom was to torture prisoners without mercy, especially males. The warrior grabbed the man's privates, sliced them off, and stuffed them in his mouth. The other man and the women looked on in panicky fear. They dreaded what would come next. The women were raped again and, as expected, the second man was tortured and killed.

Three Toes raised his hand. He looked at the two women. One seemed healthy enough, the other a bit on the scrawny side. "Enough!" He pointed to the woman he'd judged to be the weaker of the two. "Kill her." The woman was quickly impaled on a warrior lance. The other woman remained tied and would accompany them back to the tribe. She would keep her life by working as a slave in the Comanche camp. "Get horses." Three Toes had no use for the wagons or mules. "Look for food." A couple of bags of

White man's flour could prove handy, as well as a few other victuals they could conveniently carry on horseback.

War Cloud looked at Three Toes and then at the dead child lying in the dirt outside the cabin door. "You take scalp?" War Cloud rightly calculated he might be pushing his luck a little here.

This Kotsoteka Comanche warrior was getting on Three Toes's nerves. The chief looked at the warrior with the haughtiest, I-am-better-than-thou expression he could muster. "Three Toes need no scalps from children," he hissed. Then he raised the scalp he'd taken from Caleb. He was telling War Cloud that he was a proven warrior and didn't need battle trophies from defenseless children to prove his manhood.

War Cloud nodded. He'd push no more.

The chief pointed to the remaining woman. "Mount woman on horse. Burn cabin. Go to camp." He promptly turned his pony and began heading back. Three Toes's thoughts turned inward. He'd been caught up in the passion of battle. War Cloud had dredged up the old ways. Those old cultural teachings had taken over his being, and he'd succumbed to the very atrocities he was striving to overcome through his friendship with Luke. He felt a twinge of guilt at what he'd done.

He looked over at One Arrow. The young warrior had counted his first coup and killed one of the men who'd tried to escape. Despite outnumbering the settlers, there had been an opportunity for the young warrior in his first battle.

One Arrow had even been pushed into raping the women, as he barely had any idea what to do. He'd seen Three Toes and Cactus Flower once, but this was far different. He was confused that sex could be loving or violent. He looked at Three Toes as if for explanation.

The chief gave him a sympathetic look. "One Arrow fight again." That about summed it up.

EIGHTEEN

WHAT PRICE REVENGE?

"RIP FORD HAS REQUESTED that I bring Zeke Bose and Cal Withers to justice." Luke said it matter of factly as Elisa was serving up breakfast. He smiled as he grabbed a thick slice of bacon. "I don't have a clue as to where those two might be. They could be anywhere on the Nueces Strip or long gone to the north."

"What will you do, Lucas?" She watched him thoughtfully stroke his mustache.

He picked up the cup of coffee she'd set before him and took a long sip. "This one has me stumped, Lisa. Guess I'll head down to Corpus Christi and ask a few questions. I don't even think Bill Meaney knows much of anything and their lawbreaking was in his jurisdiction."

"Something else is worrying you about this one, Lucas." Elisa had a good sense for these sorts of things. "What's bothering you, love?"

"It reeks of politics, Lisa. This has Sam Houston's hands in it. He and a bunch of others are deep into this secession business that's being talked about. Rip supports it, too."

"Are you against secession?"

Luke sat back and set his coffee down. "Not sure. I do worry about too much government meddling in our affairs. I expect I'm simply not so sure that slavery ought to be the issue that drives the outcome. It's got a lot of emotion attached to it, Lisa. A lot of emotion for sure."

Elisa got up and walked over behind her husband. She placed her hands on his broad shoulders and massaged gently. "You know what I think?"

"What do you think, Lisa Dunn?"

"I think our governor is sending you after these men because he wants Texans to think he's fighting the abolitionists. This assignment is more symbolic, so he can say he's got a Texas Ranger looking into it…his very best Ranger at that." She brushed her lips against his ear. "I think you ought to saddle up Big Horse and go make an official appearance in Corpus."

"Should I do that right this minute?" He turned his head up and met her lips. Just then, a plaintive cry was heard from a newborn.

"I think a little one might be hungry. Maybe you can get to the city and back in time for dinner." She ran her hand inside his shirt and felt a shiver of sexuality course through her. Barely a week since giving birth to Michael and here she was aroused, by her man. "You hurry back, you hear?"

Jubal Strong sat at the table sipping a whiskey. He felt as though he'd just about had enough of Laredo. Texas Jack's Saloon had worn thin on his psyche. He'd already spent two days in what he saw as a godforsaken place. It was expected to be a rough winter back in Laramie, at least so far as he could tell by having observed the behaviors of wildlife before he departed. He nevertheless urgently wanted to find out exactly what had happened to his cousin.

"Did you say you were looking for a certain Texas Ranger, cowboy?"

Strong assessed the man seated opposite. "Well, I'm especially looking for a Ranger named Luke Dunn. You know him?" Strong noticed the man's badge.

"My name is Stills. I'm sheriff around here. I've met this Ranger you're talking about a time or two. He's a tough one. What's your business with Dunn?"

"I'm looking for some information."

"About what, may I ask?"

"I heard he hunted my cousin Bart Strong and brought in his dead body."

Stills chewed on that a moment as he dug into his memory. "You talking about a fella named Bad Bart?"

Strong stared at the sheriff. "You know something about it?"

Stills leaned back into the table. "Shoot, son, I buried him. I can show you his grave."

"Did this Texas Ranger kill him?"

"Nope. Rattler did the killing."

"What did the Ranger have to do with it?" Strong asked.

"From what I'd heard, your cousin tried to bushwhack Captain Dunn near Nuecestown. Wounded him, I might add. The Ranger was tracking him to bring him to justice." Stills shuddered at what he was about to say. "Dunn brought in a purplish, swollen, rattlesnake-bit body to be buried. The Ranger had apparently trapped your cousin, but the snake got him first."

Strong nodded. "I expect I'd still like to get the story straight from that Texas Ranger. Where can I find him?"

Stills had gone this far, so it was natural to continue. "I

hear tell he owns a ranch outside of Nuecestown over near Corpus Christi."

Strong started to get up from the table. "It's gettin' late. You think come morning you can show me my cousin's grave?"

"Sure. I can direct you right to it. I hope I've helped ease your mind so far as what happened to your cousin."

Jubal Strong left Texas Jack's Saloon and walked his horse out to the edge of town. He was used to sleeping under the stars and didn't fancy spending money on some fancy room just to have a comfy bed. After he roused the sheriff in the morning and visited his cousin's grave, he'd set out for Nuecestown to find Luke Dunn.

He didn't yet feel any particular malice toward the Ranger, but he still hadn't given the matter enough thought. If the sheriff was telling the truth and Dunn corroborated the story, then there was no quarrel and he'd be satisfied.

The sergeant snapped to attention before Captain Belknap's desk and handed over the pouch. He saluted and was about to turn and leave.

"At ease, Sergeant." Belknap relaxed and sat back. He pointed to a nearby chair. "Please sit." The captain thoughtfully stared off into space. "What's on the men's minds these days, Sergeant?"

"Am I free to speak openly, sir?"

Belknap turned to face him. "I'm not asking you to divulge any secrets, Sergeant. I'm concerned with the mental condition of the men."

The sergeant smiled. "They're terribly bored, Captain. They appreciate decent housing and full bellies, sir, but they need either women or battle."

Belknap laughed involuntarily. "Damn, Sergeant. That actually makes sense. To be straight, I feel the same way."

The sergeant was taken aback by his captain being so casually forthright. "Sir?"

"No Cortina raids have been reported in the past three weeks, our patrols come back empty-handed, and the Apache seem to have vacated these parts. The Texas Rangers have pulled back for the present, so we're all that remains to protect the border." Belknap smiled broadly. "What would you say, Sergeant, to letting our men visit Rio Grande City over the next few days? We'll need to be sure as best we can that they maintain best behavior, but..."

The sergeant returned the smile. "Best behavior might be a challenge, sir, but the men would certainly be up for some time in the city. It'd be a great relief from close drills and general camp chores, sir."

"Well, you're dismissed, Sergeant. Tell the lieutenant I want to see him immediately." The implication was that the lieutenant would set up a system whereby groups of troopers would take turns enjoying time in Rio Grande City.

With the sergeant gone, Belknap turned to the courier pouch and spilled its contents on his desk. One envelope was marked as classified. Belknap wondered why it hadn't been delivered by special courier?

The captain fondled it, teasing himself as to what a classified message in an unclassified courier pouch portended. He purposefully set it on his desk, got up, and put a fresh log on the fire. The weather was growing chilly, even for South Texas. He returned to the desk and picked up the envelope. He let out a thoughtful sigh before slicing open the envelope with his knife.

The official-looking letter slid easily from the envelope. It was from Texas command headquarters. Belknap slowly unfolded and read the letter. "Damn!" The word gushed from his lips just as there was a knock at the door. He sat at his desk, the letter dangling from his hands. "Come in, Lieutenant."

The lieutenant entered and saluted smartly. He didn't quite know what to make of the expression on Belknap's face. The sergeant had been rather jovial and indicated to expect good news from the captain. "Sir?"

"Lieutenant, assemble a meeting of our command staff for early this evening. You are dismissed."

"Sir?"

Belknap had forgotten the purpose of the lieutenant reporting to him. "Oh…yes. Rotate our men for leave to Rio Grande City over the next three days, Lieutenant. Tell them to maintain decorum as best they can. You are dismissed."

The lieutenant saluted and departed. He was a bit perplexed at how his captain was acting.

Meanwhile, Belknap reread the letter from headquarters. Essentially, it told him about activities going on in Texas that indicated the possibility of secession from the United States. Further orders would arrive, but for now his troop was to be on high alert for possible rebellion. By now, the captain considered himself a Texan and, while his loyalties were to the United States, he didn't look forward to the possibility—however remote—of fighting against his adopted countrymen.

Luke rode easy-like into Corpus Christi and pulled up in front of the jail. He figured his first stop would be to chat with Sheriff Meaney about the abolitionist troublemakers and what, if anything, he might know.

Meaney was ahead of him, appearing at the jail

doorway before Luke could even dismount. "Luke Dunn. Good to see you, my friend. How's our Texas Ranger captain this fine morning?" Meaney wore a suspicious grin.

"Bill, what are you up to that you're so all-fired happy about?"

"Clara and I are gonna tie the knot, Luke."

"Well, congratulations, Bill. Seems to be a bit of this marriage thing going around lately." Luke heard the back door slam, and soon enough, from his peripheral vision, he saw Clara emerge from behind the jail and hustle away.

"Yep. It was a right nice ceremony that Bernice and Agatha held for Walker Carson and Scarlett Rose. They sure seem happy."

"Well, I'm certain you'll make a great husband for Clara, Bill." In his mind he figured the sheriff would at least be making an honest woman of her. "Bill, can we talk a spell about those abolitionist fellows who murdered that slaver?"

"Sure, come on in. I don't know any more than what I put in my report. We haven't heard any more about those two." He led the way into his office, sat behind his desk, and offered Luke a seat. "They pulled that fake hanging and then lit out of Corpus. We aren't even sure what direction they headed."

Luke nodded and stroked his mustache. "Doesn't seem like they want to be found, Bill, at least not around these parts. Folks who kill for a cause generally show up somewhere and repeat their killing. It's more about emotion and far less about common sense. I saw it back in Ireland among our clan members who sought to rebel against British rule. When emotion was foremost, the rebellion failed."

"I'm of a mind you're thinking on more than a couple of crazy abolitionists in Corpus Christi, Luke."

"Lisa and I were talking about it. If there's any sort of move of states to secede, the side with their emotions in check will prevail. South Carolina has already voted to leave the Union."

Meaney sat back in his chair and propped his boots on the desk. "I'm with you there, Luke. There are some sly dogs up in Washington that could stir up emotions for their own purposes." He offered Luke a cigar. "Damned politicians. They're all liars, Luke."

Luke politely turned down the cigar. "Well, it remains to be seen how it will affect us here in Texas." He stood and leaned on the desk. "I'd best be heading back to Heaven's Gate. If you hear anything about those abolitionists, please let me know."

"Oh, Luke, don't forget about that Jubal Strong fella. He just might show up around these parts looking for you."

"I'll keep an eye out, Bill." Luke ambled toward the door. "Be sure to let us know when you and Clara are hitching up."

Luke mounted up and headed Big Horse back toward Heaven's Gate. It occurred to him that the logical place for the abolitionists to head would have been north. They'd likely be long gone in any case. Still, if they had the creativity to stage their own demise, maybe they didn't head north after all. He figured he'd lately pretty much ignored the southern reaches of the Nueces Strip and it might do to nose around down toward Rio Grande City and Brownsville. With winter fully set in, chores at Heaven's Gate weren't so heavy that his *vaquero* couldn't handle them. Elisa had the house under control. All considered, he needed to earn what little Ranger pay he could. Chasing those abolitionists might be a fool's errand, given how long it had been since they escaped from Corpus Christi, but he'd be able to honestly tell Rip Ford that he'd made an effort.

Strong was making good time on the road. He was about two days into his ride and perhaps a day out of San Diego. He found himself reflecting on having stood over his cousin's grave a couple of days earlier. He had mixed feelings, especially as he couldn't rid himself of how agonizing Bart's death must have been. He'd seen a couple of folks bit by rattlesnakes up near the North Platte River. One had been lucky, but had taken months to fully recover. If his cousin had been struck in the neck as the sheriff described, he never had a prayer of surviving.

The sound of a rifle fired to the south of him broke the spell of his ponderings. A second blast followed the first. "Dang, that's loud," he thought to himself. He had to see what sort of weapon was making such a loud report. Strong turned toward the sound, staying alert lest he be in the line of fire. Soon enough he came upon a cowboy apparently shooting at some target. He couldn't make it out, as it was several hundred yards away. He'd watch the shooter fire and then see an explosion downrange. Incredibly, the cowboy was firing from a standing position. The gun itself looked impressive with some sort of contraption attached over top of the barrel. The cowboy looked into it as he aimed and fired.

"Pardon, mister."

The shooter was initially startled. He wheeled around and brought the muzzle to bear on Strong. "Who the hell?!"

Strong didn't exactly cotton to a large bore rifle being pointed at him at close range. "Sorry to startle you. Name's Jubal Strong."

The cowboy lowered the barrel slightly.

"I heard your shooting, and had to see what sort of piece made such a booming sound."

"Name's Clay Bell. My family owns a spread near here." Bell decided Strong wasn't a threat, especially having noted the relatively ancient weapons he carried. "This here's a Sharps with a telescopic sight."

Strong dismounted. "You seem to be hitting something a long way off, Mr. Bell."

"Blocks of wood. They're about four hundred yards out." He paused to size up Strong again. "Can you see them?"

Strong shook his head.

"Come over and look through the telescopic sight." He held the rifle and allowed Strong to peer into the sight.

"Oh, yeah, I see them now. Couple of them are blasted to pieces."

Bell pulled the rifle back. No self-respecting cowboy ever gave over control of his weapons to a stranger. "Hunters use the Sharps to bring down buffalo. Expect you could call it extremely effective. The 50-caliber slug tears up meat and bone pretty good."

"You use it for hunting?"

"Yep. I don't have to get so close to my prey. With the telescopic sight, it's hard to miss whatever I aim at."

"Maybe I'll get me one of those someday." Strong eased back over to his horse. "Thanks for showing it to me. I'd best be moving on."

"Where you from, Mr. Strong?"

"Fort Laramie up on the North Platte River. I'm passing through to visit some folks near Corpus Christi." Strong mounted up. "Again, I'm much obliged."

"*Via con Dios*. If you're ever in these parts again, come visit."

Curiosity satisfied, Strong resumed his ride toward San Diego.

He was still bedding down at trailside as was his habit,

so increasingly felt the bite of oncoming winter chill despite being pretty far south. His journey had taken him through Uvalde and Laredo. He picked up stories about Texas that grabbed his interest. The area around Fort Laramie had its share of savages and rough weather, but there was that and more in Texas. A blizzard could turn to a hailstorm to sunshine and then to dark clouds and tornadoes in the space of a couple of days. The savages were every bit as fearsome as the Lakota Sioux, Cheyenne, and Arapahoe up near the North Platte. The tales he heard of Comanche and Kiowa alone were enough to know that you never wanted to be captured by them. Mix in the rough-and-tumble frontiersmen, desperadoes, and Mexican bandits, and Texas had a formula that wasn't for the faint-hearted. And yet, it held appeal for Jubal Strong. It made his life back around Fort Laramie seem almost boringly mundane.

He found himself sitting in a combination general store and saloon there in San Diego. He hoped he'd make Nuecestown inside of the next day. Meanwhile, he enjoyed a bit of indoor comfort sheltered from the Texas elements. And weather was stirring up just a bit, as dark clouds and rapidly falling temperatures portended freezing rain and possibly snow.

"Where you from, cowboy? Mind if we join you?" A friendly enough cowboy and his lady friend were looking for a place to park themselves in the unusually crowded saloon section.

Strong felt comfortable enough in his skin to welcome the pair. Besides, he figured he might learn something more about Texas. "Sure, sit on down. My name's Jubal...Jubal Strong. I'm from way north of here up near Fort Laramie."

"I'm Butch Travis and this is my friend Isabella. We're local. I'm a ranch hand. Never heard of Fort Laramie. You say it's up north?"

Strong smiled friendly-like. "About two weeks ride up on the North Platte River. I work on a ranch. Have a wife and kids."

"If you don't mind us askin', what brings you to San Diego?"

"Family business. I'm looking to meet up with a Texas Ranger named Luke Dunn. You heard of him?"

Travis laughed. "If you're on the wrong side of the law, you don't want Captain Dunn anywhere near you. He's gonna find you and bring you to justice, sure as shootin'."

"He's really that good?"

Travis nodded vigorously. "He's a good honest man, too. Has a ranch and family near Nuecestown. Raises cattle and horses when he's not hunting down lawbreakers." Travis looked at Strong as if to size him up. "I'll say this, if I was goin' to pick one man to have on my side in a fight, it'd be Luke Dunn. It's more than him being big and strong— he's savvy about how folks think."

"Thanks, Butch. So what's it like to live around these parts?"

"There's a couple of months in winter when the weather can get about as uncertain as a woman's moods, but mostly it's hot and dry." Butch's lady friend laughed at that. "It's great grazin' country for longhorns and horses, got plenty of good huntin', and folks manage to raise a crop or two 'Course, we do have occasional problems with Comanche, Apache, and Kiowa. Savages can be nasty. Mexican bandits are no trouble, as they generally stay pretty far to the south of these parts."

"Is there still land to be had?" Clearly, the lure of Texas was working its way into Strong's thinking.

"If that's what you're lookin' for, I'd say there's land aplenty. You know, our spread will be hirin' drovers in a couple of months. I could put in a word for you, if you'd like to give Texas livin' a try. The fellow I drove longhorns for is a tough Irish immigrant who's built a reputation as an Indian fighter and cattle speculator. Fact is, he's cousin to that Texas Ranger you're lookin' for."

"I'll be honest, Butch, I like what I've seen of this country. I like Laramie, too, but in a different way. I grew up in a place called Pennsylvania and worked on a dairy farm back there. Cattle are second nature, but being close to the wild country has brought it all home to me. I crave big starry skies and endless countryside. Maybe I'll take you up on your offer." Strong had never talked so much in his life. Texas seemed to pull it from the inner recesses of his soul. He earnestly hoped all would go well with the Texas Ranger. He wasn't of a mind to seek any sort of vengeance. He'd heard about the vicious cycles that such thinking could bring on. Honor was a concern, but his brother had broken the law…multiple times as he understood it.

"Damn, Cal. What were you thinking to bring us to this godforsaken place?" Bose looked around. Far as the eye could see was prairie, endless wiregrass dotted by an occasional motte of live oak or mesquite. "We shoulda headed north."

Withers kept his composure. He'd been through this conversation at least a dozen times. "Zeke, they'd have been lookin' for us to the north. We'll be in Veracruz afore you know it and catchin' a ship to New York."

"How do the Mexicans feel about slavery?"

Bose hadn't thrown this question at Withers previously. "You been thinkin' on this a bit, Zeke. Far as I know, Mexico abolished slavery back in '29. They'd had a couple of centuries of African slave labor, maybe a couple of hundred thousand slaves. How do they feel about it? Guess we're gonna find out. Hell, Zeke, it's enough that their border is a mess what with marauding Apache and Juan Cortina's rebels."

Bose thought on Withers's perspective. He was mostly looking out for their necks, as they'd likely be hung if the Texas law caught up with them. "I've heard that the underground railroad has helped several thousand Texas slaves escape to Mexico. Guess an advantage is that the Mexicans don't return the slaves to Texas. That's more than we can say for our northern supposedly "free" states."

"My bet is we'll be in sympathetic hands in Mexico, Zeke."

Bose also wished that his companion had a better sense of direction. More than once, he'd felt as though they were traveling in aimless circles on the vast landscape. Withers would say he was doubling back to be sure they weren't followed, but that excuse had worn thin. Their water had nearly run out, and Bose felt he could use a good meal. To make matters worse, Withers's horse was slightly lame owing to a loose shoe. Bose's patience was wearing thin. "If you'd been riding straight, we'd likely be at Rio Grande City already and enjoying a bath and real food."

Withers shrugged. He looked up at Bose just in time to see a bullet plow into his companion's chest. Withers reflexively dug his spurs into his horse, but it was too late.

NINETEEN
AMBUSH

ELISA WAS none too happy with Luke going away, even for a couple of weeks. She'd envisioned romantic nights with Luke huddled by the hearth. He'd promised to make up for it upon his return, but it really didn't make it any easier. On the one hand were her housekeeping duties and being mother to their children, but what she craved more than anything was the feel of Luke holding her. She marveled at how this big, handsome, well-muscled cowboy-lawman could touch her so sensuously as to quickly arouse her innermost passions, bringing her to an orgasmic climax without even being inside her. He was every woman's dream, and he was hers. Now, he'd be gone for far too long to suit her.

For Luke's part, he'd miss Elisa. He didn't figure this venture to South Texas would be more than routine, but it would take a couple of weeks. The abolitionists were gone by now, either to the north or south. The Texas Rangers had mostly cleared out the Apache and held Juan Cortina in check. He'd have to be on guard against over-confidence, stay alert, and keep his singing of old Irish ballads to a minimum. Big Horse was certainly up to the task of covering the ground about as efficiently as any horse in Texas.

He was about four days out of Nuecestown, when he came upon an unusual trail. He drew Big Horse to a halt. "Easy, big fella. We saw this track yesterday." When he was alone, Luke engaged Big Horse as though in conversation. In a way, it helped him think. There had been no rain on the Nueces Strip for nearly a month. A drought wouldn't be welcome to ranchers and farmers, but lack of rain was a blessing right now for Luke. "Looks like two horses. They seem lost." Luke shrugged. He had a feeling that he'd encounter these tracks again as he headed south.

Luke looked off to his left. "What the heck is that racket?" He was talking with Big Horse again. He found a low spot in a nearby arroyo where he could wait and see what was coming.

Soon enough, horses emerged with a US flag and an Army company banner leading the way. Right behind the banner rode a familiar face. The clatter of sabers and creaking of saddles accounted for much of the noise.

Luke gave a gentle tap of his spurs to Big Horse, and he approached the troop at a canter. "Belknap...Captain Belknap. Hold up!"

Belknap's hand went up. "Troop halt!" He couldn't believe his eyes. "Luke? Luke Dunn!" He broke ranks and rode to meet his friend. "What are you doing out here?"

"Could ask you the same, Gordon. Me, I'm looking for a couple of abolitionists. Likely as not, they've already escaped to Mexico."

"There are no army troops south of here, Luke. We've

been called back to Fort Mason. Seems there's trouble brewing. I'd be careful."

"Well, doggone, but it's good to see you, my friend." Luke sensed that Belknap was anxious to get on to Fort Mason. He'd heard rumors of trouble, too, and they were getting more difficult to ignore. "Guess we're both on missions. When you have some leave, come on down and spend some time with us at Heaven's Gate. We can relive our adventures."

Belknap was about to turn and return to the troop, but paused. He'd caught himself being rude to a former companion-in-arms. "I'm sorry, Luke. How are Elisa and the children?"

"We had a fourth. Michael was born a bit ago. Even my *vaquero* and his wife had a child same day. Shoot, Gordon, the area around Corpus is growing like wildfire. We're praying it continues."

"What about Bol Richards and those Texas Rangers?"

Luke turned serious. "Afraid Bol met his maker at the hands of some coward on the way back to Corpus Christi. He went down fighting for what he believed in. On the upside, that young Ranger he was teaching the lawman trade to wound up finding his true love in Corpus and getting hitched."

Belknap wore a mixed but somewhat resigned expression as he bade farewell and returned to his troop. With the rumors flying about, the future and possible insurrection seemed terribly foreboding to him. Seeing Luke even briefly was like experiencing a dose of reality, the reality of a saner world.

Luke watched the troop move off, gave a final tap on his hat to wish Belknap farewell, and turned Big Horse south.

He'd ridden another couple of hours when he spotted

the telltale signs of death. He could see buzzards circling about a half mile away. He sighed and headed in that direction.

As he drew close, he saw a couple of horses. From the saddles, he assumed they'd been ridden by White men or Mexicans. The horses were apparently putting off the buzzards, though some coyotes were hanging nearby. He didn't cotton to taking on coyotes, especially when it came to interrupting their potential meal.

Luke finally reached the scene. The two men had been dead for at least three or maybe four days. The bodies had been gnawed at by coyotes and stunk to high heaven. They'd been shot and scalped. Apache didn't have much use for scalping, as they apparently found it sort of disgusting. Comanche didn't usually come this far south, and they'd most likely have used arrows. It occurred to him that Cortina might be paying the Apache for scalps as proof of their killing White men. He shrugged, put his bandanna over his mouth to better endure the odor, and began the grim task of trying to find some sort of identification. One of the men had a letter in his pocket addressed to Ezekiel Bose. Luke deduced that the other man must have been his partner in crime, Cal Withers.

Luke unfastened the shovel he'd long ago learned to carry in this business and began to dig a pair of graves. He'd fix the one horse's loose shoe and be on his way soon enough.

He was bent over digging when it hit him. The butt of the rifle caught him square in the back of his neck. Stunned, he fell forward. By all appearances, he'd been knocked unconscious. To the unpracticed eye, he might have even looked as though the blow killed him.

Luke was just aware enough to feel the heavy knee

jammed between his shoulder blades as the Apache grabbed his flowing red hair, lifted his head, and began a cut across his forehead. Somehow, the Apache must have thought he'd knocked Luke out cold, maybe even killed him. The cold steel blade's initial cut across his forehead brought the big Ranger back to something resembling consciousness. No Indian was ever going to scalp Luke Dunn, whether dead or alive.

Luke flinched involuntarily, just enough to make the Apache pause in his scalp-lifting. The big Ranger managed to muster the inner strength to twist far enough to throw his elbow in the Apache's face. He heard bone crack as the Indian's nose was smashed. He turned as hard as he could, tossing the Apache from his back. Blood was flowing liberally down his face, nearly blinding him. The Apache's face wasn't much better—blood streamed from the warrior's nose. Luke struggled to one knee, but the Apache was on him in a heartbeat. Luke fended off the first assault with his forearm, sustaining a deep gash but catching the Apache's arm with his free hand. He threw another punch, further damaging the Indian's already flattened nose.

The Apache was big as members of his race went, though not nearly so big as Luke. He wrenched his arm free and readied to attack Luke again.

Luke heard laughter. Through his veil of blood and sweat, he saw two more Apache on horseback. They were pointing and laughing at Luke's attacker who, for his part, laughed back at them, despite struggling to breathe. Of a sudden, the two warriors grew serious and pointed urgently in Luke's direction. They went to grab their rifles.

The Apache turned toward Luke to find himself looking down the barrel of the Ranger's Colt Navy revolver. Luke had recovered his senses. He squeezed the trigger. The blast at close range echoed across the prairie and sent the Apache back several feet as the bullet tore into his body. The savage was dead before he hit the ground. Luke aimed with lightning speed and blew one of the other Apache off his pony. This was far more than the Apache had bargained for. The remaining warrior, if he could be called that, galloped off in a hasty cowardly retreat.

Luke stood surveying this small battlefield, blood still oozing from his forehead and arm and smoke wafting from the barrel of his Colt. So much for an easy couple of weeks on the Nueces Strip. He grabbed a spare shirt from his saddlebag and ripped the sleeves from it. Elisa wouldn't be especially happy about that. He wrapped one strip around his head and used the other to bandage his arm, pretty much staunching the flow of blood.

He didn't exactly feel up to any further grave digging. The two he'd dug were shallow, so he managed to drag Withers' and Bose's bodies into the impressions and threw enough sandy soil on them to provide cover. Realistically, he knew the coyotes, buzzards, and other varmints would likely find them and finish their meal. He forced an ironic smile as he figured the varmints could have the two dead Apaches for dessert.

Luke tethered the two abolitionists' horses together, along with one of the Apache ponies, mounted Big Horse, and began heading south. He hoped there'd be a doctor of sorts in Rio Grande City to tend to his head. All of a sudden, he pulled up and gazed up at the sky. He found himself struck with how close he'd come to being killed. Once again, he'd cheated death. He uttered a brief prayer, then nudged Big Horse forward and began humming an Irish lullaby toward soothing his soul and his headache.

Strong decided to take a break from his journey to Corpus Christi. He wanted to learn more about the region. He had it in his mind to visit the owner of the nearby ranch that Butch Travis had mentioned. It seemed to make sense to investigate the opportunity now rather than wait until spring and undertake another long journey from Fort Laramie. There was frost on the prairie grasses, but that would melt off soon enough. Strong rode eastward, following the directions Butch had given him, and soon found himself at a makeshift gateway. It wasn't exactly impressive, but it was functional so far as identifying the entrance to the property.

He rode on through the gate and soon found himself in front of what could best be described as a shack. A stocky, red-haired man was chopping wood alongside the structure. A couple of handsome stallions frolicked in a nearby corral. "Pardon me. Are you Mr. Nicholas Dunn?"

"Who's asking?"

"Name's Jubal Strong. Butch Travis sent me. I'm from up north. I work a ranch up near Fort Laramie."

"Never heard of the place."

Strong guessed the man to be in his midtwenties. Likely, he was pretty much frontier-hardened to be living out here by himself. "Mr. Travis said you might be lookin' for drovers in the spring. Just wanted to come by an' let you know I'm interested." It occurred to Strong that this rancher did indeed have the same surname as the Texas Ranger.

"Well, I am the Dunn fellow you're looking for, and this is my spread. You have family?"

That was an interesting question to be asking someone looking for work on a cattle ranch. Most cowboys were single. "Why, yes, I have a wife and children."

"If you come down here to work my ranch and drive

cattle, you'd better bring them." Dunn promptly switched topics. "You ever fight Indians? Comanche? Kiowa?"

"Yes, sir, Mr. Dunn. Up on the North Platte River, we've had to fight Arapahoe, Cheyenne, and Lakota Sioux. Haven't fought Comanche yet." Strong thought back to Dunn's concern with family. "You want me to bring my…"

"I'm building a cabin. There'll be space." Dunn smiled. "You get back here about middle of March."

"One more thing, Mr. Dunn. You kin to that big Texas Ranger folks talk about?"

Dunn laughed heartily. "We're cousins. Both immigrated from Ireland. I give him advice on the cattle business. I've heard he's a pretty tough lawman. He has a family on his ranch near Nuecestown. Calls it Heaven's Gate. You have an interest in Luke?"

"Just want to meet him."

"Well, Mr. Strong, good luck. Sorry I can't be more hospitable. I've got wood to cut and a cabin to build. Hope to see you in March."

Luke knew he was drawing close to Rio Grande City, as there were more clusters of trees. His plan was that after he saw whatever sawbones was in residence to have his wounds tended to, he'd sell the horses and possibly check in at nearby Fort Ringgold.

His head throbbed slightly, though the ride on Big Horse was slow and fairly gentle. It was as though the big gray sensed that Luke was hurting.

Several live oaks off to his left caught his attention. There was a bit of white among the tree trunks that was out of place. He reached back inside his saddlebag and pulled out his spyglass. It had been acquired as a sort of compensation to him given that the young Gascon Thorpe had been using such a device as part of his preparation to ambush him. Recalling that the sun's reflection from the spyglass gave away Thorpe's position, Luke had scuffed up the polished surfaces. He lifted the device to his eye and scanned the oaks, turning the eyepiece to bring the trees into focus. Partially hidden from view were what appeared to be two bodies hanging from a limb.

He sighed and turned Big Horse to ride over and investigate the scene. At about twenty feet from the victims, the breeze shifted toward him. The odor of death was nearly overwhelming. Luke wet his bandanna and tied it over his nose. Big Horse wasn't so fortunate and neighed and snorted to let him know. "Looks like Mexicans." If Big Horse could have talked, he'd likely have agreed. The bodies had already been stripped of anything of value. It appeared they'd put up a struggle, obviously to no avail. "Okay, Big Horse, let's go catch up with the sheriff. This'll be his business."

About an hour later, Luke pulled up in front of the Rio Grande City jail. The sign beside the door identified the sheriff as Will Thompson. "Will Thompson?" Luke called out. "Will Thompson?"

A voice responded from behind Luke. "Thompson got hisself killed. Town's electin' a new sheriff tomorrow." Luke turned to see a young man of no more than eighteen or nineteen years. He sported a sheriff badge. "I was deputy. Name's Grady Jones."

"I'm Texas Ranger Captain Luke Dunn. I've got some horses to sell, a report of an Apache attack, a burial, and a hanging to report."

"Oh, you're that Ranger they talk about. They said you were big, and damn, they weren't kiddin'." He looked up at

Luke with awe written across his face. "What happened to your head, Captain?"

Luke forced an "aw shucks" smile. "Apache. Savages tried to scalp me. Forgot to kill me first." Luke smiled at his own humor. "You got a doctor in town?"

"There was a sawbones with the soldiers at Fort Ringgold, but he left when they pulled out." Jones thought a minute. "Ma Callahan sews. She might be able to stitch you up." Jones cringed at the thought of suturing. "She lives over that way in the yellow house."

"I appreciate that, Deputy." Luke's head still throbbed, but he had one more question. "So tell me what happened with those two Mexicans hung out there among the live oaks."

"It's a messy tale, Captain. Sheriff Thompson had arrested them for comin' after the mayor's daughter. They were crazy drunk. The mayor's sons formed up a vigilance committee, forced the sheriff to release the prisoners, and hung 'em out there where you found 'em. The Mexican men's kinfolk got their pants twisted and shot and killed the sheriff for givin' up the prisoners to the vigilantes. That's kind of the way it stands today, Captain."

Luke had heard of these sorts of dramas before. "Sounds like there's a lot of sorting out to be doing in Rio Grande City, Deputy. Good luck with that." Luke started to head over to Ma Callahan's place but paused. "Say, could you look after these horses? If you can get a decent price, I'll split it with you."

The deputy smiled. "Fifty-fifty?"

"Yep, that's about the mathematics of it, son. I'll be back in a little while to write my report."

Luke rode up the road to get his head and arm tended to. About now, he was starting to think what Elisa's reaction might be to his latest brush with death. She was tolerant of this Texas Ranger business, but this event might have been just beyond the pale. He also thought on the all-too-frequent lynching that far too often substituted for justice out on the Texas frontier. The lack of access to judges and anything resembling courtrooms made people's justice more the rule than the exception. It was expeditious, though innocent men were often the victims. It deeply offended Luke. He saw no justice in it at all.

Ma Callahan stitched him up and shared tea with him before he headed back to the sheriff's office. Naturally, she warned him to be more careful out on the Nueces Strip. He repeatedly assured her that he would and headed back to see Deputy Grady Jones at the Rio Grande City jail. Jones had indeed managed to sell the horses, and he split the proceeds with Luke. Luke assumed the deputy was honest. It would have been easy enough to check who he sold the horses to and for how much. Luke laboriously wrote a brief report of the killing and burial of the two abolitionists and the Apache attack. He decided to let Rio Grande City sort out its own vigilance committee problems.

"You ever get up to Corpus Christi, you be sure to visit, son." Luke fetched Big Horse and headed up the road toward Fort Ringgold. He was a striking figure heading out of Rio Grande City despite the dried bloodstains on his shirt and around the headband of his hat.

Luke pounded on the gate to Fort Ringgold. To his surprise, a blue-uniformed guard challenged him.

"Who goes there?"

"I'm Texas Ranger Captain Luke Dunn, just paying a visit."

The gate creaked open. "Enter, sir."

Luke was struck by the fact that there really weren't any walls. The fort was situated at a great location overlooking the Rio Grande and with a view toward Mexico and the town of Camargo, which housed a garrison of Mexican soldiers. According to Captain Belknap, the place was to be abandoned, but there were at least a hundred soldiers and what appeared to be Texas Rangers in view. "Who's in charge, Corporal?"

A familiar voice responded off to Luke's left. "Damn. If it isn't Luke Dunn!"

"Rip?"

"Whew, you look like you been through the slaughter-house with the longhorns, Luke."

"I got those abolitionists you sent me to capture."

"Seriously. You found them? Damn, you're good. So where are they?"

Luke stroked his mustache and flashed one of his more ironic smiles. "Won't be killing any more slavers, Rip. Apaches got them both."

"Holy...how do you know it was Apache?"

Luke shook his head...gently. "They came back for the scalps and found me. Almost lost my own hair to the savages. Rumor has it that Cortina is paying the Apache for White men's scalps."

"Son of a bitch. Cortina gets nastier by the day." Ford shook his head resignedly. "So what happened to the Apache?"

Luke gave him a you-can't-seriously-be-asking-that sort of look. "Killed two. One ran off." Luke started to shake his head, but that was a bit too painful. "Case you don't yet know, Rio Grande City is sorting out a bit of a mess right now owing to some vigilantes. Sheriff was killed."

"We'll straighten them out, Luke. Thanks for letting me know. We just got here yesterday. Plenty more men are coming. We're to keep Juan Cortina under control. Guess you've heard the rumors about secession?"

"We'll see what happens." Luke decided not to dally at Fort Ringgold and provide Ford with an opportunity to give him another assignment. "I just stopped by to check on the fort. I'm headed back to Nuecestown. I've been told that Bad Bart Strong's cousin, Jubal, is looking for me. I'm hoping he's got more sense than Bart." Luke offered a casual salute. "Stay in touch, Rip. Watch out for rattlers and Apaches. Good to have seen you." He let out an inaudible sigh, as he turned Big Horse back through the gate. He felt as though he was escaping, and in a sense he was.

Ford watched Luke depart. He shook his head ruefully. He wished he had an entire company of men like Captain Dunn.

Riding through the night would get Luke back to Nuecestown in roughly four days. His scalp wound would be well on its way to healing, though there'd be no way he could hide it from Elisa. He was grateful for Ma Callahan's handiwork and that his head had stopped throbbing. The cut on his forearm hadn't been any problem at all. The back of his neck was still sore and bruised from the Apache's rifle butt.

Pastor Horace Rucker read and reread the letter from his son Stephen. It was deeply concerning. Before becoming a pastor, he'd had a solid if not mostly unimpressive career. He'd retired as a colonel after helping the Texas Rangers bring his commanding officer to justice. Rucker had been fortunate to retain his rank upon retirement. It had been a bonus and a matter of pride that both his sons had been accepted into West Point. Stephen and Rex were good boys, and the Army would make men of them.

Now Stephen wrote about joining the rebels should the southern states in fact secede from the Union. It was a troubling situation.

His most recent correspondence from Rex had described his concern over his brother Stephen's thinking. Rucker prayed frequently that his family wouldn't be divided. The idea of brother fighting brother was anathema to him.

TWENTY

NUECES STRIP GIVES UP ITS OWN

THREE TOES HAD MIXED feelings about having led the massacre of the settlers. He had permitted himself to be overly influenced by the Kotsoteka Comanche that had joined him. He'd felt challenged to prove that he wasn't under some White man's spell as cast on him by the necklace with its cross. On the one hand, it had felt good to once again lead warriors in a true battle, but the settlers hadn't even had a chance to defend themselves. As a victory, it rang hollow for the chief. The little massacre was too easy.

They'd finally reached the Pedernales River, and Three Toes found himself of a mind to linger longer at this site. It had good cover, plenty of water, and a great view of the surrounding landscape. Anyone intending to do them harm would need to be invisible to get anywhere close to the encampment.

One Arrow had proven himself worthy in the attack on the settlers by having single-handedly captured and killed one of the men attempting to escape. Three Toes awarded him an eagle feather at their first tribal fire in the new camp.

The chief offered War Cloud and his two sons the

opportunity to join his Penateka family. It was possible that more Penateka Comanche would join them, and Three Toes sought unity. "War Cloud, you are on Penateka Comanche lands. We would have you join us."

War Cloud admired the chief's performance in the attack on the settlers. He would have to renounce his allegiance to his Kotsoteka Comanche chief, Mow-way, but he knew it was unlikely he'd ever head back north. The Texas Rangers had inflicted heavy losses on the Comanche up around the Brazos and Canadian Rivers. Some White man named Ford had put a solid whipping on his Comanche brothers. Three Toes's stature among the various Comanche tribes had certainly risen. "I talk with Great Spirit."

War Cloud went off to meditate and pray. He'd seek guidance for this important decision.

The Kotsoteka warrior returned in the morning to find two more Penateka Comanche families in the camp. If there was to be hope for the future of the Comanche, it seemed to be lying with Three Toes.

The chief's band now consisted of seven warriors. A few more, and he'd be leading a truly battle-worthy war party capable of taking on larger prey. Both Cactus Flower and Bird Woman were pregnant, as were three of the other wives. Three Toes clung to the hope that his Comanche were regenerating their tribal heritage.

A troubling dream broke his sleep this night. He saw his people sick and dying. The dream refueled his past resentments of the White men, as there had been no such sicknesses before they appeared. Yet he was vexed by the seeming contradiction posed by the relationship he'd built with Ghost-Who-Rides. He'd been away from Luke for more than a year, and the influence that the Texas Ranger had on the chief was wearing thin. Deep within his heart, he wanted to ride out and find Luke. He felt that it would help him sort through the dilemmas he was facing.

Rip Ford figured this might be his last chance to rid the Mexican border of Juan Cheno Cortina's rebels and the ever-harassing Apache. He'd hoped Luke would hold off returning to Nuecestown, but that was not to be. With the increased prospect of hostilities between the agrarian, slave-dependent southern states and the industrial north, Ford feared most of his Rangers would sign up for the Texas cause in any resulting fight.

He doubted that Sam Houston would be able to hold off the secessionists within the Texas legislature. As much as Ford yearned to be free of the growing threat posed by the federal government, he recognized that the southern states would be at a decided disadvantage militarily and economically. It didn't bode well.

Strong rode easy-like into Nuecestown. As he reached the first couple of structures, he dismounted to better take in the ambiance of the town, such as it was. Were it not for his need for closure about his cousin, coupled with the prospect of facing the winter on a journey back to Fort Laramie, he'd simply end his search for Luke. He'd pretty much made up his mind to move his family to Texas. Meeting with the Texas Ranger would hopefully serve to cement that decision.

Bernice and Agatha's boarding house seemed to be the obvious first place folks gravitated to when entering Nuecestown. Strong was no exception. He hitched his horse and strode up to the door. Bernice opened it before he could knock.

"Howdy, ma'am. Name's Jubal Strong. Do you have a room for a tired traveler?"

"I'm Bernice, Mr. Strong." She sized him up. "A room is two dollars in advance."

"Thanks. Is there a stable an' a place where I can get cleaned up?"

Bernice pointed up the way to the livery. "You can take your horse up yonder. We have a place out back where you can bathe, Mr. Strong, and there's a mostly sharp razor if you care to shave." She further sized up her guest. "You visiting on business?"

"I'm headed to Corpus Christi, but I mostly want to meet that Texas Ranger Captain Luke Dunn. Can he be found nearby?"

"Captain Dunn is a friend. You have business with him?"

Strong smiled friendly-like. "Seems most folk on the Nueces Strip claim to be friends with Captain Dunn. An' from what I've heard, no one is lining up to be his enemy. He sounds like some sort of legend."

Bernice laughed, but her question hadn't been answered. "He's not someone you'd want to cross, Mr. Strong. Now, what did you say your business with him was?"

Strong sighed deeply. "Truth is, Miss Bernice, I want to confirm what happened to my cousin. He was a scoundrel, an' Captain Dunn brought him to justice. I hold no ill will toward the Ranger. Just lookin' for the straight story."

Bernice's instincts told her this man was no threat to Luke. "Well, I do believe he should be getting back here right soon. He didn't expect to be away for but a couple of weeks looking for a couple of lawbreakers."

"Is it best to wait here or go on to Corpus Christi?"

"Up to you, Mr. Strong. It's getting late in the day, so you might want to wait until tomorrow. Who knows? He might be back by then."

Edward Thorpe stood on the veranda of the big house at Magnolia. He thought on how much power and influence the wealth generated by the plantation and the business interests that had belonged to his father now lay in his hands.

"Joshua, are the next ones ready?" On the one hand, Thorpe vocally supported his fellow plantation owners in pushing for secession, but on the other was gradually diversifying his crop interests to be less labor-intensive. It had been a huge weight uploaded from his shoulders when he'd shared that with Captain Dunn.

"Yes, sir, Mr. Thorpe. They be loaded in the wagon." Joshua was a mulatto field hand whom Thorpe had recruited to help with his scheme. The young man seemed a bit more eager than the other slaves, so Thorpe quickly took him under his wing.

The wagon was built especially for the task at hand. It had a false floor in its bed creating a compartment within which up to four adults could be hidden. Inside were water jugs. Passengers could slip from a trap door so they could take care of natural body functions. The bed was filled with corn, which had sufficient aroma to hide any telltale body odors. "It's time to roll it out, Joshua. I fear we won't get to make too many more of these journeys. Secession is in the wind."

The journey would take better than two weeks. Blessedly, it was late winter, so travel wouldn't be in a confined space through the blazing heat of the Nueces Strip. Their destination was a ranch near what would become McAllen. The place was about a mile from the Rio Grande. Since Mexico had abolished slavery back in 1829, Thorpe's people could count on *tejanos* to help at way stations along the route and to eventually spirit the slaves over the border. It was risky business to say the least, and there was never a guarantee to successful escapes to freedom.

Thorpe had thus far freed close to a hundred and fifty of the slaves at Magnolia. If his fellow planters knew what he was up to, he'd be more than vilified...he'd quite possibly be lynched. Edward Thorpe had hooked up with the underground railroad and that alone was a threat to his fellow plantation owners.

The wagon wended its way south, trying to cast no suspicions along its route. Soon enough, it reached the Nueces River, about halfway to the border. The wagon prepared to board the ferry at Nuecestown, when trouble came calling.

"That's a lot of corn y'all are haulin'." Two men on horseback had arrived at the landing simultaneously with the wagon. "Ain't they growin' enough corn 'round these parts?"

The driver was white. He was one of the men Thorpe hired to supervise field operations at Magnolia. A mulatto freeman sat next to him. The driver wasn't too happy with this assignment in the first place, but orders were orders. "This is a special kind of corn. We are hauling it to Mexico."

"Your corn sure stinks to high heaven. Smells like cow shit. You ride through a bunch of cattle droppings?" The men were laughing and holding their noses.

Of a sudden, there was a loud sneeze. The mulatto immediately wiped his nose, as though he'd sneezed.

"You feel okay, boy?" Both men had dismounted in

preparation for boarding the ferry. As they boarded, one of them found himself especially close to the wagon. There was another sneeze. "Y'all sure got noisy corn here." The man drew a revolver from his belt. "Something ain't right with your wagon."

The wagon driver raised his hands. "We don't want trouble. Just doing our job hauling corn." He was sticking to his story.

"You runnin' slaves? Huh, are you? You tell me true."

The ferry master stood by helplessly at the front of the ferry as the scene unfolded. There was no escape for the wagon driver or his companion. He prayed that he could haul the ferry across the river before anything ugly happened. He prayed even harder that Sheriff Meaney would have chosen this day to be in Nuecestown.

"You see slaves? All we have is corn."

The ferry was nearly halfway across. The man with the revolver cocked the hammer. "I think I'm gonna find out."

"No, please don't go shooting up our corn, mister."

"You men settle down. I'll have no shooting on my ferry!" The ferry master felt helpless. There really wasn't much he could do.

"I think we need to be certain." He aimed into the side of the wagon and pulled the trigger. The gun misfired. The driver held his breath. The man cocked the hammer again and squeezed the trigger slowly this time. The shot echoed up and down the river. There was a groan from inside the wagon. "Damn! I thought so. Sons of bitches are runnin' slaves." The men stood back. Now both had their hands filled with revolvers.

"Stop. Please stop." The ferry master was beside himself.

The men had worked themselves into a frenzy of anger. They began firing into the bed of the wagon. The driver and mulatto were unable to reach their one rifle, the only weapon they had. Blood began to pour from the bottom of the wagon, splashing onto the deck of the ferry. The men had finally emptied their guns. "We oughta shoot you, too." They looked over at the ferry master. "Get this thing to shore—pronto!"

The bigger of the men grabbed a coil of rope attached to his saddle and looked menacingly at the driver and the mulatto. "Show you what we do to your kind." He began to fashion a noose.

The ferry master caused the ferry to hit the landing hard, almost causing the cowboys to fall. In that moment, the wagon driver dove into the river and swam for his life. His companion couldn't swim, but the river offered his only hope of escape. It was drown or be hung. He jumped. The men couldn't reload in time.

The men mounted their horses and lit out at a gallop. There seemed no point in hanging around to clean up the mess.

The ferry master had been an innocent bystander. He did what little he could, but it was no help to the four humans inside the wagon bed. He led the team off the ferry. There'd be a lot of cleaning up to do. Folks wouldn't appreciate blood all over the deck. He'd try to get a decent burial for the dead slaves there in the Nuecestown Cemetery. The ferry master figured this was likely the fate met by some on what he'd heard called the underground railroad.

Sheriff Meaney had missed all the action.

Thorpe would be unhappy when he learned of the tragedy from the driver and the mulatto, who had quickly learned to swim. The killing would sadden Thorpe, but it wouldn't stop him.

TWENTY-ONE
HEAVEN'S GATE

THE MOON WAS bright enough that it nearly caused the stars to disappear from view. For Luke, it was nearly like traveling in daylight. He was used to non-stop travel, as he'd caught up with more than one fugitive by sheer dogged endurance.

He figured it was near midnight when he rode into the barn at Heaven's Gate. The hoot owls and an occasional coyote drowned out the sound of his approach.

Big Horse was happy to be back in his familiar stall. And as much as Luke wanted to get up to the house, he took the time to curry and feed his best friend on the trail. The big gray nuzzled him repeatedly in appreciation.

Finally, Luke threw his saddlebags over his shoulder, grabbed his rifle, and headed up the hill to the house. He'd taken off his spurs, so he wouldn't unnecessarily awaken anyone with their jangling.

As he approached the house, he caught sight of Elisa. She'd apparently felt the need to use the privy and sought to use it rather than the pot they often used indoors during winter. After all, it was a gorgeous night, and a bit of fresh air was welcome. He watched as she fumbled with the door latch. "Pardon, ma'am, you need help with that door?"

Momentarily startled, she quickly recognized that voice. "Lucas? Lucas? You're home!"

Luke dropped the saddlebags and rifle. In a heartbeat, their bodies were merged as one. "Lisa…Lisa…I've missed you so."

Despite the brightness of the moonlight, she couldn't yet see the wound across his forehead as partially hidden by his hat. It mattered not. Her man was home safely. "Come on in. You must be hungry." She pulled him to the door, barely giving him a chance to grab his saddlebags and rifle. Once inside, they renewed their embrace.

Luke's hat came off.

Elisa saw the wound for the first time. "Lucas? What? What happened?"

"Talk about it in the morning. I'm whupped, sweetheart." The expression he saw said this wouldn't wait until morning. He sighed. "Let's sit." He urged her over to the oak table in the kitchen and waited until she was comfortable.

She couldn't divert her eyes from the wound. It gave her involuntary shudders at what it likely portended.

"I found those two abolitionists that Rip wanted me to bring in. Pure chance coming on them. Like a needle in a barn full of hay." He said the sentence calmly, evenly. "Unfortunately for them, they were dead when I found them. Apache."

His simply uttering the word Apache sent another shudder through her.

Luke took her hands in his to reassure her. "I went about digging a couple of graves for the remains." He took a deep breath. "While I was distracted with digging, an Apache jumped me. Tried to take my scalp…but I was able to fend him off. He was distracted by a couple of others, and it cost him and another Apache their lives." There, the story was out.

Elisa slumped forward in her seat and put her forehead to his hands. "Praises to God that you're all right, Lucas."

He put his head against hers, and then gently pulled back. "A nice old lady in Rio Grande City patched me up, then I met with Rip Ford at Fort Ringgold and headed home." He made it sound like just another day on the prairies of the Nueces Strip. He decided not to mention the lynching.

Elisa looked up and smiled. "What am I going to do with you, Lucas Dunn?"

He smiled mischievously. "You have to ask?"

Jubal Strong arose early. He was of a mind to ride into Corpus Christi. "I'm much obliged for your hospitality, Miss Bernice, ma'am. I'm gonna head into Corpus and see whether there's any word about Captain Dunn's return." He paused thoughtfully. "I talked with a nearby rancher named Nicholas Dunn. He wants to hire me on come spring. He said Captain Dunn has a ranch near here. Fact is, I've met a few folks in my travels. I'm taking a liking to Texas."

Bernice considered herself a pretty fair judge of human nature and had decided that this man had no ill intentions. "Actually, Mr. Strong, you might stop by Heaven's Gate. It's about five miles out of town on the road to Corpus. That's Captain Dunn's spread. Could be he's back."

Strong smiled friendly-like. "Again, much obliged,

ma'am." Soon enough, Strong was on the road toward Corpus Christi that would take him past Luke's spread. He'd ridden about an hour, thinking further on what he might say when he finally met up with Luke. The entrance to Heaven's Gate soon loomed before him. He was impressed, especially compared to Luke's cousin's place. He made the turn up the trail that led to the ranch house.

Luke sat on the gallery sipping coffee and relishing the beautiful landscape before him. He was nevertheless quite a sight with the bandage peeking out from under his hat. He thought on the bluebonnets he'd given Elisa a bit earlier and how they'd made her smile. He recalled the day he'd first seen her kneeling at her mother's grave spreading flower petals over the earthen mound. She'd been impressed that he'd recognized the blossoms. He loved everything about Elisa, about Heaven's Gate.

Elisa busied herself inside feeding the children. She was getting a few things done so she could join him in his idyll.

Luke's story the night before about his adventures on the southern reaches of the Nueces Strip had been unnerving, but he'd more than made up for it before they found their way to bed.

The steady staccato of horse hooves coming up the trail grabbed Luke's attention. This was still very much frontier, so he reflexively moved one of his Colt Navy revolvers to his lap while continuing to rock. He calmly set his coffee cup on the side table. The visitor soon emerged.

Strong recognized Luke from the description he'd been given. He approached the house, pulled up, and nodded to Luke. "Howdy. My name's Jubal Strong. My apologies for showing up uninvited."

Luke saw that the man was unarmed save for the rifle in the saddle scabbard. "Welcome to Heaven's Gate, Mr. Strong." Luke got up from his seat and slipped the revolver back into his holster. "Heard rumor you might visit. Care for a cup of coffee?"

Strong dismounted, climbed to the gallery, and shook hands with Luke. He wasn't the least surprised that the Texas Ranger had heard of his coming to visit.

"Hear tell you're curious about how your cousin met his fate." Luke didn't see any point in beating around the bush. "Have a seat, and I'll tell you as best I can recall."

Elisa stepped from the house and handed Strong a cup of coffee.

"Oh, this is my wife, Elisa. Sweetheart, this is Bart Strong's cousin Jubal come to learn about Bart's end."

Strong nodded to Elisa. "I hear you have a growing family, Mrs. Dunn. My wife and children are back near Fort Laramie. I hope to bring them here in the spring, as your husband's cousin offered me an opportunity on his ranch." He smiled and turned back to Luke. "I know that my cousin Bart had built a terrible reputation, Captain Dunn."

"My interest in him began in earnest when he bushwhacked me a way west of here. Nearly blew my hand off." He waved his scarred hand in front of Strong. "It became my duty to bring him to justice—not for shooting at me, mind you—but for several murders of which he was accused. There was a fair-sized bounty on him."

"Were you a Ranger or bounty hunter, Captain?"

"Back then, the Texas Rangers weren't funded, so our income came from bounties. In your cousin's case, I actually gave the bounty away—but that's another story."

Strong nodded approvingly. He was already warming to the big Texas Ranger.

"Your cousin was heading to Laredo, and I had no difficulty tracking him. I believe he was frustrated that his attempt to bushwhack me failed, so he wanted to lure me into an ambush. Along the trail, I met and sort of befriended a Comanche chief named Three Toes. That too is another story. Also, another Texas Ranger joined me. Now, we had three of us tracking your cousin."

Strong took a long sip of coffee. He found himself enjoying Luke's tale, even though it was about his cousin's demise.

Luke looked out onto Heaven's Gate as though recalling what happened next. "We made it to Laredo and learned he'd headed south toward San Ygnacio. We split up and did a lot of backtracking to make it difficult to be ambushed. Finally, the Comanche chief figured out where your cousin was holed up. A rock outcropping afforded Bart a great view of the road below. As I recall, he had a Sharps rifle and a revolver, so he was well-armed. Three Toes and I stalked your cousin's position. Unfortunately, we couldn't do that fast enough to keep him from ambushing our Texas Ranger partner."

Strong winced at the injustice. "Sorry to hear that, Captain."

"Your cousin made the mistake of leaving the protection of the rocks. That's when the chief and I approached him. The Comanche and I were about thirty feet apart. I had my guns and the chief had an arrow aimed at him. Your cousin was standing beside a rock outcropping about shoulder high. He didn't see the rattler sitting on it. Worse yet, the damned snake had lost its rattles, so it was coiled there silent and evil-like. I called out to Bart to not move. He had a gun in his hand and, as he began to raise his arm, the rattlesnake struck him in the neck. He fired his gun once wildly into the air. He knew he'd met his end, and that didn't take long. We buried the Texas Ranger and took your cousin's body to Laredo for burial. That's about the whole story, Mr. Strong. I sent the reward on to Elisa, so she could secure this place. It was before we married. She'd lost most of her family in a Comanche raid."

"What about my cousin's belongings?"

"Those were up to the sheriff in Laredo to dispose of. As I recall, there was nothing memorable on his person. No photos, no jewelry. I knew Comanche treasure horses, so I gave Bart's horse to the Comanche as reward for helping. Figured it was only the fair thing to do. Guess the chief was impressed. He thought I'd called the rattlesnake from some spirit world so nicknamed me Ghost-Who-Rides."

"I deeply appreciate your honesty, Captain. My cousin was not right in his head and hurt a lot of folks. There was plenty of trouble on his side of the family. His father was an abusive son of a bitch who beat Bart's mother to death before Bart killed him. His brother Sam escaped the family a year earlier, but seems he ran into you as well." Strong shook his head slowly. Luke had simply confirmed what he'd known all along about his cousin. "I guess, in a sense, you didn't even kill Bart." He looked off, as though contemplating what to do. "I do figure to move down to this neck of the woods come spring. I hope we can be good neighbors, Captain."

"In that case, you can call me Luke. You're welcome to visit any time."

"I expect I ought to mosey on back to Fort Laramie country so I can get back here in time for spring roundup. I appreciate the coffee." With that, Strong mounted up and was soon on his way.

Elisa joined Luke on the gallery. "Mr. Strong has left already?"

"Seems like he found the closure he was looking for. That's what it takes sometimes. Jubal's anxious to move his family down here and begin a new life. Can't say as I blame him…this is Texas, after all." He gave Elisa a little hug, took a final sip of coffee, looked back over his shoulder at their ranch with its grazing horses and longhorns, and led her inside.

TWENTY-TWO
DECISIONS WRIT IN BLOOD

GOVERNOR SAM HOUSTON had been right. But he had mixed feelings, as his dreams of the presidency of the United States had been rudely interrupted. A Texas State Convention voted overwhelmingly on the first of February to secede. It would later be confirmed in a public referendum. The wheels of a possible new order were gathering momentum. Word had gotten back to Austin that the soon-to-be inaugurated Abraham Lincoln had announced that there really was no crisis except an artificial one. By most Texans' minds, the president-elect needed to pay a visit to Texas.

Luke was visiting in Corpus Christi with Colonel Kinney when Walker Carson sought them out. "Colonel Kinney, Captain Dunn, have you heard?" Carson had seen the two men conversing animatedly in front of Kinney's house. He'd run up the street as fast as he could, wobbling in a pair of yet-to-be-broken-in new boots Scarlett had given him as a birthday gift. "Texas has seceded!"

Luke and the Colonel exchanged knowing glances. This had pretty much been a foregone outcome. Luke stepped toward Carson and put his hand on his shoulder to try to settle him. "Calm yourself down, Walker. Where did you hear this?"

"A courier just arrived at the post office, Captain. The postmaster nailed it up for all to see. I read it with my own two eyes. No doubt about it, sir."

"Well, Colonel, seems decision times are upon us." Luke turned to Kinney. "It's going to be a mixed bag for us in Texas."

Kinney sort of understood. "You mean the Rangers will join Texas militia and our western frontier will be defenseless?"

"You think otherwise, Colonel?"

"You're likely right, Luke." Kinney was perplexed. "There's likely to be a lot of tough decisions being made." He looked at Carson as if the young man's decision would be a bell-weather for what to expect from others. "You have any idea what you might do, Mr. Carson?"

The sheer weight of such a decision fell like a giant ox yoke on Carson's unwitting shoulders. He'd heard the rumors. He and Scarlett had discussed what might happen. What indeed would he do? "Er...I...er...I expect I'll do what every loyal Texan would do, Colonel."

Kinney understood. "It's not going to be easy, Mr. Carson. I do suggest that you start thinking about getting your affairs in order. There's fixing to be quite a fight, and we'll need every able-bodied man. Someone with your fighting experience will be critical to the cause."

A confused Walker Carson bid farewell. He was facing life-impacting decisions not of his own choosing. His seemingly perfect plans with Scarlett were in grave jeopardy.

Luke shook his head. "This is only the beginning, Colonel. I don't envy the decisions facing Texan families." Luke thought about how he had just begun to think about settling into ranch life full-time. "If Rip Ford is right, we'll still need to protect that western frontier as best we can. We'll be under-manned out there, in any case." He stroked his mustache. "What about you, Colonel?"

"We have a city to defend here. Since we're a port, I'd be surprised if the Yankees wouldn't consider it important to any trade blockade strategy." It was clear that Kinney had thought on this a bit.

"Well, I'd best get back to Elisa, Colonel. As you say, there'll be a lot of decision making ahead." Events had happened far too quickly to suit Luke. He slowly made his way to the hitching post and walked Big Horse up the street toward the jail. He figured he'd better have a few words with Sheriff Meaney before heading back to Heaven's Gate.

Meaney was sitting on the front steps of the sheriff's office. The fact that he was smiling caused Luke to wonder whether he'd not heard about secession. "Bill, what's put you in good spirits?"

"Clara and me...we're getting hitched." He smiled even more broadly.

"You've heard about secession?"

"Hell, yes, Luke. Shoot, I'm nearly fifty years old and sheriff of a city that's likely to get a lot of attention from the federals. I ain't gonna join any army again, so I expect I'll be doing the best I can to keep order here. We still need to keep the peace."

Luke couldn't really argue with Meaney's logic. "You're likely right, Bill." He stood there, thoughtfully stroking his mustache as he held Big Horse's reins and pondered what lay ahead for him and Elisa. "Seems I'm in a similar situation. I could likely get an officer commission, but I'm concerned for what's likely to be our defenseless borders. The Comanche and Kiowa to the west and Apache and Mexicans to the south won't be wasting time waiting to attack our citizens. The folks in Austin won't fund the Texas Rangers with a war brewing."

Meaney nodded in agreement. "Soon enough, Luke, folks will realize what goes on to sustain a war. Texans will have to support an army, feed it, clothe it…and they'll expect their lives to be safeguarded from violence. I'm not liking that Lincoln fellow they elected. He says there's no crisis, but you just watch how he plays the political game, Luke. You just watch."

"You really think it's going to go badly?"

"I've fought in two wars, Luke. It never goes well."

Luke nodded. "Well, you've likely made the right decision for you and Clara, Bill. I pray all goes well." Luke mounted Big Horse. "I'll let you know what Elisa and I decide."

As he rode out of Corpus Christi on the road to Nuecestown, he brought Big Horse to a halt. Luke had a lot on his mind as he considered his choices for the future. He gazed out across the gentle prairie with its seemingly endless grasses. A ball of brush caught in a breeze aimlessly tumbled across his path. He wondered whether the tumbleweed held wisdom he'd not yet grasped. The darned things seemed to show up just about every time he found himself facing life-impacting decisions. His consternation with the tumbleweeds was that they seemed to disappear about as quickly as they appeared. Were the goldarned things real? Was there some message in the vision? What would the future bring? He pressed his spurs lightly to Big Horse's sides, just enough to shake the tumbleweeds from his thoughts.

"You can't just up and leave, Stephen. It'd be desertion… treason."

"They're forming up an army in Texas, Rex. I'm going to join the cavalry."

"There might not even be any war, Stephen. You can't throw away your career over something that might not happen."

"You heard about Fort Sumter? Federal troops and South Carolina militia are staring each other down. If there's a spark that ignites a war, it'll be coming from there."

Rex ruefully shook his head. He seemed helpless to turn his brother's mind. It was likely to break his father's heart. Worse yet, what if he had to face his own kin in battle? They'd likely both wind up with officer commissions, but would that really matter in the total scheme of things? He was a diligent student of the military arts, and he saw no way that the southern states could defeat the industrial might of the north.

"I'm sorry, Rex. I love you as a brother, but I don't agree with you in this matter. I'll leave secret-like so they won't give you demerits for not reporting me. I'll stop by in Nuecestown and let Father know."

Rex reached out for his brother's hand but then drew him close for a final embrace. "May God's mercy and protection be with you, Stephen." He turned away with tear-laden eyes. This wasn't how life was supposed to be. Anger seeped into the inner recesses of his soul as he cursed the politicians who had brought the nation to this state. How would it all end?

★★

The major leaned forward with clenched fists pressed against the desk. The expression on his face spoke volumes. Frustration, anger, loyalty to his country seemed etched in its sunbaked crevices. "Captain, our orders are to secure this fort from anyone who attempts to take it over. Sounds contradictory, but we are to avoid any armed resistance, if at all possible."

Belknap couldn't help himself. Fort Mason was a vulnerable outpost and was likely to be easily overwhelmed by Texas troops. His jaw dropped. "Yes, sir." He wanted to ask who had come up with such cowardly defense of federal property. He'd spent the past three years patrolling the vast prairies of the Nueces Strip, journeyed so far as Utah, fought Comanche and Apache, fended off Mexican rebels, and more. Was it all to come down to this? He saluted the major. "Sir?"

"What is it, Captain?"

"May I...?"

"No!" The major put his hands on his hips. "Look, I know this doesn't make sense. If someone's looking for a fight, I'm not the officer that'd run from it. We've got orders, Captain. I don't like them, either, but I'll follow them to my last breath."

Deep in their guts, the two officers knew they'd have to surrender the fort at the first sign of any threat.

Big Horse seemed to sense that Luke was deep in thought. A creature of habit, the big gray stallion turned through the gate and up the lane at Heaven's Gate. Luke rode up to the barn with his mind pretty much made up. Despite his being distracted, he never short-changed caring for his beloved horse. Man and horse shared a critically important bond on the wide open spaces of the frontier. Once Big Horse was settled, Luke threw his saddlebags over his shoulder, grabbed his rifle, and strode easy-like up to the house. Elisa was standing on the gallery, smiling in her winsomely attractive way. Her reddish-gold hair fell in sensuously disheveled cascades across her breasts. The twins, Peter and John, were hanging onto her legs and she held Andrea Ann on her hip. Baby Michael was wrapped in a blanket like an Indian papoose. Indeed, the entire family had turned out to greet him. Luke found new energy as he bounded up the final few steps to the house. How did she manage to look so incredibly desirable with four children hanging on to her? "Lisa…"

"Yes…yes, Lucas, you're home."

He'd have had her right then and there were it not for the children. He shook from his head at the vision of the two of them drowning in passion. "We've got a lot to talk about."

She'd caught the look in his eye. The first one, not the serious we've-got-to-talk one. "It'll just take a few minutes to rustle up some dinner, cowboy."

He was used to her calling him Lucas or Ranger, but the cowboy moniker was unusual. He sensed something was going on. He caught sight of an unfamiliar horse tied to the post. She gave him the *we've-got-an-unexpected-guest look* and from her expression, he assumed there was no problem. "Don't have to twist my arm, Lisa." He scooped up the twins, and followed Elisa and the youngsters into the house.

"Captain Dunn, howdy. Name's John Dunn." The distinct Irish brogue caught Luke off guard.

Luke was totally surprised. He'd only met his cousin Nick's father once before, and that was by chance when he was on his cousin's ranch getting advice on buying and selling livestock. "Mr. Dunn, *céad míle fáilte*." Luke rarely used the old Irish tongue anymore. He almost surprised himself as he offered his cousin a hundred thousand welcomes. "Welcome to Heaven's Gate." Luke extended his hand in welcome. Now, despite his empty stomach, he felt a burning need to find out exactly what it could be that brought this highly respected elder statesman of the Dunn family to Heaven's Gate. Luke hung his hat and leaned the Sharps rifle against the wall near the door.

Elisa went about fixing dinner. The aroma of cornbread and sounds of sizzling steak soon filled the confines of the kitchen and wafted into the dining room. It served as a sensory reminder that dinner would soon follow. Luke and his cousin sat at the table while the twins toddled around and under.

"So what brings you to Heaven's Gate, Mr. Dunn?"

"I appreciate the respect, but you can call me John." He smiled friendly-like. It was an awkward smile, as a long-horn had hooked his cheek a couple of years back and left him with a crooked jaw. "I fancy myself a fair judge of folks, Luke. With all that's brewing, I'd have to guess that you've likely made a decision about the future. I don't figure you to be joining any army, at least not with your lawman experience. Plus, you saw firsthand back in Kildare what happens with rebellions."

Luke nodded. "So far, you've got me figured out, John."

"Nor do I see you avoiding a conflict that might very well be raging not far from your family. I also figure that Indians and Mexicans are likely to take advantage of the situation, not to mention foraging troops, federal and otherwise."

Clearly, Luke's cousin had given whatever he was going to propose a lot of thought. "Go on, John." Luke politely encouraged him to get to his point.

Elisa had just about finished fixing dinner but kept an ear to the conversation. She'd already pulled John Dunn's proposal from him before Luke's arrival, so anxiously awaited her husband's reaction.

"I'm expecting a good cotton crop this year, Luke. But I suspect the Yankees are going to try to interrupt our normal trade route through Corpus. Likely even seize it. I'm thinking that we must adapt, so my plan is to load the cotton bales on wagons and drive them by oxen to Veracruz. Looks as though the Mexicans are willing to help, despite their own conflict. The folks in Austin are making nice with Mexico for a trade deal." He waited for this information to sink in. "I expect we're going to need an armed escort, Luke. Federal troops will be looking for us and Indians and bandits are likely to harass us. So my question is, will you assemble an escort for us and accompany our shipments to Mexico? We already have some family that will help, and you know the Dunn family is as tough as they come."

By this time, Luke was stroking his mustache enough that Elisa thought he might rub it from his face. He glanced up at Elisa and caught her almost imperceptible nod. Escorting his cousin's cotton meant he wouldn't be donning any military uniform nor would he likely be roaming the far reaches of the Nueces Strip looking for troublemakers. "Anything else I should know, John?"

"I can offer up some land as payment, Luke. I'm not confident in whatever script the new government issues." John Dunn was an Irishman to the bone, which meant that he was right careful about money and anything else of value. "I'd say two hundred acres per trip would be fair. Likely be a couple of trips."

Luke's own Irish blood crept into a haggling spirit. He glanced again at Elisa. She smiled and nodded. She had a pretty good idea what was running through his mind. "You know, John, if I leave Heaven's Gate for any length of time, my family is at risk should the Yankees start foraging to supply any troops they're able to station in Corpus." He looked again at Elisa. "Three hundred acres and five beeves per trip, and you've got a deal, John."

John gave thought to countering. Then he reached his hand across the table. "*A déileáil!*" Indeed, it was a deal. John Dunn hadn't forgotten the Irish mother tongue either. It was as though the purity of the Gaelic sealed the deal.

They shook hands, and Elisa began serving a scrumptious meal as though on cue. Smiles, laughter, and general good humor filled the Dunn household. John began telling leprechaun tales describing rainbows and little people much to the delight of the twins who were just about old enough to understand. The boys would spend their next few days trying to find the mischievous little men in green hats.

After dinner, and with their cousin headed home and children put to bed, Luke and Elisa finally had a chance to relax. They lay back in each other's arms before the hearth. The immediate future seemed settled enough.

"What aren't you saying, Lucas?"

"I worry that, despite all the political blarney, the south is getting into a fight it can't possibly win." He thought on that for a moment. "It will surely get ugly, Lisa. It conjures up images of my time with the rebels back in County Kildare. We strove to resist the power of the British empire and paid dearly."

Elisa chose to ignore his fretting. She leaned to him, kissed his cheek, and took his hand. She pulled him toward the bedroom, gently at first…then with an aroused urgency.

"Just what are you trying to do, you little tart?" he half-laughingly whispered as he nuzzled her neck?

She pushed him onto the bed. "Oh, Mr. Texas Ranger, what indeed do we have here?" Her hand explored the growing bulge between his legs and soon freed it. A delightful nearly orgasmic shudder coursed through her body, as she lifted her dress, mounted him, and took him to her innermost core.

Their rapture reached incandescent heights as hands and mouths explored as though for the first time. Love surely knew no bounds.

And he kissed her...all over her body, exploring her nakedness. He ran a finger along the scar that traced from her sternum to her groin.

She shuddered at the reminder. "It's so ugly, Lucas."

"No, Lisa, it's not ugly. It's beautiful. It's a reminder that God was looking out for you...for us. The cut delayed the evil long enough for me to arrive and save you from a worse fate. It will always be beautiful to me. It says you are a fighter...and gives me ever more reason to love you."

Elisa wrapped herself in Luke as closely as she could. He was indeed the real man she'd always dreamed of. He'd never disappoint her. She pushed him onto his back, and her lips explored every inch of his hard-muscled body. She felt his manhood respond and once again slipped on top of him and sated their sexual desires. No words were spoken. There was no need. Their passions spoke volumes. The morning would arrive all too soon.

The masked horsemen had ridden up the long magnolia-lined lane, stopping at the very steps of the manor house. Edward Thorpe stood legs akimbo on the porch, dressed in his best gentleman's suit, black riding boots, and broad-brimmed planter's hat. He held two large-gauge shotguns casually at his sides. Thorpe looked very much the lord of the manor.

There were all told about a dozen well-armed men. One of the riders edged his mount forward. "Mr. Thorpe, we hear tell you've been running your slaves to Mexico. Is that true?"

"What I do with my slaves is my business."

"Afraid you're setting a bad example, Mr. Thorpe. If you persist, be assured that you will regret it. Consider this your first and only warning."

There was a long silence as the two sides stared each other down.

The horsemen were losing patience. "Damn it, Carney, what we giving him warnings for?" Three of the men moved their horses forward and lowered their rifles at Thorpe. It all happened in the blink of an eye.

There was a huge explosion one of Thorpe's shotguns blasted and left a crater in the dirt directly before the leader's horse. "You men ought to think twice. You may get me, but are any of you prepared to die tonight?" With that, three Magnolia plantation overseers armed with rifles stepped from behind the white Georgian columns. Thorpe stood firm. "There's likely going to be enough for y'all to get into fighting federal troops. You start shooting here, and some of you aren't going to make it to enjoy that fighting."

An unearthly quiet now settled over the scene. The leader considered the situation. "Men, I think we've finished our business here. Goodnight, Mr. Thorpe. Be advised of our warning." They all turned and headed back up the lane from Magnolia.

Thorpe breathed a sigh of relief. He turned to one of his overseers. "How did they know?"

"Couple of cowboys attacked the wagon down on the Nuecestown ferry. Our driver and the mulatto escaped but, as the killers lit out, they identified your father's brands on that mulatto. The other ones were trapped in the wagon and shot to death."

Thorpe watched the riders as they rode through the gate and left Magnolia behind. "Seems like our days of freeing slaves have suddenly become a bit more dangerous." He shook his head in dismay. "Time doesn't appear to be on our side, men." He thought on how the area around the Nueces ferry had not been kind to the Thorpe family. The only upside had been getting acquainted with that Texas Ranger, Luke Dunn. He looked up at the leaden sky beginning to fill with dark gray clouds. "Looks as though old man winter is going to send us his last hurrah." He waited until the first raindrops fell before turning and entering the manor. It was a lonely place at the moment. War loomed, and he had no one to share his fears with.

Three Toes found himself flush with pride as his band of Penateka Comanche had now grown to nearly twenty warriors. There was no way to fully camouflage their encampment any longer. The warriors were growing restless, tiring of hunting and the labors of day-to-day life, such as they were. The Comanche were a warrior people by nature. War Cloud, despite his Kotsoteka Comanche roots, had become a sub-chief to Three Toes. This forced the chief to be ever vigilant for tribal insurrection. War Cloud seemed to have the ear of several warriors, likely owing to his being a little younger than Three Toes.

The chief sat in his teepee this morning and admired how the bellies of Cactus Flower and Bird Woman had grown. Perhaps there'd be a respite from the predations of the White men.

Three Toes emerged from his teepee into the damp of the morning. His enjoyment of the tranquil sounds of the rushing waters of the Pedernales River was rudely interrupted by none other than War Cloud. The Kotsoteka warrior didn't speak but stood next to the chief.

"You have something to say, War Cloud?"

"My chief, bluecoats leaving forts. White men soon fight each other." Even the Comanche were aware of the looming War Between the States. It did not matter why they would fight, just that it would serve as opportunity for the Comanche. The warrior's implication was that there would be easy pickings to steal horses and cattle, chances to count coup, and opportunities to rape and kill the hated Anglos.

Three Toes knew it was inevitable. He sighed resignedly and looked out at the river. "Take six warriors. Scout two days' ride. No warpaint." The chief couldn't help but agree with the warrior's proposal, but his admonition about no warpaint sent a clear message. So long as War Cloud was in camp, he'd have to deal with the warrior's demands, whether he agreed or not. The chief sighed resignedly. "At new moon, we attack Whites."

War Cloud smiled broadly. He understood that the chief would not tolerate his jumping the gun. If he were to engage Anglos while scouting for targets, it must be strictly self-defense or look that way.

The anticipated message from Rip Ford finally arrived. Nearly all the Texas Rangers were joining the Texas Army, mostly as members of Terry's 8th Texas Cavalry, and others joining McCulloch's 1st Mounted Volunteers and the 3rd Cavalry. The units had been divided into regiments throughout Texas.

Luke had been sitting on the gallery sipping a morning coffee when the courier arrived. It was pouring rain, so he was not especially anxious to ride out and patrol the ranch. The livestock could mostly take care of themselves, though flash flooding was always a concern. He sat thoughtfully fondling the envelope as he listened to the patter of rain on the roof and splashes in the puddles scattered before him. What if his arrangement with his cousin didn't work out? Finally, he sighed deeply. "Lisa! Rip Ford sent us a message."

Elisa was feeding baby Michael. Her shoulders reflexively slumped. Michael seemed to sense it, as he began to fuss. "Just a moment, Lucas. I'll be right out." She wished he'd come inside, but she appreciated her husband's preference for the out of doors. There was something in the Texas air and the sight of its vast prairies that freed mind and soul.

Luke cut the seal with his knife and slit open the envelope. He'd wait for Elisa before pulling the message out.

At last, Elisa emerged and stood behind him with her hands on his shoulders. Memories of the impassioned love-making of the evening before yet lingered, as she whimsically turned a lock of his hair with her fingers. "So what does Mr. Ford have to say?"

Luke opened the letter. There was what appeared to be a formal invitation and a second sheet of paper with personal notes from Ford. The former Texas Ranger had accepted a commission as a colonel commanding a cavalry regiment in the Rio Grande area. It made sense to Luke, as Ford was familiar with the area after having taken on Juan Cortina a couple of years earlier in what was called the Battle of Rio Grande City. Luke reread the invitation. "Looks like the Texas Rangers won't officially exist, Lisa. But Rip wants me to maintain civil order between Corpus Christi and San Diego."

Lisa felt a mixed sense of relief and guarded fear sweep over her. Luke would still be in harm's way, but he'd mostly be near Heaven's Gate. She appreciated that Rip Ford knew that a military uniform, regardless of rank, wouldn't suit Luke or his talents. "What about your cousin?"

"Appears I can do both, Lisa. Lord knows, there are enough lawbreakers round here as it is. Bill Meaney will have his hands full, and I doubt he'll get outside Corpus, much less Nueces County."

"Doesn't appear that they're able to pay but with government script, Lucas. If the south loses, it'll be worthless."

Luke knew she was right. There was already strife within the Texas government. He'd learned that Governor Houston didn't want to join the Confederacy. The majority of secession supporters were calling for his ouster. "It's all pretty shaky, Lisa. I'm inclined to accept Rip's offer."

Elisa had known from the moment the courier had arrived that he would. He could never give up being a Texas Ranger, even if it were, in essence, an illusion. They knew that the region was a hotbed of crime from land and insurance fraud to livestock rustling to robbery to murder. With Texas fighting men distracted to fight the Yankees, Luke would have his hands full. If being a Texas Ranger was illusory, so peace might be a fleeting hope.

"Don't know how long this mess might last, Lisa. It's going to be like a twister that doesn't know its own mind but sets down now and again to wreak havoc. I'm thinking we should all head to St. Patrick's in Corpus Christi this Sunday and be listening to Father O'Reilly." Dublin-born Father Bernard

O'Reilly was the first resident priest in Corpus and was highly respected, especially among the Irish community. At the worst, it would offer a patina of comfort over the stresses that lay ahead. Their biggest challenge would likely be trying to maintain some sort of normalcy for the sake of the children.

Elisa nodded. "I hear Peter and John stirring, Lucas. Seems our future is settled for now."

"May God have mercy on all our souls, my sweet."

"But what of our business?" Scarlett stood with hands on hips.

Carson had never seen her like this before. "It's my duty, Scarlett."

"What about your duty to me…your duty to us? The Army needs uniforms. We can make them. You needn't go get shot at."

She was right, and Carson knew it. Sheep raising was flourishing in the region, making for a ready supply of raw materials to make tunics and trousers aplenty. He looked into her eyes. There was toughness but with a hint of vulnerability.

"And…and I'm pregnant."

Carson's jaw dropped. "Well…I…er…oh, my god, Scarlett." His mouth broke into a broad grin. "Are you sure?"

She gave him the look. Of course she was sure. "Yes. Now, are you going to run off and soldier or stay and support the Texas Army from here?"

Carson was fit to be tied. He was now an experienced fighting man. He'd proven himself fighting Apache and Mexicans. He'd led Texas Rangers. Was he to stay at home with his pregnant wife and weave cloth? Might it be seen by some as a cowardly choice? Then an idea came to him. "What if I sign on as a deputy sheriff to help Bill Meaney?"

Scarlett looked him up one side and down the other. Carson's proposition had male ego written all over it. What was she to do? "Okay, Walker Carson."

"I love you, Scarlett." He swept her into his arms. She didn't resist. He placed his hand on her belly. He put his mouth near her ear. "So Margaret's gonna have a sister or brother." Carson couldn't suppress a broad grin. He was bust-a-button proud.

Better than a week had passed with no sign of War Cloud and the scouting party. Three Toes was none too happy with the possibilities that swirled through his mind. Had they been attacked and wiped out? Had they simply been delayed? Or the worst, had they decided to do what the chief had warned against? Were they attacking ranches and villages? He didn't want to appear paranoid, but he felt increasingly justified in trying to find the Kotsoteka Comanche warrior.

Three Toes gathered his remaining warriors and explained his fears. He put it in the context of the possibility of something evil having befallen War Cloud's party. They would need to pack supplies for possibly several days of travel. Three Toes judged that the warrior would have traveled south into a warmer climate. He felt fortunate that he had the advantage of knowing the territory from his previous travels.

The chief bade farewell to Cactus Flower and Bird Woman. Their bellies were growing, and they would likely give birth by spring. He prayed to the Great Spirit that he'd return for that event. "I return before next moon, Cactus Flower."

Call it something in the air or a spirit, but Cactus Flower and Bird Woman felt a foreboding. They feared this might be Three Toes's final adventure into the White men's territories.

As he sat on his best pony with five warriors in his band, he was the image of the regal Comanche chief. The scars and even triumphs of battles past mattered not. He sat straight and proud with his lance, bow with its quiver of arrows and old Colt revolver stuck into his waistband. He gave Cactus Flower and Bird Woman a look that held just a touch of forlornness. It said he had a premonition.

The party turned to the south and rode from the encampment. The chief looked around at the rushing waters of the Pedernales River and the surrounding oak trees and strove to take into his very soul the breath of freedom it represented.

TWENTY-THREE
BEGINNINGS & AN END

LUKE HAD BROUGHT his family to Corpus Christi to attend church. It wasn't something they did so frequently as they might, owing to his extensive travels throughout the Nueces Strip. While Elisa and the children visited with Scarlett, Luke, and Carson had slipped away to the Longhorn Saloon. To Luke's way of thinking, he figured he had pretty much covered his backside so far as dealing with these uncertain times. Now he found himself sparing a few moments of time with Sheriff Bill Meaney, Carson, and a couple of Nueces County ranchers. All were focused on the impending civil strife that was sure to come. "I've heard that Lincoln is arresting anyone who disagrees with him. Something called *habeas corpus* that the man is defying."

"Ain't that just like a Texas Ranger." Meaney chuckled as he looked over at Luke. "That *habeas corpus* thing is supposed to protect folks from being thrown in jail without just cause. Gonna have to get you to do some reading, Luke."

Carson weighed in. "How can he do that?"

"Something about fear of rebellion." Luke was already

deep in thought and stroking his mustache. "A fellow passing through from New Orleans told me Lincoln had arrested a couple of newspapermen for anti-war reporting."

"Even before fightin's begun? Ain't right! Just damned ain't right!" One of the local ranchers was getting his blood up.

"Calm down, Jack. Not much we can do about it here in Corpus. The damned politicians are going to do whatever they please." Meaney strove to keep a lid on any vitriol.

Luke leaned forward in his seat. "That fellow said several armories have been captured by state militia. The pot is near to boiling, folks." Luke leaned back as his eyes scanned the small assembly. "This is going to make the rebellions back in Ireland seem like child's play. I fought back in Kildare, and it was a nasty business." He stroked his mustache, signaling those gathered that a pearl of wisdom might follow. "Tell you what I fear, my friends." Luke had their rapt attention. "I fear loss of freedom. Seems to me that every time the government comes to impose a solution to a problem, they take our freedom. That *habeas corpus* thing is just the beginning. It happens almost so slowly we don't notice. Like I said, I saw it in Ireland." Luke eased back in his chair, still stroking his mustache. "Seems there's a war brewing, and it looks to me that the politicians' cure will be far worse than the sickness." They hadn't been used to hearing Luke opine on such matters. The gathered folks looked one to the other and nodded in agreement. A silence enveloped the room.

Meaney broke the spell. "Whatever happens, we've got to stand together. My loyalty is with Texas first. I don't like the idea of one man enslaving another, but I don't think violence is going to solve the problem." Meaney was sort of putting his heart on full display. "May God rest our souls if we have to fight. We all have families to defend."

Luke did a sort of double-take. "You've got no family here, Bill. Right?"

"Clara's got a bun in the oven." Meaney blushed. "Thought we were too old." He and Clara had gotten secretly married. His announcement signaled a decided shift in the conversation.

"Well, congratulations, Bill." Luke stood and nodded to the men seated around the oak table. "I'll be around these parts to do the best I can to help keep peace. From what I've heard, the Texas Rangers are mostly joining the Texas Army. Carson here is going to help the sheriff as a deputy. You folks need to keep an especially watchful eye on your live-stock. If this becomes a real fighting war, there's going to be nasty things happening. Armies must be fed and housed. They'll think nothing of stealing us blind with their forag-ing. And folks that you thought of as friends could now be enemies." Luke paused to let his words sink in. "I think I'd best be getting my family back to Heaven's Gate. Y'all take care." Vulnerability hung heavy in the air. It was late after-noon, and Luke figured he could make it home well before evening.

Three Toes nearly missed it. The little homestead has been burned to the ground. The cabin was little more than a mere pile of black coals. A man, a woman, and two young chil-dren had been mutilated and killed. It was clearly a Comanche attack, and it confirmed what the chief had feared.

There was nothing he could do at the site. Scavengers had already feasted. The burned-out remnants of the cabin had cooled. Angrily, he wasted no time and easily found War Cloud's tracks. Flush with satisfying their blood lust, the Kotsoteka Comanche and his warriors had gotten careless. Three Toes and his band now sped up their pursuit. War Cloud had a head start, but the chief was fully resolved to catch him. The rebellious warrior had now become prey.

The five warriors in his own party were Penateka Comanche, so Three Toes could be assured of their loyalty to him. They fully shared his anger over War Cloud's indiscretion and more so his defiance of their chief. Tribal loyalties hung thick.

They rode southward, then turned southeast. War Cloud seemed to be heading toward the area that the great Comanche chief Buffalo Hump had attacked a decade earlier. Whereas Buffalo Hump had a veritable army of nearly 1,000 warriors, War Cloud was not likely to mimic the chief's accomplishments of burning Linnville to the ground or devastating Victoria. Blood lust played with men's minds, and the Kotsoteka Comanche warrior was no exception. Three Toes was developing a fuller grasp of what was driving his prey.

By Three Toes's count, the rebellious warriors had counted plenty of coup and taken more than a dozen scalps in ravaging four ranches. On their current route, they'd reach the Gulf of Mexico at Corpus Christi. Of course, half a dozen warriors wouldn't stand up to a city of nearly three hundred. The questions became when would they have satisfied their blood lust and head back toward the Pedernales River. They were bypassing even the smallest towns and villages, so War Cloud wasn't making especially foolhardy attacks.

Three Toes and his band arrived at the fifth ranch attacked by War Cloud and began looking for sign. He examined the fresh wounds of the victims. The blood on the corral post had barely dried. The cabin was still a mass of smoldering hot coals. He turned to the warrior next to him. "Half-day ahead."

The warrior nodded. "They turn toward morning sun."

Three Toes had feared this outcome. They were following a trail eastward along the Nueces River. War Cloud was closing in on the ranches near Nuecestown. "One, maybe two prisoners." The prisoners were likely women who'd be discarded once the warriors were done having their way with them. The chief smiled. "They go slow now." The warriors were getting excited by the prospect of wreaking vengeance on War Cloud for disobeying their chief.

Three Toes waved the band forward at a brisker pace. The prey was within reach.

"I'm going to patrol along the river into Nuecestown this morning, Lisa. I'll be sure to send your best to Doc, Bernice, and Agatha. I should be back by early afternoon."

Elisa knew that was optimistic. "Just come back in one piece, Mr. Texas Ranger." She smiled and hugged her man.

As he began to leave the house, he paused. He felt a strange chilling sensation. He walked over to the mantle and took the Colt repeating rifle from its rack. He inspected it and made certain it was loaded. He placed it back on the mantel.

"You worried about something, Lucas?"

"Just can't be too safe these days, sweetheart." He kissed her and strolled easy-like down to the barn. He waved to Jaime along the way. He appreciated the *vaquero's* work more than ever these days.

The day had begun with plenty of cloud cover, and the last vestiges of winter were mostly gone. Worst they'd get now so far as rough weather would be rainstorms. In fact, the winter on the Nueces Strip had been quite mild, with virtually no snow and merely a couple of hailstorms. This day held promise as the sun had begun to break through and would soon dry out the landscape.

As he neared the road that ran from Corpus Christi to San Antonio, he saw a lone rider headed toward Nuecestown. The man wore a military uniform. He was too far away for Luke to easily hail him. He thought he recognized the rider as Stephen Rucker. Why wasn't the young man at the military academy? Then it occurred to Luke. Stephen was going to fight with Texas in the upcoming hostilities. He shook his head in dismay. Would it be brother versus brother? Would families be torn asunder?

Luke headed Big Horse down toward the banks of the Nueces River. It offered plenty of cover for anyone wanting to avoid being seen. They weren't very far from where the meandering river emptied into the Nueces Bay on its way past Corpus Christi to the Gulf of Mexico.

Perhaps fifteen minutes had elapsed at most, when he heard the snap of a piece of dead tree branch. He turned just as a gun fired and a bullet whizzed past his head. In fact, it knocked a piece from the edge of his hat. "Who the...!" His hands were instantly filled with his Colt revolvers. He fired.

Luke's third shot elicited a holler of pain from nearby bushes. "Drop your gun and come out of there, you damned bushwhacker!"

The bushwhacker turned out to be a young girl of no more than fourteen years old. "D...d...don't shoot." The girl was sobbing uncontrollably.

"Get over here. Did you know who you were shooting at?"

"Indians. Indians attacked." She was not hearing all of

what Luke was saying. For one thing, Luke had put a bullet clean through her hand and it hurt terribly.

"What about Indians?"

The girl finally realized that she was talking with a White man who meant her no harm. "My name is Sarah… Sarah Duncan." She was in obvious pain from her wound.

Luke recalled a family named Duncan that had a small farm several miles upstream along the river. "Come over here." Luke dismounted and grabbed a strip of cloth from his saddlebag. He'd been carrying bandages ever since his near-scalping by Apache. "They attack you?" He began to gently bandage her hand.

"They ran off. My mommy and daddy shot one of them. I was in the fields and was afraid they'd seen me. I ran like blazes. My daddy always taught me to take a gun out with me to the fields. I'm so sorry I shot at you. I was scared."

It struck Luke that the Duncan place was no more than ten miles west of Heaven's Gate. What if these Indians were heading toward his place at this very minute?

"They aren't going to bother with you now, Sarah. You head on back to your farm. Your folks are likely worried sick over you. I've got to go see to my ranch." With that, he remounted, pivoted Big Horse, and headed to Heaven's Gate at a full gallop. From about a mile away, he could just barely hear whooping and hollering.

The delay caused by the attack on the Duncan farm had been enough to enable Three Toes to catch up with War Cloud just as the Comanche warrior was preparing to raid Heaven's Gate.

As War Cloud shouted war whoops and began working up his courage for a charge at the house, Three Toes and his small band moved in from the warrior's left. The chief kicked his heels into his pony's sides and led a charge toward the house. Three Toes began with his own war whoops but soon was yelling in War Cloud's direction. "Coward! War Cloud coward!" Three Toes's yelling was also aimed at alerting Elisa.

Three Toes leaped to the gallery and crashed through the front door. "Hide...hide!" He waved his hands to signal urgency.

Elisa was stunned at the chief's entrance. She'd heard War Cloud and already grabbed the Colt rifle.

Three Toes hustled Elisa and the children into the cubby hole under the floorboards, before running back onto the gallery. "No one here!" He motioned War Cloud to leave. "You go!"

War Cloud ignored Three Toes's orders. To the warrior's thinking, the chief was obviously not telling the truth. Three Toes was certainly protecting Anglos inside the house. The warrior turned his pony, took careful aim, and put an arrow into the chief's chest. A look of utter surprise swept across Three Toes's face as he fell mortally wounded. How could this happen? War Cloud's unhinged anger now knew no bounds. He charged the house, leaped from his pony onto the gallery, determined to see for himself who or what was inside. He disdainfully stepped over the body of the dying chief, pausing but a moment to give a final derisive look at Three Toes.

Elisa would have none of hiding for herself. With the children safe in their hiding place, she readied the rifle. Flashes of defending her family's homestead against Comanche five years back flashed through her mind. She'd shot and killed a savage then, and she was fully up to the task now.

War Cloud, filled with a rage akin to insanity, took but a

single step through the threshold. His eyes grew wide with battle-fueled lust as they met Elisa's. With a leering smile, he walked full on into a bullet from her rifle. He lurched forward. Took one more step. Coughed up blood. A second bullet finished the warrior's life on earth.

Ignoring the fearful cries of her children, Elisa stepped over the lifeless warrior and began firing at the attacking Comanche, pulling the trigger even as she ran out of ammunition. The grimace on her face and grit in her demeanor were part of every bullet fired at the Comanche attackers.

Meanwhile, Jaime opened fire from the cabin.

The remaining Comanche had enough. Caught in a deadly crossfire and seeing that their leaders were dead, they rode off at a gallop.

Luke arrived in a cloud of dust just in time to kill one lagging attacker as the Comanche retreated. He leaped from Big Horse to Elisa's side and surveyed the scene. The battle had been quick. They usually were, as the savages didn't tend to like sieges.

Elisa was flush with the excitement of the battle but remained all too aware of her circumstances. She felt secure in the grasp of Luke's strong arms. But then she slipped from him, dropped to her knees, and cradled Three Toes's head in her lap. To her surprise, the chief wore a peaceful smile. His bronze skin had become smooth. In his semi-consciousness, his life-roughened hands fondled the cross on his necklace. In the mind of this savage, this warrior of the prairies, he sensed some sort of greater good from the gift she'd given him so long ago. It gave him peace.

The chief looked up in his semi-consciousness at Luke. "Ghost-Who-Rides...have great medicine. Cross strong. Helped me...save your family." He coughed up traces of blood. "You...save...you save mine...Pederna..." They'd be his dying words, his deathbed wish. He smiled as though at peace, wrinkles and crevices fully left his face, and the great chief took his final painful breath. His Comanche thinking would never grasp the meaning of the cross around his neck, but had only understood it in terms of spirit power. Perhaps it was enough. The chief's final thought through the fog of death was for Luke to protect his Penateka Comanche family up on the Pedernales River.

Tears traced through the dust on Luke's cheeks. His shoulders began to heave with sobs of heartfelt grief at the loss of his friend. He sank down next to Elisa as she still held Three Toes. "He knew, Lisa. He knew."

Jaime and Julia appeared. "They are gone, *Señor* Dunn. All gone." He spoke the words slowly out of respect. Jaime knew Three Toes was no ordinary Comanche, and he could sense Luke's anguish. Would men ever stop fighting over things they couldn't control? He heard the cries of the children and motioned to Julia to see to them. Like Luke, he prayed that his son would grow up to see peace. "*Señor* Dunn, can I help?"

"Ah, Jaime, thank you. We must give this chief a burial respectful of his heritage. He was a great friend, a great chief." Luke stood, lifted Elisa up to him, and looked deeply into her eyes. "Thank God you are all right."

As he held her close, he looked out over the clearing in front of the house. Four Comanche bodies littered the area around the house. A tumbleweed, one bigger than most, went bouncing by, lifted on the air currents that decided where its destination might be. Luke was done with contemplating tumbleweeds. He decided he was who he was. He had Elisa, young children, a thriving ranch, and plenty of family and friends. Even an impending war was not going to rob Texas Ranger Captain Luke Dunn of his destiny there on the eastern edge of the vast reaches of the

Texas Nueces Strip. The taming of the frontier beckoned. Freedom needed to be preserved and justice had to always prevail. His lot was to pursue justice, to race the wind and chase the sun. He leaned down and buried his face in the flowing cascade of Elisa's golden tresses, closed his eyes, and prayed.

They gave Three Toes a funeral worthy of his status as chief and friend. Luke placed a stake carved with the chief's name at the head of the burial mound. The mound was actually placed near the live oak where Elisa had buried her own family. She tied the chief's bone beaded necklace with its cross to the stake. They hadn't felt it appropriate to fashion a cross marker, but hoped Saint Peter would give due consideration to Three Toes.

War Cloud and four other dead Comanche were buried near where Luke had planted the three attackers of the Corrigan homestead years before.

After the brief ceremony, Luke stood arm in arm with Elisa and looked out over the expanse that was Heaven's Gate. They were blessed despite whatever might come. War did indeed loom on the horizon.

One Arrow and the two remaining Penateka Comanche began the slow journey back to the encampment. It would be his duty to tell Cactus Flower and Bird Woman how Three Toes's bravery had saved his friends. He'd also deal with telling War Cloud's squaw of the warrior's treachery and how the rogue warrior met his end embarrassingly at the hands of a small White woman.

Above all, and nestled deep within One Arrow's thoughts, was a growing need to better understand Three Toes's friendship with the Texas Ranger Captain Luke

Dunn. Deep in his bones, he sensed that Three Toes had arrived at some understanding of the White man. It was as though the chief had found more than accommodation. It was deeper and couched in respect and especially friendship. He fondled the carved cross on the necklace Three Toes had given him and resolved to seek out the chief's white friend and find for himself what was great enough for the Penateka Comanche chief to give his life.

Rip Ford sat across from former Governor Houston. He held a deep respect for the man, even though he disagreed strongly about the issue of joining the Confederate States of America.

Houston sipped a whiskey, perhaps one too many, as he slurred his words ever so slightly. "Rip, this Confederacy thing is leaving our backside terribly exposed. All our soldiers are looking to the Sabine. Hell, that fool Yankee General Butler already took our measure at New Orleans."

"We didn't have a choice, Sam. I know where your heart laid on this, but our treasury is weak. Jefferson Davis promised what we need to defend Texas."

"Tell that to that Mexican Juan Cortina...or the Apache...or the Comanche. And we've got all sorts of lawbreakers ready to threaten our citizens. Our strongest men will be off fighting Yankees. Too many Texans won't be sleeping well, Rip."

Ford wasn't inclined to drink, but poured himself a shot of whiskey. He gulped it down. Rip nodded respectfully to Houston. "It'll work out, Sam." As he turned and departed, he thought on how they'd have to rely on the likes of Luke Dunn to do whatever could be done to protect settlers and keep the peace. Of course, Ford had contributed in a big way to the likelihood of war with his newspaper articles and influence among legislators. It had been a price that had to be paid.

As he watched Ford depart, Houston shook his head ruefully. Texas was swarming with Mexican bandits, Indians, and other human vermin. He hadn't the funds anymore to pay Texas Rangers. He still had hopes of Texas avoiding joining the Confederacy, but realized it would be an uphill battle. The vote to secede had been overwhelming, and he intuitively knew his days as governor were likely numbered.

Luke sat tall in his saddle about three miles off from Heaven's Gate. He was becoming painfully aware that they'd had no rain in nearly three months. The creeks were drying up, and he was figuring that he'd surely have to deepen their well. Luke had noted on a visit to Nuecestown a couple of days before that the ferry across the Nueces River, despite its shallow draft, was scraping bottom as it approached the landing.

He had a feeling in his bones that an extended drought was coming, and there was no way of knowing how long it might last. He'd do his best to get water in the cistern and store what crops he could, but he began to resign himself to the loss of livestock.

Luke strove to be as resourceful as he could. It was a blessing that Elisa joined him in such pragmatic thinking. They wasted very little of the precious resources they had. With the real possibility of war looming on the horizon and the strong likelihood of drought, they'd have to redouble their efforts at conserving precious resources.

He watched appraisingly as a couple of longhorn beeves

trotted across his path. To his practiced eyes, they already seemed to be feeling the effects of an inadequate water supply. They were certainly leaner. He'd need to get them to market as best he could while they still had value. He knew there'd be other ranchers selling stock, so prices would tend to be driven down. Still, he really had little choice. He might be able to keep enough breed stock until the drought broke.

It hadn't taken Luke nearly so long as he'd expected. The escaping Comanche had left a pretty plain trail to follow, especially in the dry arroyos and among the tall grasses they'd ridden through.

Elisa had approved of his commitment to Three Toes's final request. The chief had asked Luke to look after his remaining family up on the Pedernales.

The morning of the fourth day on the trail, Luke found the Comanche encampment. The only sounds were the rustling of leaves.

One Arrow had just emerged from his teepee when he found himself face to face with Ghost-Who-Rides.

Luke had appeared as if from nowhere. He sat astride Big Horse, veiled in the early morning mists that had rolled in from the river. It could hardly have been more ghost-like.

One Arrow's jaw dropped. He was frozen in place. Here was Three Toes's friend. Here was the man whose ranch he'd just attacked. The young warrior's face revealed deep-seated fear.

Luke raised his hand as a sign of peace.

One Arrow exhaled an almost-audible sigh. Luke could easily have killed him. "You Three Toes's friend…Ghost-Who-Rides?"

Luke shook his head affirmatively.

One Arrow stood helpless at what to do next.

Luke nodded reassuringly and dismounted. He held his hands out at his sides. "I come in peace."

Cactus Flower and Bird Woman emerged and stood by One Arrow. The warrior remained fearful but was beginning to grasp what Luke was doing.

Crouching Lion, easily the most respected warrior in the encampment after One Arrow, suspiciously poked his head out from a nearby teepee.

Luke drew a bag from his shirt. It was the bag that contained items Three Toes had used in his prayers to the Comanche spirits. "In his final breath, Three Toes asked me to be sure you were all right." Luke hadn't a clue as to how much English they understood, but hoped the symbolism of his offering would transcend language. "Three Toes…my friend." Luke pointed to his heart as he handed over Three Toes's bag.

One Arrow had learned a few English words from Three Toes. "Where Three Toes?"

Luke pointed to the sky. "With spirits." Luke wasn't sure how much One Arrow might understand. "You are welcome at my home." Luke pulled a pouch of tobacco from his vest pocket. "You will be safe." He handed the pouch to One Arrow. Good tobacco was a precious commodity, and it was obvious to Luke that he'd struck a positive chord with Three Toes protégé.

Just as One Arrow had begun to feel comfortable with Luke's peaceful intentions, Crouching Lion and the two remaining Comanche in the camp came forward with arrows nocked and bows at the ready. One Arrow was quick to forcefully dissuade them. "*Kee.*" As accompanied by a grimly fierce facial expression, his "no" was emphatic. One Arrow let them know in no uncertain terms whom Luke was. "*Haits*." He was firm. Luke was a friend.

Luke smiled friendly-like at the warriors and raised his hands to indicate peace.

To warriors trained from birth to think of other humans as enemies, One Arrow's actions were antithetical. But One Arrow had proven himself in battle and taken charge upon their return from the homestead raids. He was unquestionably the protégé of Three Toes and, despite his youth, was to be respected for that if nothing else. Torturing and killing the Texas Ranger would have to wait for another time. They put their bows and arrows down and awaited One Arrow's next command.

Luke had begun to doubt the wisdom of his coming to this Comanche encampment, but he was in their midst and had little choice but to stick it out.

One Arrow was beginning to get a grasp on his newfound power over this small Comanche band. "Ghost-Who-Rides eat?"

The invitation for Luke to join them for a meal was a very good sign. Luke nodded, then turned to Big Horse. As the Comanche watched suspiciously, he walked over, reached into his saddlebag, and pulled out a carefully wrapped package. He walked back over to One Arrow and presented it to him.

One Arrow couldn't help but notice the sweet aroma wafting from the package. It might have been better than four days old, but Elisa's cornbread was the best around. A broad grin swept across One Arrow's face, as he handed the gift to Bird Woman. "We eat." He motioned the others to join in what was now to become a tribal meal. It was warm and a bit crowded inside the teepee, but good food, warm smiles, and a bit of sweat would make for building closer friendships and the accompanying mutual trust.

It hadn't taken very long: a few minutes at best. The bandits rode up to the cabin. They were nine dregs of Mexican society sitting astride tired-looking horses, caked with trail dirt from boots to sombreros, bandoliers askew, and rifles pointed at a man nervously begging for his life.

For their part, the bandits were nurturing a sort of blood lust as fed by successful attacks each of the preceding two days. As they'd approached from a distance, they'd seen a woman and child run into the house. They relished what they would do to the woman. These bandits could be nearly as sadistic as the Comanche as concerned the horrors they were inclined to wreak on a woman. Their perversions knew no bounds.

The sun bore down with a relentlessly searing heat. The homesteader sweated profusely, as he fell to his knees. "*Por el amor de Dios, no nos hagas daño.*" He begged in God's name desperately for he and his family to be spared.

The bandit leader gazed hatefully at the whiteness of the homesteader. "*¡Eres un ladrón, gringo! Muy blanco!*" He considered the homesteader and all their kind as thieves, *ladróns*, interlopers on land belonging to Mexico.

"*¡Por amor de Dios!*" the man pleaded.

The bandits could see two small frightened faces peering through the front window of the cabin as well as a woman with abject horror written large on her. The Mexicans laughed at the fear they were wreaking upon the family. "*¡Cobardes! ¡Estas cobardes!*" The words were spat derisively from their mostly toothless mouths. To them, all Anglo homesteaders were cowards.

The bandit leader gazed around wildly. He wrung his hands with a perverse sort of glee.

ACKNOWLEDGMENTS

Book writing simply doesn't happen in a vacuum. The author provides the creative talent and crafts the stories, but there's so much more that demandment. I've been blessed with many friends and family who have supported my writing of The Tumbleweed Sagas. My wife Carolyn's reviews and encouragement were a huge help, along with very important tech support from our sons Mike and Matt.

Other supporters have included Cara Miller, Jim May, Ernie Angell, and cousins Jim and Cindy Holmgreen and Johnny Dunn. Many more friends have contributed support at some level to the creation and publication of Nueces Blood, be it encouragement or advice.

Naturally, I am grateful to the great folks at Wolfpack Publishing. The team they bring to publishing is first rate from promotion to editing, cover design, narration, and the myriad tasks that lead to successful book sales.

Most of my authoring has occurred in my office as decorated to channel my inner Texan, but my creative juices have often been inspired and imagination stoked in cafés and coffee houses across America. My favorites were Hester's Café & Coffee Bar in Corpus Christi, TX; Nueces Café in Robstown, TX; Java Ranch Espresso Bar & Café in Fredericksburg, TX; PAX Coffee & Goods in Kerrville, TX; Ragged Edge Coffee House and Bantam Coffee Roasters in Gettysburg, PA; 1889 Coffee House in Helena, MT; Dunn Brothers Coffee in Rapid City, SD; Postmasters Coffee &

Bakery and Brio Coffeehouse in Waynesboro, PA; Birdie's Café and American Ice Co Café in Westminster, MD; Deja Brew Coffee House, New Oxford and Deja Brew at Miney Branch, Carroll Valley, PA; and Baltimore Coffee & Tea Co., Frederick Coffee Company & Café, and Dublin Roasters in Frederick, MD. I must admit to also frequenting a few Dunkin Donuts and Starbucks around our fine nation. The décors and easy listening music in these fine establishments combined with savory cups of coffee tended to set me in the right creative frame of mind.

Last but not least, I'm especially thankful for the many folks who have read and enjoyed my books.

I do believe it's important to acknowledge how the old west represents the brave pioneering spirit of settlers that met the challenges and transcended mere survival to enable America to achieve exceptional growth. The settling of the American frontier west is replete with tales of leveraging freedom for individual achievement. I hope you'll agree that reliving our past—even through history-based fiction— often has the effect of pointing the way to an ever-brighter future. Might we be up to it? I hope that the inspiration I've drawn from my having walked the very earth my characters have trodden coupled with my extensive historical research will enable readers to fully experience the grit, adventure, and passion of my characters while sensing aromas of gunsmoke, trail dust, leather, and bluebonnets.

A LOOK AT BOOK FIVE
NUECES GRIT

War rages across the Nueces Strip.

As the War Between the States engulfs the nation, Texas Ranger Captain Luke Dunn finds himself on a perilous frontier. With the Nueces Strip stretching from Corpus Christi to Laredo and south to Brownsville, the once-lawless prairies are now war-ravaged battlegrounds. Union cannonballs rain on the coast, Mexican bandits raid unguarded settlements, and rogue soldiers abandon their posts for lives of violence and greed.

Known as "Ghost-Who-Rides" to the Comanche, Dunn's commitment to justice is pushed to its limits. Murderers, swindlers, and hired killers conspire to rid the Strip of his influence, while the chaos of war threatens to undo all he has fought to protect. Even as his love for the spirited Elisa strengthens his resolve, new enemies and old savages rise to challenge him at every turn.

With loyalty scarce and the horrors of war closing in, Luke must decide: can justice endure when the very fabric of Texas is at risk of unraveling?

AVAILABLE FEBRUARY 2025

ABOUT THE AUTHOR

Award-winning author Mark Greathouse's love for the Western genre draws upon his deep family roots and love of the outdoors, honed from teen years spent hiking the Appalachian Trail and family travels across America's frontier. He hopes his work reveals his passion for America's western history.

A member of Western Writers of America and the Wild West History Association, Mark also contributes articles on the history of America's west to Western-themed magazines. He was recognized as a 2024 Finalist in the Western genre by the American Literary Book Awards for his sixth Tumbleweed Saga, *Nueces Truth: Texans Face War's Realities.*

Mark began writing full time after a successful career as a business executive and later as an entrepreneurial investor and advisor. His service as president of several business and community nonprofits led to their extraordinary growth. He holds a BA in English and MBA in marketing.

Mark also donates time and books annually to support wounded military warriors. He was a Boy Scout leader (Eagle Scout) and served on a local school board earlier in life.